THE LAKE

ALSO BY NATASHA PRESTON

The Cellar

Awake

The Cabin

You Will Be Mine

The Lost

The Twin

THE LAKE

NATASHA PRESTON

DELACORTE PRESS

Delacorte Press is a registered trademark and the colophon is a trademark of Penguin Random House LLC.

GetUnderlined.com

Educators and librarians, for a variety of teaching tools, visit us at RHTeachersLibrarians.com

Library of Congress Cataloging-in-Publication Data
Names: Preston, Natasha, author.
Title: The lake / Natasha Preston.
Description: First edition. | New York : Delacorte Press, [2021] |
Audience: Ages 12 and up. | Summary: Seventeen-year-old best friends Esme and Kayla return to Camp Pine Lake as counselors in training, but the dark secret they have been hiding for nine years is back to haunt them.
Identifiers: LCCN 2020028605 (print) | LCCN 2020028606 (ebook) |
ISBN 978-0-593-12497-0 (trade paperback) | ISBN 978-0-593-12499-4 (ebook)
Subjects: CYAC: Camps—Fiction. | Secrets—Fiction. | Best friends—Fiction. |
Friendship—Fiction. | Camp counselors—Fiction. | Mystery and detective stories.
Classification: LCC PZ7.P9234 Lak 2021 (print) | LCC PZ7.P9234 (ebook) |
DDC [Fic]—dc23

The text of this book is set in 11-point Janson MT Pro.
Interior design by Jen Valero

Printed in the United States of America
20 19 18
First Edition

Steve, Kyra, and Abbi. Thank you for visiting my books in Barnes & Noble while you were on holiday in NYC! You guys are the best. Steve, you'll be missed always and remembered forever.

1

We're returning to camp, to new friendships, to songs and s'mores around the campfire . . . and to the scene of our crime.

I lean between the front seats to get a better look out the windshield. "There it is," I say as we drive under the large CAMP PINE LAKE sign. It's exactly as I remember it, the name carved into the wood.

Glancing down, I trace one finger across identical bold lettering on the pamphlet I received earlier this year. Kayla and I both got letters asking us to consider becoming counselors-in-training.

We're back.

My best friend of fifteen years glances at me as the cab crawls to a stop. She pouts her glossy lips, which makes her eyebrows pull together. "Does it seem, I don't know, *smaller* to you?"

"Everything seems bigger when you're a kid, Kayla," I remind her. The last time we were here was nine years ago.

Compared to the other camps nearby, which really aren't that near, we're the smallest. But the best. Camp Pine Lake takes girls and boys ages seven to ten. Kayla and I spent two epic summers here when we were seven and eight.

We didn't come back when we were nine or ten.

We didn't dare.

But we're seventeen now. It's time.

Kayla squeals as she opens the cab door. "Yes! This summer is going to be amazing." She winks at me. "We can even stay up late this time."

"We stayed up late when we were campers."

The very second I open the other passenger door and we lose the AC, I feel like I'm going to melt. At least our uniforms are shorts and T-shirts. Texas summers can be brutal. I forgot how insane the heat is.

"Yeah, but this time we're actually *allowed* to."

Kind of. "We have to stay in the same cabin as the kids," I remind Kayla. It feels like more of a lateral move.

Kayla grins. "Esme, we'll be in our *own* teeny room, though. A bedroom in a bedroom. We'll have some privacy." Her eyes flit over the grounds. "I hope they have some cute counselors here."

There's my bestie. Kayla is boy crazy, loves pink and heels, and falls in love about every three minutes.

We thank the cabdriver, then pay and tip him as he removes our bags for us.

I lick my lips, swallowing as I take a look around. *I'm really back.* I feel a little ping in my stomach. I reach for Kayla's arm as she goes to pick up her pink camo suitcase. "Kay . . . are we doing the right thing coming back?"

She groans. "Don't overthink it. We're going to be fine. Everything is going to be *fine*."

Nodding, I pretend to agree. "We're not kids anymore."

"Exactly. No one here knew us back then, so no one knows what happened. Chillax."

"Do people still say 'chillax'?" I let go of her and smile as she glares. "All right. I'll *chillax*. We'll be fine. The last of my nerves have officially gone, *I promise*."

What a stupid promise.

"I did not miss the Texas heat," she says, her shoulders slumping.

I wave my hand in front of my face like a lunatic. "Can air be on fire? Because I think it is. Why has no one put more research into outdoor AC? . . . Look, there they all are. The counselors and the other CITs."

Kayla squeals and we drag our suitcases across the grass to the group gathered outside a cabin. How can they stand to be exposed in this heat?

"We need to find Andy," Kayla tells me.

Andy Marson is our boss. His name is on all the starter paperwork we were sent. He's the one in charge. Kayla and I have been paired together and assigned a counselor we'll do most of our activities with, along with our small group of campers.

"Which one do you think is Andy?" she asks.

I scan the group. "My money is on the redheaded guy with the clipboard."

He lifts his chin as we approach, and his pale eyes light up. "Ah, our final CITs are here. Kayla Price and Esme Randal?"

"Kayla," she says, lifting her hand.

"I'm Esme," I say.

Andy scribbles something on his clipboard. "Glad everyone is here. We're going to have a blast this summer, but first we need to get to know each other. Then I want to run through some rules and safety information."

He motions to two girls behind him. "This is Rebekah and Tia. And over there are Olly and Jake. They're all CITs too. You'll have your free evenings with them." Andy then rattles off some rules, but I know Kayla isn't listening. Her eyes are firmly on the two *very* cute guys standing behind Andy. Olly and Jake.

Camp just got a lot more interesting.

Rebekah and Tia step up to us with identical toothy smiles. That's the only thing similar about them. Rebekah is tall, with pale skin and shoulder-length ash-brown hair. She looks kind and a little bit lost, with her gentle, nervous blue eyes. Tia is petite, with black skin and large brown eyes. Her silky dark hair is so long it almost touches her butt.

"Hi," Rebekah says with a Southern twang.

"We're going to have the best summer," Tia says.

"Absolutely. Do you know which cabin is yours yet?" I ask.

"Rebekah and I are in Verbena. You're in Bluebonnet, the one right next to the food hall." Tia leans in, and I realize we're about the same height. "They're kind of small, but the beds look comfortable enough. Me and Rebekah are sharing a cabin with those two, and they're a little scary."

Tia points at two older girls who are full counselors. They both have dark heavy bangs and short bobs. One is pale like me, and the other has a gorgeous olive tan, the kind that Kayla pays for every six weeks.

"Mary and Catalina," Tia tells me. "Otherwise known as the Buttercups. Like the Powerpuff Girls."

I laugh. That's exactly who they look like. "Why are they scary?" I ask.

"Kind of intense when they're talking to you. You'll see what I mean."

"I wonder who we'll report to," I ask, looking around.

"Oh, I heard Andy talking. You guys report to Cora. She seems supernice. I think she just went into the food hall. It's kind of a mess in there, with a lot of equipment that needs sorting before the campers arrive. Final checks apparently."

"You get the impression that this is, like, the tenth final check?" I ask, watching Andy rushing from cabin to cabin with his clipboard.

Tia laughs. "Oh, for sure."

Rebekah and Kayla are chatting, having a similar conversation to ours, but Kayla is doing all the talking. My bestie can *talk*. Rebekah seems kind of overwhelmed, with her arms curled around her body and her eyes darting everywhere like she's trying to figure out all the escape routes.

Tia laughs and pulls me to the side. "Rebekah's from Kansas and applied to be a CIT because she wants to gain confidence before college. She's so sweet I feel like I'm getting a cavity just talking to her."

"Well, we can definitely help her out," I say. "We get our evenings off together. I wonder if we'll be allowed to leave camp."

Tia groans. "Apparently not. But I did a little research before I arrived, and there's a shortcut through the forest, right by the bramblebush at the side of the lake. It takes you to the edge of town, and there are no lights up that way."

I remember the shortcut. . . . But I don't want Tia to know I was a camper here. My eyes widen. "I have heart palpitations already."

"You don't want to come?" she asks.

"Oh no, I'll come."

She smirks. "Do you scare easily?"

"No, but it's not often that I walk through an unfamiliar forest at night. Kayla is going to freak out."

"We'll be fine. Why is Kayla going to freak out?"

"Shh," I hush Tia, and tug her closer. "I'll tell you another time."

Kayla is *so* scared of any kind of danger. It's a fear that not even extensive therapy has managed to calm. She doesn't need to be worrying about sneaking through a dark forest yet.

Rebekah glances at us both like she knows exactly what we're talking about. Tia has already had this conversation with her.

"CITs, if you can finish unpacking and then head back out to the fire for lunch, we'll eat and then go to the multiuse cabin so I can assign you a job!" Andy shouts, looking at something on his clipboard.

Tia cuts me a look. "He's going to be a nightmare."

Yeah.

Kayla and I head to our cabin to unpack. Kayla stands in front of the full-length mirror in our little room. The separate room gives us a little privacy while also making it easy to keep an eye on the campers.

We'll be sharing a bunk bed and a minuscule dresser since the cabin is so small. Cora, full-fledged camp counselor, has the other tiny room in the cabin.

Kayla and I will be rotating nights off with Cora so there is always a counselor in the cabin with the campers. I remember being so jealous of the counselors and CITs whenever it was their turn to sit by the campfire after hours. Now I get to do it.

I take the top bunk because Kayla doesn't like heights.

The cabin smells like wood and pine trees. Big surprise, right? The bunks look new, not like the old ones with names and private jokes scribbled in Sharpie on the sides.

"Which one do you like?" Kayla asks, and because I know her, I know she's referring to Jake and Olly.

"That didn't take you long."

She arches one perfectly shaped eyebrow in the mirror and fluffs her blond hair. Kayla is gorgeous, with fake tanned skin, huge blue eyes, thick lips and a killer figure with curves in all the best places. I'm pretty sure I'm going to look like a middle schooler—petite, skinny and pale—in the camp uniform, especially next to her. Texas might give me a nice tan, though.

"Which one, babe?" she asks.

"Hos before bros," I tell her, shoving my few belongings in the closet. I place my parents' picture on top.

"Fine. I like Jake."

Like I didn't know that. Tall, sandy blond hair, blue eyes and built like a football player, Jake is definitely Kayla's type.

"Shocker," I say sarcastically. "Go for it."

Kayla has unpacked all her clothes and hung them neatly.

"Summer's going to fly by, Esme. We have to move fast."

"So does that mean you'll sneak out with me into town one night?"

Her eyes narrow. "Seriously? Nothing good ever happens when you sneak into a forest at night."

I give her a nudge. "Things are going to be different this summer. Please, you baby, there's nothing scary in the woods."

2

Another minute slowly ticks by on my watch. Lunch is dragging.

I'm sitting under a pine tree with Kayla, Tia and Rebekah.

Olly and Jake are close by, a couple of trees over with the other male CITs, Marcus and Lorenzo. They seem more interested in spending time with each other than getting to know us. They might be a little older.

We've been here for about an hour and the counselor cliques are complete.

On my little paper plate there is a hot dog smothered in ketchup and charred corn. The second I take a bite out of the hot dog, I'm eight years old again. The taste brings me back to long summers swimming in the lake, and Kayla and me as skinny kids with dirty knees and wild hair. We'd eat hot dogs almost every day at camp, along with mac and cheese.

I loved it so much, and I can't wait to give the campers the same experience.

"He keeps looking at you," Tia sings.

"What?"

"Olly. He's talking to the guys, but about every three seconds his eyes wander your way."

I'm not even going to pretend I'm not interested in tall, dark and handsome. I would have to tilt my head up to talk to him, but I have to do that with almost everyone.

"What about you, Tia?"

She shrugs. "I'm not really into guys."

"There are girls here."

Her cheeks turn pink. "Well . . . Cora."

"How old is she?"

Tia sighs. "It's just a crush. I think maybe twenty? And *straight*."

I pat her arm. "Are you seventeen?"

"Yep. All of the CITs are sixteen and seventeen except Lorenzo, who's eighteen."

"You know everything. How long have you been here?"

"I arrived early this morning. I work fast." She taps her head. "Knowledge is power."

"You here as a CIT or as FBI?"

That gets a laugh. "You stick with me, girl."

"I'm going to talk to them," Kayla says, standing up and taking her plate to the boys.

Andy watches her from where he's sitting by the campfire. His expression is hard and his head tilted. Oh, come on, he can't possibly want to separate us. This whole camp is coed.

I'm not spending the entire summer pretending that boys don't exist.

"Shall we?" Tia asks.

Rebekah looks up and her eyes widen. "You wanna join them?"

"Yes, come on," I say, standing up. With one hand I hold my plate and with the other I offer to help Rebekah up.

"All right, I'll go with y'all." She places one hand in mine and I tug her to her feet. She towers over me. "Thanks, Esme."

Tia, Rebekah and I take a seat on a log bench. I strategically sit next to Olly. He *has* been looking at me, and he is totally cute. He looks athletic. I'm betting on football.

"Hey," I say.

He glances sideways and smiles. "Esme, right?"

"Should I be flattered that you remembered?"

Laughing, he says, "You should actually. I forgot my cousin's name once."

"How do you do that?"

"I have fourteen. Most of us live on the same street."

"Yeah, I only have five. Where are you from?"

"Missouri. You?"

"Pennsylvania. So, what made you want to be a CIT?"

He rips the end of a hot dog bun off. "I went to a camp when I was thirteen. It looked a lot more fun being a CIT. I guess I'll find out. How about you?"

I think of the pamphlet, now buried away in my tiny dresser. "Pretty much the same as you."

His insane green-blue eyes drift to the bramblebush that is probably going to shred my skin. I hope we don't have to go through it to take the shortcut.

"Tia told you, too?" I ask.

He grins. "I think before she even said hello."

"All right, guys, let's finish up and organize the multi and the food cabins," Andy says. "There's lots to do before the campers arrive the day after tomorrow."

Olly doesn't move. He does glare at Andy's back, though.

I sit straighter. "I guess we should . . ."

"Finish eating, Esme," Olly replies.

My glance drifts between him and Andy. "Did you know him before you came here?"

"Kind of. Only through one of my cousins. They went to college together and I met him at their graduation. He talked to me a little about camp. When I got a pamphlet about becoming a CIT earlier this year, I figured he was the one who sent it."

"He really likes this job, doesn't he?"

Olly laughs. "Yes. He spends about ten hours every day promoting it. You should see his social media, it's nothing but camp."

"I don't think I want to see his social media."

I finish eating. The Buttercups—Mary and Catalina, I need to use their actual names!—follow Andy, almost tripping over themselves to get in first.

Is there a prize for best counselor or biggest suck-up?

That's not a medal I'm likely to win.

Kayla and I dump our plates in the trash and head into the hall with our newly formed coed group.

Jake and Olly have broken away from the guys to stick with us four girls. We really don't mind.

Inside the multiuse cabin is a sea of equipment. Tents, canoes, kayaks, sports gear, ropes, camping stoves and pans are spread out. It smells like a gym.

"Er, we have to check *all* of this?" Kayla mutters to our group.

"What qualifies me to assure anyone that a kayak won't sink?" I mutter.

Olly chuckles, but I'm being serious.

Andy claps his hands. "Right, CITs can start by putting tents up and checking that they're intact. I want to know if anything is missing or if there are rips, et cetera, et cetera. Counselors are to check outdoor equipment, and I will check the cooking equipment."

We pair off and get to work. Kayla makes a beeline for Jake, so I end up with Olly. Not that I'm going to complain when his crazy shiny eyes keep making my tummy flip. I smile as I grab the first tent and try to hide my face with my long hair. My cheeks are probably tomato red.

The first tent goes up without a problem. It's a small, simple four-person one.

We walk around it checking for rips, and Olly ducks inside, checking there too.

"It's fine," I say.

"Yep," he agrees, poking his head out of the opening. "On to the next one, Esme."

I like the way his rough voice says my name.

Enough, you weirdo!

The day rolls on, and we keep making good time with organizing. It's nonstop work, but I'm enjoying it.

Nerves are swimming lengths in my stomach, though. What if I'm not good at this? What if my little team of campers doesn't like me? I have to guide them and make them feel safe as well as learn new skills and have fun.

This isn't just something that will look good on my résumé. I want to be good at it. I loved it here. I loved *almost* every part of Camp Pine Lake. There was just one thing. One night picked from a horror movie that still freezes my heart.

By nightfall we're officially ready for the campers. Or at least the camp and equipment are.

We pushed on and got everything done. I'm a hot, sweaty, gross mess of a human, but because we finished, it means tomorrow we can have some fun. Then, it will be all about the young people we're caring for.

After a refresh in the communal showers, we gather back outside. The air is a lot cooler, though I'm still in shorts and a T-shirt.

Tia grabs my elbow and I startle. "Let's take a walk."

I do a double take as she pulls me in another direction. "What?"

"Around the lake."

She doesn't wait for me to agree, but all right.

"What are we doing?" I ask when she lets me go.

"Walking."

"I got that. Why?"

Grinning over her shoulder, she replies, "We're checking out the shortcut. You just go straight along a man-made trail right through the trees. We should wait a week before we sneak out."

Her voice is animated, and she waves her arms as she speaks. Her hair is tied in a messy bun.

"Make Andy think we're good little CITs and following the rules," I say.

"Exactly."

"What happens if we get caught?"

"We'd be in a lot of trouble, I think. I doubt we'd get kicked out, though."

I take a breath. "I hope not."

My mom and dad would be *so* mad.

"Don't worry, Esme, we won't get caught."

I mean, the chances are high. If someone else is outside, too, they will see us disappear into a bush and not come out for a couple of hours. Maybe they all do it.

We walk along the edge of the oval lake with trees to our left and water to our right. It's beautiful, peaceful.

In a couple of days, we're going to be swimming out here. We even have an inflatable obstacle course for the water. We didn't have that when I was a camper, so I can't wait to try it. I can get a bit competitive, so I need to remember to play fair with the children.

"Are you going to college after summer?" I ask.

"Yep, in New York. Big change from Oregon. I can't wait. What about you?"

I nod. "Denver. I'm from Pennsylvania, so a big change for me, too. It's so pretty in Colorado. I can't wait to see mountains."

"We'll have to keep in touch."

"Definitely. Is this it?" I ask.

"Yep. Must be."

Thankfully, the track is just behind the bramble.

Tia and I continue to walk around the lake. It's dark over here without camp lighting, but the moon is bright, so there's enough light to see where we're walking. The scent of pine is stronger away from the cabins and campfire. I breathe it in.

It takes about ten minutes to walk all the way around the lake, probably quicker now that I'm not eight.

"Next week," I say with a bubble of excitement. This summer is going to rock.

≋

Back at camp, some of the CITs are down by the lake, while others are playing cards.

"I'm not jumping in the water tonight, I've already showered," Tia says.

"I'm with you," I say. We take a seat with Kayla, Rebekah, Jake and Olly. They are sitting to the side of the campfire in a little circle.

"Campfire games," Tia says. "We can play Which One Is the Lie. You have to tell two facts about yourself, but only one can be an actual fact. The rest of us have to guess which one is the lie."

Rebekah interjects. "I have a better one for y'all, a way for us to really get to know each other. But we have to all agree to be completely honest and no one can judge."

I'm not sure I like the sound of that.

“I’m game,” Jake says, rubbing his hands together.

Good for him.

Kayla and I share a look. There are some things we won’t *ever* be telling anyone.

“Come on, it’ll be fun.” Rebekah sits taller if that’s even possible. “It’s something I’ve played before with my best friends. It keeps us close.”

“All right,” I concede. I don’t have to lie to anyone. Kayla and I just won’t tell *everything*.

Kayla’s eyes snap to mine and I see her body visibly stiffen. *We’re obviously not going* there. I subtly shake my head, telling her it’s okay.

“I’ll go first,” Rebekah says. “My greatest fear is that I will never be happy. Really, truly happy.”

Her confession knocks the air out of my lungs. “You’ve *never* been happy?”

She shakes her head, eyes downcast. “I don’t think I know how. Since I was young, I knew there was something wrong with me.”

Well, this got dark fast. I want to ask what she thinks is wrong with her, but her eyes fill with tears and I don’t want to make her cry.

Olly purses his lips like he’s deeply uncomfortable and doesn’t know what to say. Jake clears his throat and looks longingly at the lake as if he wishes he was in it.

He’s not alone.

“You will be happy,” Tia tells Rebekah, giving her shoulder

a squeeze, and then quickly moves on. "So, my big confession is that my parents still don't know I'm gay." She laughs. "In fact, no one does but you guys."

"What, no one at all?" I ask.

She shrugs. "I guess being here and being out will give me the kick in the ass I need to live this way back home, too. What's yours, Esme?"

I clear my throat.

My biggest fear is that someone will find out what I did ten years ago.

3

I wake in the morning in the top bunk with a crick in my neck. The beds aren't too bad, but the pillows are. Tilting my head from side to side, I kick off the thin blanket and climb down the ladder.

Kayla is still asleep. I don't want to wake her, so I take my clothes and toiletries and go to the bathroom to get ready.

When I get back to the cabin, I notice how eerily quiet it is this early in the morning. Every bunk bed in the main room is neatly made, blankets and sheets tucked in, ready for the campers tomorrow.

I dump my bag back in our room and shake my head at Kayla's soft snore. She could sleep in for hours. Getting her beauty rest, she calls it. She doesn't need it, though; she's naturally model material. Her Insta following grows with every selfie.

I take the few steps to our dresser and open my drawer. From it, I pull out the pamphlet Kayla and I received a few months earlier asking us to consider positions as CITs. They arrived at our houses on the same day. We assumed most ex-campers received them. I run my hand over the laminated cover. It's a picture of the lake at sunset, campers jumping off the dock. Inside is a bunch of information—about schedules, pay and benefits. I flip the brochure over and a chill runs down my spine, just like it did the first time I read it.

In big block letters are the words **COME TO CAMP PINE LAKE . . . YOU'LL REGRET IT IF YOU DON'T.**

The first time I pointed this out to Kayla, she told me it was nothing. Just cheesy copy. But something about it rubbed me the wrong way. By the time I realized why, Kayla was already in love with the idea of coming back. I agreed to come too, but for different reasons. I had the feeling this pamphlet was a threat. That if I didn't come back, something bad would happen. Like maybe someone would reveal my and Kayla's secret.

But who would do that? Only one other person knows what happened the last time Kayla and I were here. A girl from town named Lillian Campbell. I remember her being a little bit . . . off. Kayla would use the word *weird.* But Lillian would want to keep what happened a secret just as much as we do. Unless . . .

No. I shake my head, clearing away the thoughts. I am just being paranoid. Being back here must be having a stronger effect on me than I had anticipated.

I put the pamphlet back in the drawer and head out the door.

The landscape takes my breath away for a second. Blue sky at first light, with lush pine trees surrounding us and a peaceful lake in the middle.

I'm not the only one up early. Rebekah is with Andy and a

couple of other counselors who I haven't had a chance to speak to yet. They're standing by the lake, on the beach area. I quietly close the cabin door and take the steps down to the grass.

Last night I learned that Tia is scared her parents won't accept she's gay, Olly won't be as successful as his cousins, and Jake won't make it in football.

I told them I'm scared of disappointing my parents because of how seemingly perfect they are, always doing the right thing and advocating for 100 percent honesty. They totally lied about Santa, the Tooth Fairy and the Easter Bunny, but whatever.

My confession wasn't technically a lie. The thought of disappointing them does actually make me nauseous. They can never know what I did. No one can.

My personal favorite revelation was Kayla's. She told everyone that her greatest fear is she'll need Botox before the age of forty. Now, I have no doubt she *is* worried about that, but I'm pretty sure her *greatest* fear matches mine.

I slide my sunglasses down over my eyes and walk to the little group. "Morning," I say.

"Mornin', Esme. You're up early." Rebekah looks relieved to have someone else she knows up. She stands and takes my wrist. "Let's go get coffee. Do you drink coffee?"

Another one of my fears is people who don't drink caffeine. Like, how do you function?

I nod. "Absolutely. Too bad there's no Starbucks here."

"Did you sleep okay?" she asks as we walk.

"Okay. My neck is hurting, though." I tilt my head from side to side.

"Mine, too. I'm on the bottom bunk and had to listen to Tia toss and turn above me. We're on the lake today, right? I'm kind of nervous."

"It'll be fine. I think Andy will make us wear life jackets even though we could stand up in it."

"The middle is deep. Be careful." The middle of the lake is cordoned off. There were lots of wild rumors and ghost stories about it when Kayla and I were here. One was that some hybrid shark was down there. The other part of the hybrid was never mentioned.

"Have you been here before?" I ask.

Rebekah flattens her straight hair. "No. I did spend a lot of my childhood in summer camps, though."

Maybe it's because she seems so nervous that I decide to open up . . . a little. "I was a camper here with Kayla when we were younger. My parents couldn't afford to send me every year, unfortunately."

The truth is, I *couldn't* come back.

Rebekah scoffs. "My parents are more than willing to pay to get me out of their hair for a summer."

Wow, okay. Her parents don't sound like fuzzy, loving people.

"Why did you decide to train to be a counselor here?"

"I wanted something different. As soon as I looked the camp up, I fell in love with the lake. It's got such a traditional camp vibe, right? Like this place could be used as a set for a movie."

Yeah, a movie where you either swap with your twin you didn't know existed or you get murdered. Both are super farfetched, but, yeah, this place would totally make a great movie set.

"I heard you're from Kansas," I say.

"Yep. How about you?"

"Lewisburg, Pennsylvania. Kayla is too."

"Have you been friends for long?"

"Yeah, we met in preschool, actually."

Her smile doesn't touch her sad eyes. "I wish I had a good friend."

Didn't she say she played the game of fears with her friends? "There's no one back home?"

"Not really. I have a few friends, but we don't confide in each other."

Nope, I'm calling her out on this. "But I thought you said you did the secrets thing?"

We walk into the hall. A few people are milling around, eating cereal and fruit. Rebekah and I go straight for the coffee.

With a sigh, she admits the truth. "Okay, confession time. The game last night. It didn't exactly come from my friends, it's what my cousin does. Her and her friends are tight, and they tell each other their deepest, darkest fears. I tried it once with a group back home in the hopes that it would tie us together and we'd be close."

"What happened?"

"They were the wrong people to try it with; we weren't tight enough. We grew apart, but we all know each other's secrets so we're all fake nice to each other, talking about the weather and how lame school is. I don't even think school is lame."

I pour two mugs of coffee. "So why did you do it with us?"

She shrugs. "I just felt, like, I don't know, that we clicked. Our little group of six. I've never had that. The only thing I had in common with my high school 'friends' was that we were all running from the same bully."

"I'm sorry high school sucked." I was never bullied, but I know it's traumatic, never being able to get away from the people making your life a misery, not even at home thanks to social media. Feeling alone is awful; feeling alone *and* hated must be unbearable. "You have us now." I hand her a coffee. "And soon you'll be in college."

"Thanks. I sure hope college is different."

From what my mom has told me about her office environment, I don't think anything is too different from high school. But I don't tell her that.

Kayla and I weren't part of the popular group. Well, she could have been, but she stuck with me. We were somewhere in the middle. It was the best place to be. We didn't have to pretend the way the popular people did, and we didn't have to fear anyone like the unpopular people did.

Rebekah and I grab some breakfast and sit down. I sip my coffee and dig my spoon into my cereal.

Over Rebekah's shoulder I see Olly walk in. The khaki shorts and white T-shirt look great on him. He scans the room and his bluey-green eyes settle on us. I get a mild electric shock.

"Olly's here," I say as he makes his way toward us.

Rebekah takes a quick look and turns back. "He so likes ya," she sings quietly.

I wide-eye her, telling her to shush as he approaches.

"Morning." He sits down next to me. "You two okay?"

"Yep," we reply at the exact same time.

His smile widens. "How's the coffee?"

"It's fine," I reply.

Rebekah adds, "It's no Starbucks, right, Esme?"

I groan. "Don't remind me about Starbucks. I would kill for a vanilla latte."

"*Kill* is a little strong, isn't it?" Olly asks, lifting his eyebrow.

"No, I don't think so."

Rebekah eats her banana in silence, watching us like we're in a play.

"We have a whole day to hang out . . . and do final *final* checks, apparently. I'm going to grab some food, and then we'll head out there, yeah?" Olly says.

"Sure," I reply as he heads for the cereal.

Rebekah smirks.

"Don't say a word." I'm pretty sure I'm blushing a very unflattering shade of red.

She puts her banana peel in her bowl. "Okay, I'm going to see if Tia is up. Meet you at the dock?"

I know exactly what she's doing.

"Rebekah!"

Laughing, she adds, "Enjoy breakfast."

She leaves just as Olly puts down a bowl and coffee. He sits. "Hey, where's she going?"

"To find Tia."

To leave us alone. Why? What does she think is going to happen over breakfast? He kisses me? Announces love at first sight? No. Insta love is dumb.

"Do you know what jobs we have to do today?" I ask.

"I don't think we've been assigned anything yet. Andy did say we could get on the lake, explore the camp and the forest if we want, get to know the place before the campers arrive."

We have a grand total of seven cabins. I don't think anyone is getting lost.

I nod. "Good. I'm going to spend the whole day chilling around camp. There won't be much chance for that later."

"That's true. What have you and Rebekah been doing this morning?"

"Not much, I haven't been up long. She seems really nice."

Nice and . . . something. I haven't figured it out. It's probably her shy nature and desire to please. When someone is like that, it's hard to know the real them.

4

My eyes are saucers.

That is a lot of children.

Today the campers are arriving—all fifty-six of them. Although I knew how many were coming, actually seeing them all in one place makes it seem like a lot more.

I tie my hair on top of my head and smell the coconut-scented SPF 50 on my skin.

I'm both excited and nervous. Then I suddenly realize that I'm one of the people responsible for keeping all these kids alive for six whole weeks. My chest tightens.

What if I lose one on a hike? What if one drowns?

They're everywhere, hugging parents and chatting enthusiastically with their new camp friends. Andy and his clipboard are out in force. He's frantically ticking people off and telling them where to take their things. No one else has been trusted to do that. He's a bit of a control freak, I think.

The camp is buzzing with excitement and nerves.

"What were you expecting?" Kayla asks, taking in my panicked expression.

I shake my head. "I don't know."

She laughs, wrapping an arm around my shoulders. "We're going to be fine. We'll have a small group each and be with counselors the whole time."

"You look like you're going to pass out," Olly says, stopping beside Kayla and me. "Second thoughts, or Andy's cooking last night?"

"No, I'm good. Got a little worried there, but I'm over it now. I will not lose a child," I say.

He dips his chin. "Good. That's good."

While the campers get settled and say their final goodbyes, half of the counselors stay outside and half are in the cabins helping. We want it to look like there are plenty of CITs and counselors. The parents of these children are trusting us.

My eyes drift to the shortcut through the woods. Are we terribly irresponsible to sneak off? I mean, we're not on duty every night.

Stop overthinking!

A little girl, probably eight or nine, clings to her mom's waist. Her big green eyes shed tear after tear while her mom tries to reassure her that she'll have a good time.

A lot of the parents are leaving or have already left.

In the clear blue sky, the sun shines down, making this the most beautiful day for the campers to arrive. The whole camp looks bright and inviting.

“Hi,” I say, walking over to the little girl and her mom. “I’m Esme.”

The mom looks up. “Oh, Esme. Andy just told us that you’re Isabel’s CIT.”

I smile, trying to look friendly and reassuring. “Hi, Isabel. This is my first time being a counselor here, so you’re not alone, okay? It’s new for me, too.” Her eyes meet mine, but she still keeps a tight grip on her mom’s T-shirt. “We’re going to have the best summer ever. Remember you can write your mom anytime you like, so you’re not saying goodbye right now, you’re only saying see you later. Would you like to come with me?”

Isabel presses her lips together, completely unsure.

I add, “I think we’re going to do some ‘getting to know you’ games before we cook a welcome lunch on the campfire. You could help me until you feel like joining in, if you like?”

“Go on, Isabel. You’ll be fine, my darling,” her mom prompts.

“The trees are scary,” Isabel says.

I shake my head. “I promise you, there is nothing scary in the woods.”

“Okay.” Isabel lets go of her mom, giving her one last kiss on the cheek before she leaves.

“Let’s go find the rest of our group. We’re looking for Maisie, Addison and Audrey,” I tell her.

“Do you know who they are?” Isabel asks.

“Not yet, but we can find them. They’re also part of the E Team.”

Isabel follows me as Andy shoots off more instructions, calling out names and telling children which staff member to go with.

I find the three other girls, then stand with Kayla and her group.

There are a lot of children. I hope I can remember them all. Or at the very least remember the ones I'll be spending the most time with.

I wipe my forehead as the heat scorches my skin. None of the campers care how hot it is.

I don't know why Andy insists on cooking on a fire in this heat.

Tia rocks on her heels, grinning at her little group like she wants to corrupt them all. I'm sure she won't. Well, I'm not *sure*. She's standing next to a petrified Rebekah, who periodically glances at one of her campers, a girl with makeup, glossy, straight hair and low heels. A queen bee type. She's going to have to change into tennis shoes soon.

I can't help feeling sorry for Rebekah as she glances worriedly at a girl nearly ten years younger than her. The kind of girl who probably made Rebekah's life miserable in school. That's unfair, though. The girl isn't necessarily a bully just because of her stereotypically popular-girl appearance. Kayla isn't.

We're split, Kayla and me with Cora's group. Three adults and twelve children. Olly and his group head toward the lake, but we're staying near to the tennis court to play our "getting to know you" games.

Cora takes over, but Kayla and I stand with them. Cora explains what we're going to do. We're playing All About Me tennis. Each time you hit the ball, you have to call out something about yourself, like your favorite vacation destination, animal, color, food, class at school, celebrity, etc.

I remember playing the exact same game when I was a camper.

The girls split easily into groups of two, each twosome taking a tennis racket. I stand on the sidelines with Kayla. The girls call out random facts with every hit of the ball. Laughter fills the stifling-hot air, and none of the campers seem to care about the heat.

"They're all so adorable," Kayla says.

"Remember when that was us? You spent the first few hours crying because you missed your mom and then forgot to write to her the rest of the summer."

"Oh, but she wrote to me. *All* the time!"

"She's your mom."

"And you," Kayla says, "were so cute, the smallest one here with the biggest green eyes that matched the leaves on the trees. You looked around as if you'd never seen a lake or forest before."

"Okay, so I didn't get out much. I was way less tragic the second year we came."

But we don't need to talk about that second time.

Kayla laughs. "All right, I'll give you that. I'm so excited these girls get to experience this. They're already making friends."

"So are you," I say, arching an eyebrow.

"You're talking about Jake."

My smile widens. "Ding, ding, ding."

"He's hot." She side-eyes me. "Almost as hot as Olly."

"Don't start."

Andy calls an end to the games after an hour. Most of the kids have swapped partners and met new people. The rest of the afternoon is spent splashing in the lake, and the evening toasting s'mores on the campfire and telling crazy stories about killers in the woods.

There aren't killers in the woods, but I did lie to Isabel.

Bad things do happen there.

5

Yesterday was tiring, yet here I am, wide awake at five a.m. Below me, Kayla's deep breathing vibrates through the room. If I didn't love her, I'd throw something at her.

No one is getting up anytime soon, and I'm bored. There is no rule about me leaving the cabin in the morning. I won't go far, just outside to see if anyone else is up. Besides, Kayla and Cora are still here.

Twisting my body, I carefully climb down the ladder, holding my breath as if breathing is the part of my escape that could wake Kayla. I don't think a marching band could wake her this early.

My feet touch the cool wood floor. I quietly change into my camp T-shirt and shorts and creep out of the room. The door creaks when it opens and I wince. I'm sure it doesn't do that during the day. After a quick head count—every camper is still in their bed—I leave the cabin.

Even though the sun won't rise for at least another hour, it's not too dark.

I pull my jacket on and walk down the few steps to the grass.

Rebekah is up early again. She's sitting on the beach, by the firepit. She has a blanket around her shoulders and her eyes are fixed on the center of the lake.

"Hey, are you okay?" I ask, walking toward her.

She jolts and looks over her shoulder. "Hi. Esme. Yeah, I've just never been able to sleep late when I'm away from home."

I sit on the sand and curl my arms around my legs. Me neither, apparently. "Nothing beats your own bed."

"How come you're up so early?"

I shrug. "I can't sleep. Excited, maybe?"

"I wish the hall was open so we could at least make coffee."

"Andy probably sleeps with the key on a chain around his neck."

That gets a laugh out of her. "He loves it here. He's not so bad, though."

Rebekah seems like the type of person who would bite her tongue so that she doesn't end up in the middle of any kind of conflict. Hopefully, that's something she will leave here. It doesn't seem like she stood up to her bullies.

"The lake is eerie first thing in the mornin'. Dark and quiet, like it holds a lot of secrets," she says.

Okay . . .

"Have you been all the way around it?" I ask.

"No, not yet. The other side is owned by the camp, right?"

"Yeah, about a full five-minute walk past the lake. After that, it's a public forest and the locals use it to hike and camp. I remember when I was here last, an old couple wandered onto camp land. I think they put up even more signs around the perimeter after that."

The land is far too big to put a fence around, so signs are necessary.

Rebekah nods. "Didn't something happen over there, past our site? I overheard one of the counselors mention there was a fire or something."

I shrug and swallow acid at the same time. "No idea."

"So, Esme"—she sits straighter—"tell me more about you. What's the plan after college?"

"I'd love to be a journalist. I love the hustle and going out on the hunt for stories."

Her light eyes watch me carefully. "But you seem too honest to do that."

I laugh and hope it sounds normal. "I want to write facts. There are still some news outlets that do that." And probably four times as many that don't.

"You might be the first."

I raise my eyebrows. "You don't like journalists?"

Rebekah turns away, her eyes settling back on the middle of the lake. "I don't like lies."

"What's your plan, then?"

She blows out a breath. "I wanted to swim in college."

"Not anymore?"

Shaking her head, she replies, "No. Now I don't know what I'll do."

"What made you change your mind?"

She hesitates. "I didn't get a scholarship. I like where I'll be going, but there's no chance for swimming. I'm going to take all the classes I can and see what I like."

"That's cool. You can go wherever your heart takes you."

"Do you have siblings?" she asks. "I only have a brother."

"I'm an only child, but Kayla feels more like a sister than a friend."

"Well, you're not missing much."

"Don't you get along with your brother?"

"We'd do anything for each other, but he's twenty-eight, so we don't have a lot in common."

"I always wanted a protective older brother."

Rebekah scoffs. "Trust me, you don't. Hey, do you think Tia is going to make us sneak out tomorrow?"

"She can't *make* you do anything, but I think we're going next week. We need a couple of nights to figure out what happens after lights-out, make sure no one sees us breaking out."

"By that you mean when Andy goes to bed."

Nodding, I say, "Precisely."

"Do you even know where we're going?"

"Apparently there's an arcade and bowling alley on the edge of town. Tia looked it up. So we're basically sneaking out to be thirteen again."

With a soft giggle, Rebekah stands. "Andy is up."

I follow her gaze over my shoulder. Andy walks from the staff cabin where he has a room next to the food hall.

His step falters as he spots us. "Rebekah, Esme, what are you doing out here?"

I stand and head toward him. Rebekah follows, staying a step behind me. "Neither of us could sleep. Do you need us to do anything?"

He nods. "I could use some help setting up for breakfast," he says as he lets us into the hall.

That's in two hours. This summer could pass very slowly if I keep getting up before the sun. Though I like the peace first thing. The lake is quiet, like it's sleeping.

The key is returned to his pocket. Not around his neck, then.

I wonder where he keeps it at night. In his shorts?

I'd love to be able to get in a late-night snack, but the thought of going through his shorts is nasty. They're a little shorter and tighter than they need to be. Ew.

Rebekah and I begin to bring tubs of cereal into the dining hall. There will be pastries too, but we don't need to get those out until closer to eight.

Andy hums as he works and pushes one hand through his red hair.

"I was impressed with how you both performed yesterday. You made your groups feel welcome. Were there any issues last night? Homesickness?"

"Nothing," Rebekah replies.

"I've never seen anyone fall asleep so fast," I say.

He laughs. "The first night is always like that. I assure you it won't be the same tonight."

"When Kayla and I were campers, we never fell asleep before lights-out. We'd whisper for hours," I say. It seemed like midnight back then, but in reality we were probably all asleep before ten p.m.

Rebekah adds, "The same with my camp."

Andy shakes his head. "It's been a long time since I was a camper."

"You came here?" I ask, surprised.

"Yes, probably before you two were even born."

"How old are you?" I ask.

Rebekah's eyes go round as if I've just asked Andy to strip.

"What?" I mouth at her.

"Almost thirty," he replies, not taking his eyes off the notice board where he's pinning up camp expectations.

See, he didn't care. He knows how old we are anyway.

"The boys snore."

Rebekah, Andy and I all startle at Olly's voice.

He walks into the hall, rubbing his eyes. "Is there coffee?"

Andy laughs. "Not yet. I've opened the hall so you can make some. I moved the coffee maker into the kitchen now that the campers are here."

Olly frowns like that was a dumb idea.

"We don't want a bunch of seven- to ten-year-olds caffeinated to their eyeballs," I tell him. And I don't want to share with even more people.

Andy nods. "The coffee is for the staff."

I'll never get used to that being me.

"Please hurry," I tell Olly. "I'm dying for coffee."

"Well, if your life depends on it . . . ," he says, smirking at me as he walks past. His eyes are playful, and I turn away before I blush brighter than the bottles of ketchup on each table.

Rebekah's gaze moves between me and Olly. When I look up, she turns around as if embarrassed to be caught looking.

6

You know what sucks?

Volleyball in thirty-thousand-degree heat.

All right, I don't know the *exact* temperature, but thirty thousand feels pretty damn accurate.

The campers still don't seem to care. They all have water and hats and are young enough for extreme heat to take a backseat to fun. I can't remember being like that, but I must have because I definitely didn't complain about the weather when I was here as a kid.

Maybe I really *am* an almost-adult. Is that what seals your grown-up fate? Being too hot or too cold?

"Well done, girls," I say to my group as they play against Cora's.

Kayla and her group are off with Tia and Mary's. They're swimming in the lake, where normal people are in high temperatures. There's an instructor teaching the campers the butterfly stroke.

We're in the lake after lunch, and I cannot wait.

Cora calls another point for my team and the girls play on.

Cora blows out a breath and wipes her forehead with the back of her hand. "I'm dying."

"I know the feeling," I say, sucking on the straw of my water bottle. "I should have picked a cooler state to be a CIT."

Laughing, she replies, "Yeah, it's *hot.* Stick to the shaded areas and drink plenty of water. As far as I know, we've never had anyone suffer sunstroke."

"The first will probably be me."

"Take a drink." She turns to the girls. "All right, great game. Let's wrap it up and go inside for lunch."

There's a collective cheer as we head to the hall for food.

Cora and I follow the girls inside.

We're a little late. Everyone else is already sitting down. The air-conditioning welcomes me, making the skin on my forearms pebble.

It's loud, with dozens of conversations merging together to make one big chorus of noise.

The girls get food and head to a table together. Cora and I wait until they've gone to get ours. I add some salad to my plate of mac and cheese and sit at the table with Kayla, Tia, Rebekah, Olly and Jake.

"Tomorrow night, we're going around the lake and into the forest on the other side," Rebekah tells me, her eyes wide like she's not at all comfortable with this.

I don't like it around there, but I say, "Sounds good."

I look over at Kayla. She has a brilliant poker face, but her anxiety shows physically. She will trip on air or fall up steps. Basically, she turns clumsy when she's anxious.

Kayla stabs her fork into her pasta, but the fork slides and she flings a noodle into the center of the table.

And there it is.

She looks up and her worried eyes meet mine.

A couple of the others chuckle. No one but me picks up on her nervous energy.

"Slippery?" I ask.

She clears her throat. "Mascarpone sauce."

She worries about me overthinking and blurting the wrong thing out. I worry about her clumsiness giving us away.

I want to ask her again if we're sure being here is a good idea.

We're guilty of a crime that no one even suspects us of.

My parents are superbig on honesty. "The truth always comes out, Esme."

Cold cases get solved. Not many—2 percent according to TV documentaries I've watched—but better technology means criminals are being caught years later.

Could our DNA *still* be at the scene ten years later?

Unlikely.

7

The next morning is filled with excitement. It's like the kids think we're going to Disney World, not hiking.

Kayla and I will be with Cora. I don't think we're trusted to take a group off into the woods alone yet.

Despite being a competent map reader, I'm really okay with this. I don't remember the trails from before. Back then I was messing around with Kayla and the other girls from our cabin.

The campers chow down on breakfast like they're fed only once a day. I'm sure they eat about as much as the staff.

I'm sitting at a table with Olly and Tia. The rest have finished and gone back to the cabins.

"We have the night off," I say with a grin.

Tia's dark eyes light up. Her hair is tied back in another sleek bun today. "Oh yes. Remember, we're going around the back of the lake tonight."

"Sure."

I look out the large window in the hall, my eyes following

the dock, then out across the lake to the line of trees that hide a secret.

I gulp down the last of my water and pick up my plate, the half-eaten croissant now unappealing.

"You're already done, Esme? You've barely eaten anything," Olly says.

"Too hot," I reply, as if it's perfectly reasonable to go hiking on a few bites of pastry. "I'll see you guys outside."

I dump my food and put the plate on the trolley.

Andy raises one hand as I walk past him. He half covers his mouth, chewing at the same time as he says, "Esme."

I stop beside him. "What's up?"

He stands. "Are you feeling okay? I noticed you throwing away your breakfast."

I blink. Is there anything he doesn't notice? When we leave camp, I hope he's not as sharp-eyed.

"Um, I'm fine, just not very hungry."

"Perhaps you should take something? We're going to be hiking all morning."

I nod. "I'll grab an apple."

I know he said to keep an eye on the campers and make sure they're all eating enough and especially drinking enough water, but I didn't think he would be policing me, too.

Weird.

Andy smiles and moves out of my way. I duck past and leave the hall with a Granny Smith apple in my hand.

Kayla is ready when I get back to our room. She's sitting on her bunk chatting to Cora.

"Esme, good. We were just going over a few things," Cora says, leaning against the wall.

"What's that?"

"You and I will walk at the front of the group; we'll try to keep them in twos, but it doesn't always work. Kayla will be at the back."

"Okay."

"We need to check their backpacks and make sure they have the appropriate gear: a compass, map, sun hat, sunscreen and water. If we each check bags, that would be great."

"I think they're ready," Kayla says, laughing and nodding toward the sudden noise in the room adjoining.

"Let's do it." I grab my bag and we all head into the main bedroom.

The girls are stuffing things into their bags. I go straight to the two bunks right at the end that sleeps the four girls in my group.

I take Isabel's bag first and look inside. "Okay, everyone make sure you have the map and compass on your bed and put it in." I run through the final few things and double-check that we're all set.

Once we're done, we meet up outside with the other groups, and Andy assigns trails to us. There are four trails in total.

I pull my cap on my head. Cora and I lead the group along the red trail. Inside the forest there is welcome shade.

The girls behind us are superexcited for a little trek in the woods. Getting away from the camp for a while was one of my favorite things as a camper; it kept it exciting rather than seeing the same campsite and activities for weeks.

"How long have you been a counselor here?" I ask Cora.

She smiles. "Three years full, one CIT. Do you think you'll be back next year?"

"I'm not sure yet. I am enjoying this, but the responsibilities counselors have scare me a little."

"By the time the campers are picked up again, it won't seem scary at all. It's like that for everyone. You'll realize soon that the kids actively prevent themselves from starving, and drowning too."

Laughing, I reply, "Well, that's good to hear."

I don't know why I worry so much. At eight I was relatively independent and fairly good at knowing I shouldn't run toward danger.

But then I got tangled up in something bad . . .

"You should definitely consider coming back next year," Cora says. "You're great with the girls and they love you. It's always easy to figure out who will make it. I can tell ten minutes after they've met the campers."

"Are you ever wrong?"

She straightens her back with pride. "Nope."

"So, you've worked with Andy a lot." I want to ask about the Buttercups, but I don't want to seem nosy, and I don't want her to know that we've nicknamed them.

"Yeah, Andy, Mary and Catalina have been here for years."

So they have all been here before.

"Cool."

She side-eyes me and lifts one dark eyebrow. "What do you want to ask? I can tell there's something."

"No . . . Yes. Well, it's just that I can't figure him out," I say, stumbling over my words.

"Andy's cool. A little old school sometimes, and he loves rules. I don't think he has broken one. *Ever.*"

I nod and step over a fallen log. Ahead I see a red rag tied around a tree branch.

When we get past the trail, the girls will have a go at orienteering, leading us away from the mapped-out path to get back to camp. At least, that's the hope.

"Are the other groups near us?" a girl asks.

"Not really, we're all spread out," Cora replies.

"I saw someone."

Cora stops and everyone else does too. I turn around with Cora and see Ava's big eyes looking up at us.

"What's going on?" Kayla calls from the back.

"What did you see, Ava?" I ask.

I don't like this.

With a frown, Ava steps up to me.

"Someone in the woods. They were really far away, so I can't be sure, but I think it was a boy."

"It was a child?"

She shakes her head. "Um, no, a grown-up. They were tall."

My heart sinks.

Cora tells the girls to sit down and take a water break.

Kayla joins us, her face full of worry.

"Ava, are you *sure*?" Cora asks.

"Yeah. I was going to point the person out, but when I looked back, he was *gone.*"

The girls are all chatting about who it could have been. The word *killer* almost makes my eyes roll. They'll be telling campfire stories about this all summer, imaginations going wild.

Cora and I look at each other. Some trees have fallen; others have been cut down. Ava could have seen one and thought it was a person. When she looked again, she saw nothing because there are only trees.

The land we're on is private. It belongs to the camp.

"Ava, what did the person do?" Cora asks, wrapping one arm around her.

Her head tilts all the way up. "He was just standing there. I'm not making this up."

"No one thinks you are," I tell her, glancing back in the direction she said "he" was. I point. "Do you think it could have been a tree? You see there, the tree stump with no branches nestled between the normal ones?"

Ava frowns as she looks. "You think it was that?"

"It could have been," Cora says. "I've done the same thing. Some of the trees are cut down for firewood, which makes a few of them human size. You did the right thing telling us, though."

"So there's no crazy guy out there?" Isabel asks.

"Definitely not!" Cora says. "All right, girls, everything is fine. The forest sometimes plays tricks on you, so remember you can come to us if you're ever unsure of *anything*. Let's get going again or we'll be the last team back. I might have heard Andy saying there's a surprise for the first team home."

The girls leap to their feet, the madman in the forest forgotten as they try to guess what the treat will be.

We've just stopped for five minutes to play Find the Human-Looking Tree. We might not win.

Cora and I lead the girls, with Kayla taking her place at the back.

I look at the trees, toward where Ava thought she saw something.

It would be very easy to hide.

8

Cora doesn't seem to give the idea of a person running between trees watching us a second thought.

I've given it a third, fourth and fifth thought.

I know what Ava saw wasn't really a person the way I know that I won't be instantly killed the second I turn off my light. But does that stop my imagination from trying to convince me otherwise? Nope.

My eyes dart back to the woods, getting lost in the density of the trees.

Why would anyone be watching us? It could have been someone passing by; we're close to the camp's perimeter. Perhaps they veered off course, saw us and realized where they were, then dashed back onto public land.

Cora has switched from small talk with me to singing with the girls. I wish she would stop that and ask me random questions again. I don't much feel like joining in with their poor rendition of "Alice the Camel."

They finish the tenth song and Cora takes a breath. "Okay, I don't think I can do another one," she says.

She doesn't need to. The girls start to sing their own, "Baby Bumblebee," which has to be one of the oddest and grossest camp songs. Why would anyone lick a smashed bee? You deserve to throw up, in all honesty.

"We're almost to the orienteering point," I say, glancing at my map. The red trail curls back around, but we're not going there. We're going to go off course and find our own way home. Hopefully, we should arrive back at camp in time for lunch. That's if the girls don't get us lost.

Five more minutes of walking through shaded heat and we reach a clearing. It's a man-made area with a firepit. It belongs to the camp and we'll use it for building dens and cooking later in the summer.

The girls cheer from behind me.

"Thank goodness for that!" Cora says. "Okay, everyone have a drink and then we'll let small groups of you lead at a time. Make sure you have your map orientated. If you start off wrong, you will never find where you want to be."

Isabel stops in front of me, her big eyes as worried as the day she had to say goodbye to her mom.

"Esme, was that really a tree Ava saw?"

My heart pounds. "Of course. It's easy to assume something perfectly innocent is something really scary in situations like this. Don't worry."

I smile to load up the reassurance. All the while my mind is going, *Killer in the woods.*

Isabel smiles, her posture relaxing as she takes a breath. "Okay. Good. Can you help me with my map? I don't know which way it's supposed to be."

"Sure," I reply, really hoping it will be obvious. With few landmarks, it's not likely to be straightforward.

Isabel holds out her map. My three other girls shuffle over to us, and I take a look at the map.

"Ah," I say, pointing to the trail. "This is where we've come from, look. We took the red trail to this clearing. Straight ahead is where it continues, but we're not going to go that way. We want to head directly back, so where would you go to do that?"

I peer up from the map and all four girls are staring at it with matching frowns.

Maisie points. "Well, this would be a straight line back to camp." She looks up. "I'd go between those two big trees with curly branches."

"Good, Maisie."

Cora, hearing us, calls, "Girls, Maisie has figured it out first, so we're going to let Esme's team lead for the first part. Make sure you follow on your maps as you'll all get a chance to take over. Now, the little crosses along the map represent landmarks. Where those crosses are on the map is where red ties will be on trees."

"Score for the E Team," Isabel says.

"Let's rock this," I cheer.

The other groups walk behind us. We have an hour before lunch. If we don't go wrong, we should make it back on time.

Kayla and Cora switch places. I think that shows Cora trusts us if she's willing to fall back and let us little CITs lead. Not that we're leading, four seven- and eight-year-olds are.

"How's it going, May-May?" Kayla asks, using my very old nickname.

I think she stopped using it after the last time we were here.

"Feeling pretty good, actually. I can't wait for tonight." I'm absolutely not thinking about someone else in the woods.

My group leads us through the forest, and we find each flag shown on the map. They have confidently chosen the correct path. I give each girl a high five as we hand the map reading to Cora's group.

"You guys did so good," I tell my group. Four toothy smiles beam at the praise.

I fall in line with Cora, who's leading now.

"How many of these hikes have you done?" I ask.

"I'm pretty sure I could do this without a map. Well, not this route; I'm usually on the north side. The flags aren't spaced too far apart, though."

"Yeah, I noticed that."

"The next hike we do, we remove every other flag to make the girls rely more on the map rather than just walking and looking for a colored rag."

"That's the all-day hike?"

Cora nods. "They'll all make their own shelters. Sometimes the shelters even last the whole night."

Great, I'm going to sleep under the stars and get eaten alive by bugs.

Cora laughs at my expression. I'm sure I look like I want to run home. "You'll be fine. Don't worry."

"I'm not sleeping in a tent without my hair straighteners," Sophia says. She is in Cora's group and although she is sweet, she's high maintenance and kind of a princess. It came as no surprise to learn that she's an only child and here purely because her parents wanted her to experience something different.

I'm glad the girls in my group don't mind getting their hands dirty and their hair messy.

"You'll survive too, Sophia," Cora replies, laughing.

"Are we doing anything fun this afternoon?" she asks, running her fingers over her long black plait.

"We're on the lake."

"Do we have to do anything on the lake?"

Cora's smile tightens and I can tell she wants to roll her eyes. "No one is going to make you do anything."

"You might enjoy it if you try," I tell her. "You can always get out if you don't."

Sophia shrugs. "Maybe."

She has probably lost where we are on the map now.

Cora takes a deep breath. She's makeup-free and wears shorts and T-shirts exclusively, so I can't imagine she has a lot in common with Sophia.

The girls ahead stop and look around.

"Where are we, girls?" I ask.

My group turns to me, their foreheads furrowed. "Er . . . I have no clue," Audrey says. "There should be a flag here.

Look"—she points to the *X* on the map—"the flag should be right in front of us."

I walk up to her and look at the cross. She's right, we should be standing beside a flag on a tree that Kayla is currently scowling at.

"Are we lost?" Isabel asks.

Cora looks up, alarmed. "No, we've just gone wrong a step, but don't worry, we have the map and there are plenty of flags. If we pick up another color flag, that's fine. We'll just take that route."

Cora sounds so sure. She is right to be—I'm sure too. But the girls do not look convinced.

"Hey, it's fine," I tell them. "Cora is right. There are plenty of paths out here and they all lead back to camp."

They nod, satisfied with my answer. For now.

"Okay, we're going to go east and pick up the other trail," Kayla says, scanning her map. "It looks like the flag is gone . . . or we've detoured."

Cora gives her a thumbs-up. "See, girls. We'll be back on track in a few minutes."

Cora and I resume leading and take us east.

I lick my lips and take a sip of water.

"You know this new trail?" I ask Cora as we get a few steps ahead of the girls.

"Kind of."

I frown. Her "kind of" is not at all selling it to me. "Why would the flag not be here?"

All we can see around us are tall trees. The flags are the landmarks.

Cora shrugs. "It probably is. I think it's most likely that we've veered off course. We might see it in a minute and pick up the track again. If not we'll move to green flags—those are on the trail nearest to us. It doesn't matter how we get back."

It only matters that we get back. We've been walking deeper into the forest for about an hour now, without knowing where we are on the map. How do we find our way back if we don't see another flag? We could go in circles until we pass out from the heat.

I swallow the hysteria conjured by my own damn imagination, and push forward.

Our bodies would decompose quickly in this heat.

Shut up!

Kayla is always telling me to calm down. I'm terrible. Whenever someone is late, I assume something bad has happened.

Because sometimes bad things *do* happen.

Cora's lips press into a thin line. Her eyebrows knit together. She's getting worried.

She is not alone. No one is saying anything negative, but we're all wondering why we haven't seen a red or green flag yet.

Kayla, Cora and I don't want the girls to be alarmed. They're young and they're likely to be scared if they knew the truth right now. We don't know where we are.

Cora has very cleverly started a conversation about Roblox. Most of the girls play it or want to; they chat incessantly about the game, telling each other what they've done on it and what they want to do. They swap tips and tricks and it leads them away from our reality.

We are lost in the forest.

9

Cora chews her lip, visibly uneasy now.

Her head swings around every few minutes, making her hair sway. She's scanning the trees for evidence of ripped flags.

"How much longer?" Ava asks.

I make myself smile. "Shouldn't be too long now. Are you getting hungry?"

"I'm starving!" Sophia answers for us all.

Lunch was supposed to be fifteen minutes ago.

When will Andy begin to worry? We have a phone for emergencies. Cora has placed her hand over her pocket a few times. She's probably considering when the right time to call would be.

I know what she's doing. She wants to show the girls how to orient yourself when you're lost.

But there's a reason we haven't found a single flag landmark yet.

Someone has removed them.

It's so obvious. Why else would they be missing? Colored rags do not untie themselves from tree branches. I'm no wildlife expert, but I do know that squirrels can't work knots.

"Esme," Cora calls, and she comes to a stop. Her voice is sharp, and a cold shiver ripples down my spine.

Her eyes, round and brimmed with defeat, stare back at me. With a quick nod, she gives me the answer we've all been longing for. Yes, we can call for help now.

"Hey, look!" I say, my eyes catching something red. Cora is a step behind me as I jog to the scrap of material on the ground by a tree.

"Is that the flag?" Maisie asks.

I swipe the flag off the ground and hand it to Cora.

"Someone ripped this off the tree and left a piece behind. Who would do that?" Cora says.

I shrug one shoulder. "We're on track, though. Just a shame we don't know which cross this relates to on the map."

"Yeah. I think we should still call Andy."

Kayla catches up to us.

The girls are whispering about what's happened. Hushed voices are spurting all sorts of crazy stories.

"It was definitely ripped off," I tell Cora and Kayla, keeping my voice low. The girls are already suspicious and pretty much think there is a madman after us, especially since Ava thought she saw someone watching us.

Did she?

"Do you think that Ava could have seen a person?" I whisper. "The same person who's taken the flags off, so we got lost?"

Cora shakes her head, frowning like I've just asked if she believes all of those Area 51 conspiracy theories.

I do not. If I'm an alien visiting Earth, I'm going to the Bahamas, not Nevada.

"Drink some water, Esme," Kayla tells me.

Now she thinks I'm delirious.

I take my water bottle out of my bag and pretend I can't see Kayla's tight lips and tense eyes. It's her way of telling me to get ahold of myself.

That would be wonderful, but I can't until we're safely back at camp.

"All right, girls. It looks like we've veered off course, so we're going to make a call to Andy for some assistance," Cora tells them. "For now, take a break and hydrate. You should all have a protein bar, so have at it."

"Wait, what is that?" Isabel asks.

Ava stands on tiptoes. "Yeah, why is the flag on the ground?"

Cora tucks the marker into her pocket. "It's made of thin cotton, so it isn't a flag. Must have been left by someone."

She's quick with the lie there. She didn't even blink.

I should take lessons from her. When I lie, I'm sure my face is as red as a London bus. Kayla says it isn't, though. She has told me I'm quite a good liar. I've never quite known how to take that.

"Really?" Isabel asks.

I step up to her. "Really. I checked it myself. Take a seat with everyone else and rest. Once we have our bearings, we'll set off and go get some lunch."

She does as I say and takes a seat with the others. All of them look suspicious as hell.

"How do we know you three haven't taken us out here to do something?" Sophia asks.

Cora tilts her head. "Seriously, Sophia? I know you might be worried right now, but we're here to take care of you. Everything is fine and soon we'll be back at camp."

She huffs and sits down next to Ava.

I sip my water as I walk back to Cora and Kayla.

"Doesn't that thing have Google Maps?" I ask Kayla.

She smirks. "I asked the same thing. We won't get service, but Cora's going to ask Andy to message our location and the direction we're supposed to head."

"How's he going to do that?"

Kayla shrugs. "Do I look like a tech geek?"

With her glossy hair, manicured nails and hot pink sunglasses, no, she does not.

Cora is still talking on the phone. Her voice is as calm as always, as if she's letting Andy know we're almost there, not that we got lost in the forest with twelve young girls.

This isn't going to look good on my CIT record.

"Yes, that's correct . . . Looks like it was," Cora says into the cell.

I'm guessing Andy is asking about the ripped flags.

"All right, Andy has tracked the phone number and is sending us the directions back to camp."

"He tracked us?" I ask.

"Camp cell phone," she replies, holding it up.

Okay, that's less creepy.

"Good," I say, sliding my water bottle back into my bag.

"Looks like we need to go southeast and we'll be back shortly," Cora says after the phone beeps. "We're minutes away!"

She puts the phone away, opens her compass and starts to walk slowly.

"All right, we know where we are, and we're off. Up we get, girls," Cora says, waving her arms as she passes them.

"Are we close?" Ava asks.

"Ridiculously close," I reply. "Despite the lack of flags, we almost got back."

Sophia's shoulders drop. "But we didn't."

"But we will. Come on, do you want a big bowl of mac and cheese or not?"

Her eyes widen. "I do."

"Then let's go!"

Four minutes. That's how far away we were. If everyone was out on the lake or outside, we probably would have heard them.

"Mac and cheese," Ava cheers, followed by whoops and squeals from the other girls.

It's funny the psychology of being lost to post-lost.

The girls had been hunched, looking around, whispering, worrying. I was convinced we were goners and now I can see us splashing around in the lake this afternoon without a care in the world.

Now it's no big deal. The knowledge that we're almost back and there's mac and cheese waiting has them forgetting one very important thing.

The fact that someone wanted us to lose our way hasn't changed.

Whatever they think they believe because Cora told her white lie with conviction, they'd realize the truth if they thought about it for a second.

Red material dropped by someone else at the same time our red flags go missing? Unlikely.

Kayla falls in line with me. This time Cora trusts both of us to be at the back and make sure none of the girls decide to run away. As if at this point they would be so stupid.

What with a flag-stealing stalker maniac out there and all.

"Something is off, right?" I whisper.

Kayla shrugs. "Think about it logically."

"I have."

"Who could it be?" she asks.

"I don't know who!" Not *exactly.* "People do all kinds of crazy stuff for all sorts of reasons. Some just because they're bored. Maybe someone from town is trying to make it an eventful summer."

"Then don't worry about it, Esme. They've had their fun."

"Yeah, but what if they're just getting started?"

"Babe, stop. You're going to fry that big brain of yours if you don't stop thinking."

I'm not usually this bad. It's being back *here.*

"Okay, I'm done," I tell Kayla, mostly to stop her from thinking too much about who could be out here. And I'll do my best to ignore what my mind is trying to convince me of. It's like my mind and I are separate entities sometimes. The battle of staying sane versus letting hysteria take over.

I don't want to think the worst. This summer is supposed to be fun and I'm letting what is probably some innocent prank get to me.

Kayla and I pulled pranks when we were here. Everyone does. It usually starts with the counselors once the campers have settled in. Then it goes back and forth.

The most likely culprits are teens from town who have wandered onto camp property and stolen some flags from the trees.

A cheer from the girls jolts me from my incessant thoughts.

My muscles unlock.

We're back.

The trees give way to open land and a glorious body of water. I am so freaking happy to see the lake!

The girls run for the food hall chanting about mac and cheese. Andy laughs and steps out of their way before they trample him.

He waits for us to catch up.

"Thank God we're back," Cora says. "Thanks, Andy."

"What happened?"

She takes the scrap of red material out of her pocket. "Looks like someone has been having fun on camp grounds."

Andy takes it from her hand. "Someone has taken the flags off?"

"Yeah."

Muttering something under his breath, he straightens his shoulders. "I'll deal with this. We'll have Garret and Ward come in and set the flags up again. Go eat. And well done on staying calm and getting help when you needed it."

I smile at Andy, feeling like a bit of a fraud for accepting his praise along with Cora and Kayla. I didn't show the girls that I was worried, I suppose. That's what counts.

"You good?" Kayla asks me.

"Yep. You?"

"I'm fine," she replies, and trips over the threshold of the food hall.

Yeah, me neither.

10

It's nine at night. I'm outside with Kayla, Tia, Rebekah, Olly and Jake. We're going for a walk.

The campers are tucked in bed and it'll be lights-out soon. Not that they'll stop whispering and go to sleep. It's such a relief to be able to relax after all of the lost-in-the-woods excitement. Except I didn't find it very exciting.

Kayla has stopped being clumsy, so I'm pretty sure she's moved on. She's very good at pushing something out of her mind if she doesn't like it. I wish I could do the same.

It was probably someone from town messing around. At least, that seems to have won the whodunit votes. It's not the first time that teens have wandered onto camp property and messed around, according to Andy; occasionally they've been caught and cautioned by the cops.

Now that we're out of the woods and I've eaten, I can see how over the top I was being. Kids have been hauled away by cops and taken back to town. The path through the forest leads our way, so it's easy for townies to reach the camp.

The fear of being lost and thinking that Ava saw someone got to me in a big way.

Just because the camp looks like a horror movie set does not mean it is one.

I don't know exactly when we're going to sneak into town. There was talk of next week, but after we got lost today, I think the others are hesitant.

It better be worth it. I'll probably stress the whole damn time that we'll be caught.

"Almost to the other side," Rebekah says as we walk around the lake.

I hate being this far away from camp.

Every day after the accident I would almost hyperventilate being so close to where it happened. I still remember taking this very route, then Kayla and I veered left into the woods and things got . . . bad.

But that was years ago. I'm not the same person I was back then.

It was easier to be on this side of the lake earlier, when we finally arrived back from the hike. Everyone was so relieved to have found camp again, I didn't think about how close we were to the accident site.

After getting lost in the forest, I don't much feel like being very close to that place again. But that doesn't mean I need to fear it.

The others turn, and I follow them between the trees, my stomach tightening.

"Will you stop stressing," Kayla hisses in my ear. "I can see those dark eyes filling with anxiety."

"Kayla, I don't like this—"

"Stop. You always look on the negative side whenever something is even slightly suspicious. Or not suspicious at all!"

"This isn't about the forest thing. I get what that was now, okay?" I shake my head. "It's passing that place. . . ."

"Don't. We're not talking about that ever again, remember? We made a pact. A *blood* pact."

It can hardly be called a blood pact. We both cut ourselves while we were running through the edge of the forest to get back before the counselors woke up. We promised not to tell and shook on it. There was blood on our hands.

"Fine. Okay, you're right," I tell her. "I thought it would be easier to be back here after so many years."

"It freaked me out too at first, but you have to get over it. What happened wasn't our fault. We were kids, Esme."

Smiling, I nod. "I'm forgetting it. Let's join everyone else; they're ahead."

Olly looks over his shoulder as Kayla and I speed up.

His frown is wiped away by a smile. "Come on, Esme, we're almost there."

"Almost where?"

"To the fire damage."

Kayla's steps falter at his words and she trips. I grab her elbow, holding her upright. "Tree roots," I say aloud to cover up the real reason Kayla almost wiped out.

That's where we're going?

No way.

"You okay?" Jake asks, jogging back.

Kayla blushes. "I'm so clumsy!" Jake holds his hand out and she takes it.

Can't she pretend to faint and get us out of this?

Jake and Kayla walk ahead of Olly and me.

"Why are we going there?" I ask, trying to keep my voice even and not Minnie Mouse high. Olly doesn't so much as blink, so I know I sound normal.

"Andy won't say much about the fire. I think he's embarrassed on behalf of the camp that it happened. Kids alone in the woods, starting a fire, almost burning the place down . . . It doesn't look good."

"Huh? How do you know?"

"People talk, Esme," he says.

Do they? No one was caught. There were rumors circulating, but no one talked. Kayla and I have never talked.

"What happened?" I ask, trying to figure out how much Olly knows. He thinks the fire was started by someone at camp?

"Word is a group of kids from town snuck into the woods and their campfire got out of hand."

Yeah, that's what everyone thinks. The fire department and police. I remember the cops the morning after the fire talking to the counselors.

Kayla and I were petrified that they'd come for us, but the damage wasn't to camp property.

"There's another theory, however," Olly continues.

I hold my hands behind my back. "About campers?"

He nods. "Some people think a group of campers snuck out of the cabin and lit a fire in the woods in the middle of the night. It got out of hand, but by the time counselors were alerted, the campers were already back in their beds."

I lick my lips. *Diffuse, diffuse, diffuse.* "How could they sneak in and out during a fire and not be noticed?"

Olly shrugs. "Kids are sneaky."

Play. It. Cool.

I gulp down what I think will come out as manic laughter. "True. So, we're going to look at burned wood. We've really peaked on the boredom scale, huh?"

Olly laughs. "All right, there's not a lot to do, I'll give you that. We're out of here soon and heading into town."

"What happens if we get caught?"

"Andy will likely tell us how disappointed he is. Then we'll never be allowed out of our cabins in the evening. We'll have to be asleep by nine like the campers."

"We're not getting caught, then."

He laughs again. "No getting caught."

I'm good at that. So is Kayla.

I take a deep breath. Everyone still thinks the fire was caused by kids from town, which means Lillian never spilled either. I just need to get through these six weeks and never return.

"Here it is," Tia says, bouncing up and down. She shines her flashlight around. There is a large clearing. A five-minute walk from camp.

I stand at the edge of the forest and do a three-sixty, looking around in every direction. This is crazy.

My heart thumps against my rib cage. My chest tightens. A lot of work has gone into these woods to make sure forest fires don't get out of hand—strips of land between the trees, large circles of rocks around campfires, and fire prevention signage.

Those rocks saved the woods that night. We accidentally set fire to only three trees. It was contained.

But that wasn't the worst thing that happened here.

11

Today we're going to the lake for swimming lessons. Thankfully not taught by me. I'm confident I could swim to save my life, but I'm nowhere near good enough to be able to teach. Besides, I'm not qualified.

We also have water volleyball. The lake is very deep, and dark, in the middle, but about three-quarters of the way in, there's a ring of rope that we're not supposed to go beyond.

"I remember being excited for a day on the lake," I say to Kayla, and take a big gulp of my second coffee.

"Yeah, it was so much fun. The kids are going to love it."

This is our first full day in the water and around it. We're having a picnic lunch on the beach and dinner around the campfire. Andy had a *lot* of burgers and hot dogs delivered early this morning to feed hungry children.

I can almost taste the lightly charred hot dogs just from thinking about them.

"I can't wait to get in the water. Texas is so hot," I say.

Kayla smirks. "You're getting in?"

"Totally. I can referee volleyball or something." I haven't been able to focus on anything since last night. Not even sleep. I see angry orange flames consuming three trees so clearly that it's as if it's happening right now. The screams are imbedded in my memory, refusing to leave no matter how hard I try.

"Ready to go get changed?" Cora asks, stopping by our table.

I nod and grab my empty bowl and mug.

"See you out there," I tell Kayla.

Cora and I head out. As we walk, she asks, "Where did you go last night? I saw you guys walking around the lake and into the woods."

I lick my lips. "Tia wanted to see the old fire damage."

"Gosh, that was so bad. It was lucky the fire didn't take hold."

"Seemed to be held up by the rocks," I say as if I have no idea.

"Yeah. The trees in the middle of the clearing were the only ones that burned, thankfully."

Cora knows a lot about this.

My heart skips a beat. "Were you here then?"

I don't remember her.

"No. I had a good look around when I first came as a CIT, though. It's such a nice man-made campsite, shame the dead trees ruin it."

That's all that's left. The forest has recovered; new growth has long hidden the mess left behind on the ground. But the burned trees are still there, one of them just a stump. I'm hit with a pang of guilt whenever I think about it. Which has been often lately.

If the site hadn't been man-made and the ground cleared to

protect the forest when campfires were used, the whole woods could have gone up.

Kayla and I almost destroyed acres of forest and the campsite.

Cora heads down to the lake while I return to the cabin to change into my bathing suit. I tie my long hair up on my head, pinch my pale cheeks to give them some color and stare into my green eyes. They really are the color of leaves on a tree. As if I need more reminders of what I've done.

Grabbing my towel, I head to the lake. Some of the campers are in the water already, with the swim instructors taking groups of eight each. The other campers are by the two volleyball nets and split into teams. The Buttercups, who aren't actually twins or even related, are in the water near the volleyball nets, as are Olly and Jake. I bet Kayla regrets her decision to be on swim watch now.

Out of nowhere, a young girl from Cora's group runs in front of me and trips on a large rock. She lands on the ground with a thud. For some reason, when she falls, I startle more than I should.

"Alana, are you okay?" I ask.

She's a shy girl. She looks up from the ground and I can tell she's holding back tears.

I sit down next to her. "Let me see."

With trembling hands, I inspect her knee. There's only a slight scrape and it's not bleeding. Still, I can hear my heart beating in my ears.

"I'm okay," Alana says.

"Do you want me to get you an ice pack?"

She hesitates, then shakes her head. "I want to get in the lake."

"Great. Our groups are doing volleyball first. Shall we go?"

She stands and her eyes dart to the swimmers. "I can't swim. I've never had lessons."

"You'll be able to by the end of the summer. There are lessons three times a week."

We walk around the lake to the others.

"Most of my friends can already swim," she says.

"You'll be able to tell them you can too when you go back to school."

Alana beams, her big eyes alight with the excitement of such a simple skill. She doesn't want to be the best swimmer in the world or go for the Olympics, she just wants to be able to do it like her friends.

She seems to have already forgotten about her fall. But I haven't.

"Stay waist-high, Alana," I tell her as she splashes into the lake.

She shouts a very quick okay over her shoulder and joins her team.

"All okay?" Cora asks.

"Um, yeah. Just a small scrape," I say.

Cora nods. "Thanks for taking care of her. I'll follow up later and see how she's doing."

"For sure."

I barely hear Cora tell me she is going to check out the water. My mind is still elsewhere. Back at the night of the fire. Only now, new memories are surfacing. They came to me the minute Alana hit the ground and have only grown clearer since. Kayla and I had snuck out. When we reached the clearing, we built a small fire, but we used too many logs. Only after the fire was burning did a young girl come out of the woods. She told us her name was Lillian and that she had run away from home. She wanted to show us something. Something . . . horrible. Kayla called her a freak and pushed her. Lillian fell, knocking the wood from the firepit. The flames started to spread, hot and vicious, and we all ran.

Or at least I thought we all ran.

But now something nags at my mind. The image of Lillian sprawled on the ground.

Did she run?

And if she didn't, what happened to her?

Where is Lillian now?

12

Kayla and I are sitting on the bottom bunk in our room. The campers are having s'mores after dinner and we've come inside while Andy tells some of his "infamous" ghost stories. I haven't heard any of them yet, but Cora says they're pretty lame, though highly entertaining.

"So, you don't think Lillian ran?" Kayla asks. Her fingers knit together and then she unfolds them like she's performing jazz hands.

Her back is straight as a board and I don't think she's blinked in the past few minutes.

"I can't be sure. But I don't remember seeing her get up," I say.

"That doesn't mean she didn't."

"I know that."

Kayla shakes her head.

"She could have." I take a breath that feels like I'm swallowing razors. "But she was already hurt."

"Maybe she was still there when the cops arrived and they picked her up?"

I kick my feet up on the mattress. "Maybe. But last night Olly said that no one knows who started the fire. If the cops picked Lillian up, then surely they would've pinned it on her."

"What if the cops couldn't say anything publicly because she was a minor?" Kayla says.

"Okay, I'm not really interested in what the cops think."

"You should be, Esme!"

"We know she didn't light the damn fire—we did! What I'm worried about is what happened to her after we ran. Were we the last ones to see her? Did she get into some sort of trouble?"

Kayla and I panicked and ran, flattening ourselves against trees and watching to see whether any lights came on in the cabins. We never bothered to look back.

"Why didn't you tell me any of this before?" she says.

I shake my head. "I guess because I wasn't sure. But every time I think about it, I hear the roar of the fire and those screams."

"Okay. Okay." Kayla sits even taller. "Right. Okay. Right."

Ugh, I want to throw something at her. "Kayla, use other words!"

"I'm thinking! You know, it wasn't our fault. We weren't the ones who started the trouble that night."

That sounds like something you say to justify your actions. Are you guilty because you didn't stop something from happening? Yes. We had the power that night to help and we didn't do *anything*.

"We need to find out where Lillian is," I tell Kayla.

I can't stop thinking that maybe she was injured more than we thought.

"I'm going to Google her. There could be an article about it, right?" I say, pulling my phone out of my bag on the floor.

Kayla leans forward to look over my shoulder as I type *fire, Texas* and *Lillian Campbell* into the search bar.

I shake my head, scrolling as I pass names and faces that don't match.

Come on.

I bite my lip in frustration. No one looks familiar.

Please.

"None of these kids look like Lillian," I say.

"Well, that's good. We don't want to find her in the news."

"True," I mutter. I sigh and drop my phone in my lap when the internet comes up empty. "Okay, I've got nothing."

"Good." Kayla brushes her hair over her shoulders. "That means we didn't do anything."

I side-eye her. "It only means it's not online. What we did was very real."

"Esme." Kayla says my name like all of this is exclusively my fault.

We were so dumb that night, thinking we were cool for sneaking out like the older kids. Kayla was so excited as we left the cabin, thinking about how she was going to tell them the next day.

But when we got into bed that night, we vowed to never tell anyone.

That night she also lost her desire to be popular. Mostly.

Kayla wants this to all go away, for it to be a buried memory that she never digs up.

Something is wrong here. I feel it in the skittering of my heart whenever I think about that night. Lillian was a little girl alone in the woods. We had no idea who she was; we only spoke to her for about five minutes before the fire got out of hand.

"Come on, let's go join the others before they get suspicious," I say, sliding my useless phone back in my bag. This is getting us nowhere.

Kayla hops up and knocks her water bottle off the dresser at the end of our bunk. It rolls under her bed.

"Damn it," she hisses, kneeling on the floor to reach under the bed and pick the bottle up.

At this point, we don't even need me to state the obvious. Kayla is worried too.

She ducks her head, refusing to meet my eye. I wasn't going to say anything to her anyway.

"Let's get a s'more," I say as we walk outside.

That's code for "let's act normal."

"All right, campers," Andy says. "We need you to get a good night's sleep tonight because tomorrow there is a summer school exam you're required to take."

A rumble of unhappy conversation tears through the groups of kids.

Kayla and I look at each other.

"What's this about?" I ask Cora as we sit next to her.

She shrugs, her mouth failing to hide a smile.

Oh, I get it. Andy's pranking them.

"Settle down, settle down," he says, waving his arms up and down. "This will be the only test you have to take and it's for us to see what math group to put you in."

"Math!"

I don't know who said it; I only know that the sound pierced my freaking eardrums. Wincing, I plug my knuckles into my ears and rattle them until the ringing stops.

Andy laughs and addresses the loud child. "All right, Cady." He turns to the group. "I was, of course, joking. There are no tests at camp."

The children grumble at his lame attempt to prank them but cheer for the lack of tests.

"We're going to get you back, Andy!" Zak from Olly's group shouts.

Andy smirks. "I invite you to try."

The mood lifts. A tinge of excitement makes my heart leap. I loved getting involved in silly pranks. Some of my favorites were putting food coloring in the milk dispensers, icing cleaning sponges to look like cake and stuffing counselors' shoes with tissue.

Now it's on.

Kayla rubs her hands together. "We need to think of something to do to them."

"There is plenty," Cora replies.

We sit and plot pranks by the fire, eating s'mores and chatting about how much fun the next few weeks are going to be.

I only forget Lillian for a second.

We don't know that she was *really* hurt that night. She probably ran away too. There is nothing to suggest that she didn't get home safely.

I am letting this thought reassure me when I look up and find Rebekah staring me down from across the campfire.

13

Three guesses for who didn't sleep well last night.

I hug my mug of coffee in my hands and wish I could have it in an IV.

The girls are learning how to make safe campfires on the edge of the forest. The counselors have got this one since they're trained. That means the CITs are free for the morning and we're in the hall having a late breakfast.

I'm sitting at a table with Kayla, Tia, Olly, Jake and Rebekah. After I caught her staring at me across the fire last night, Rebekah quickly looked away and it hasn't come up since. I was probably overreacting anyway, considering the state I was in last night. A leaf falling on my shoulder would've made me jump ten feet.

"I've missed sleeping in," I say, yawning behind my mug.

Olly laughs. "It feels like it's been weeks. Hey, do you want to take a walk before we have to build dens with the campers?"

I nod as the back of my neck heats. A walk in the woods is

about as close as you can get to a date here. Not that he's asking me out.

Is he?

Don't act weird.

"Sounds good," I say.

The very last thing I'm about to do is make eye contact with Kayla. She will absolutely be giving me *the look.* That goofy expression your friends give you when your crush talks to you. It's a dead giveaway.

"You ready now?" Olly asks.

He keeps eye contact so casually, like this is no big deal.

Because it isn't a big deal. Chill out!

"Uh-huh," I mutter as words fail me.

I sip the last of my coffee and Olly takes my bowl, stacking it on top of his.

My stomach flutters.

"Have fun," Kayla sings. Tia and Rebekah giggle behind their spoons, dropping cereal onto the table.

I ignore them and get up. Olly dumps the bowls and we leave the food hall. The heat hits my face. I'm glad I tied my hair up this morning and applied the standard thick layer of sunscreen.

"They've gone east, so let's go west," he says.

I turn and smile. "Okay."

"You cool, Esme? You haven't been yourself the last couple of days," Olly says after a minute. We walk into the forest, where the air is slightly cooler, more bearable.

Not been myself? He's only known me for a week. "I'm good. A little tired."

"Did sleeping late this morning help?"

Nodding, I say, "Yeah, it was awesome." It wasn't. I stayed in bed but didn't sleep in. "Hey, what's your favorite movie?"

"Are you going Ghostface on me, Esme?"

A twig snaps under my sneaker. "I didn't ask your favorite *scary* movie."

"Horror isn't my thing. My favorite is *The Godfather Part II*. What's yours?"

"You're going to think I'm superlame."

He chuckles. "It's a chick flick, isn't it?"

"I'm a total sucker for them. *Pretty Woman* is genius. And *27 Dresses*."

"You're a romantic."

We head deeper into the forest, keeping camp just in view. "Guilty. My parents have always been supersweet to each other."

"You're lucky. Mine divorced when I was a kid."

"I'm sorry," I tell him.

Olly shrugs like it's no big deal. "What pranks do you think the campers are going to pull?" he asks, changing the subject.

"I don't know, but always check the toilet thoroughly before you pee."

"Saran Wrap?"

I nod. "Would make a hell of a nasty mess."

"I'll be checking."

I grab his wrist when something crunches deeper in the forest. My gaze flies in the direction the sound came from. "What was that?"

"What?" Olly looks around. "Esme, what did you hear?"

"Twigs breaking."

Olly's shoulders relax. "It's probably an animal."

I slide my eyes to him. "Animals usually don't come too close with all the noise at camp."

It's bright this morning, but the trees block the sun. The forest is swallowed by darkness.

"Whatever it is, it's probably gone. Why are you freaking out? Seriously, I didn't hear anything, Esme," he says.

You won't if you keep talking!

I drop his wrist. "You're right. It was probably an animal. Sorry, it just spooked me."

"I've never minded hot girls grabbing hold of me."

His words light up in my mind like the Las Vegas Strip.

He called you hot. Don't cackle like some nervous witch. Play. It. Cool.

"How often does that happen? Or is that your tactic?"

Laughing, he starts walking again. "You mean do I take girls into the woods so they'll get scared and jump me?"

"Seems to be working for you."

"I live in a city, but I'm considering moving."

I shake my head. "Cities are way worse, just take them to a bad part at night."

"You can't get lost in a city," he says. "I mean, you can lose someone, but you'll always be seen. Deep in the forest, you could live the rest of your life with only the birds and squirrels."

"Can someone survive on their own like that? I'd starve in a week."

Olly laughs again. "I'm sure you'd make it. Just don't eat any berries you're not sure of."

"It's kind of scary to think that there could be a whole bunch of people living out here."

"You think people aren't? There are whole tribes who live in the Amazon."

"Yeah, but that's not on my doorstep."

"You want to go and see if we can find them? I'll get a map."

"Nope," I say, playfully slapping his arm. "When are we going to town? It's been a week."

Olly arches an eyebrow. "You itching to play arcade games?"

"I have a lot of pennies I want to exchange for a crappy plastic Slinky."

"Tomorrow?"

Okay, that's soon. But it gives me a thought. When we go into town, maybe I can find Lillian. She's the one who can put my mind to rest. If she's okay, then I can forget all about the fire.

Olly and I get back to camp just as we have to join the campers in the food hall. They're baking cookies.

Each group is at a table, with all the necessary ingredients and equipment in the middle of it. The room is a cloud of flour.

"Esme, Kayla is in the kitchen getting extra bags of chocolate chips. Can you join her and get another bag of flour? Catalina's group is missing one," Andy says.

"Yeah, sure."

I skip into the kitchen, still high from my walk with Olly. Pushing the door open, I stop dead in my tracks as Kayla almost slams into me. The door clicks shut. "Whoa, Esme!"

"We need more flour," I tell her.

"How was your date?"

"It wasn't a date, but it was nice."

Kayla hands me the chocolate chips and pulls at her sweater. "I'm too hot in this now."

"Why are you wearing a hoodie?"

"I was helping Andy print the recipes for the cookies in the staff cabin and he has the AC on ice-cold." She whips the hoodie over her head and a piece of paper falls to the floor.

I bend down and pick it up. Thick black writing catches my eye.

"Kayla," I breathe.

YOU'VE BEEN VERY BAD GIRLS

"What the hell!" Her eyes widen and she snatches the paper from me.

"Who put that there?" I ask.

"I don't know." She throws the hoodie on the floor. "Someone put that in my pocket!"

"While you were wearing it?"

"I've only had it on for, like, ten minutes. I was alone with Andy in the staff cabin, but he didn't come that close to me."

I close my eyes and take a breath. *Stay. Calm.* "Someone put it there when the hoodie was hanging up in our room."

"Ew. No way. That's *not* possible."

"Should we be freaking out?" I ask. "Because I'm thinking this is all about Lillian."

And I am so freaking out.

Kayla's wild eyes meet mine. "No . . . it can't be. This is just someone pranking me," she says.

"Then why does it say *girls*? Plural, Kayla. If it was just for you the note would say 'You've been a very bad girl.' Read it again. Read it!"

She shoves the piece of paper in her shorts pocket. "I don't need to read it again and we don't need to obsess over some stupid prank."

"Prank? You think this is one of the kids' pranks? Kayla, this is—"

"Over," she snaps, cutting me off midsentence. "Grab what you need and forget this. Please." She snatches the chocolate chips from my hands.

I watch her with my mouth wide open as she storms out of the kitchen. What did I do?

I gasp for a deep-enough breath and brace my hands on the wall.

Someone out there knows what we've done.

14

Kayla isn't my biggest fan right now.

Yesterday she thought I was being crazy and obsessive. It's clear from the silent treatment I got this morning before she left for breakfast that she still does. She stomped around our tiny room getting ready, making as much noise as possible, letting me know that she's not happy with my Lillian theories.

Kayla doesn't want there to be anything wrong, so she pretends everything is fine.

I don't want there to be anything wrong either, but we can't ignore a creepy note.

"Esme!" Cora whispers as I leave the cabin. She runs toward me from the staff cabin. Her eyebrows are pulled together like she's stressed.

"What's wrong?"

"Come here!" She beckons me, waving one hand in circles like she's about to take off.

I jog toward her. She instantly spins and runs toward . . . whatever she wants to show me.

"Cora, what are we—" The words die on my tongue. Painted on the back of the staff cabin is THE LAKE NEVER FORGETS.

My mouth parts and my fingers curl into my palms.

An ice-cold chill ripples down my spine. First the note, now this.

I shake my head, willing the message to change, but I haven't read it wrong. "Who could have done this?" I ask.

"I know we're all pranking each other, but if one of the campers managed to get out of their cabin and do this, we have a big problem," Cora says.

"Yeah," I agree.

This wasn't one of the kids.

"Should I get Andy?" I ask.

Cora's shoulders sink. "We have to tell him. He's going to be angry and he's going to want to keep this under wraps."

I clear my throat. "Right. The campers don't come around the back of the staff cabin, it's too out the way, so if we don't make it public knowledge, we either catch the culprit when he or she mentions it, or the rest of the campers go home unaware of what happened."

Cora smiles. "You're good at this, Esme."

"Thanks."

"You go get Andy, I'll get some cleaning supplies and paint so we can try to remove this crap. Whoever it is, they get points for creepiness."

The lake never forgets.

How much trouble could Kayla and I even get into over something that happened ten years ago? I don't want anything to go wrong for us . . . but maybe it should. Karma could finally be coming for us.

"Esme?"

I jolt. "Sorry. I'll go get Andy."

What if Lillian *was* hurt worse than we thought?

What if she didn't get up in time and was burned?

Or worse.

Shut up, Esme!

I run around the cabin and jog into the food hall. Rebekah almost bumps into me. "Sorry," she says, laughing and stepping back.

"Me too." I scan the hall. "Have you seen Andy?"

"He left a minute ago. Is everythin' okay? You look . . . pale."

I'm so not okay.

I pull on her hand. "Come with me, we need to find Andy."

"Huh?" Rebekah dashes after me. "This sounds a little ominous."

"It's more than a little."

"Officially intrigued."

"Andy!" I call. He's standing by one of the boys' cabins, digging his foot into a floorboard. A creaky one, maybe. He's very big on keeping the camp in top condition despite its age.

He looks up. "Everything okay?"

"Could you come with us for a minute, please?"

"Of course."

"Where are we goin'?" Rebekah asks.

They follow me around the food hall to the back of the staff cabin. "Cora found something."

Andy's eyes tighten in alarm.

"What the . . . ?" he says, and his jaw hits the ground.

"I saw this about five minutes ago," Cora says. She already has a bucket of soapy water and three sponges. Will that even work? There's a tin of brown wood paint and a brush, so I guess we'll be painting over the graffiti if it doesn't wash off.

"Who would do this?"

"One of the kids thinks they're funny," Rebekah says, shaking her head.

Yeah, only problem with that theory is the writing is at my height. A kid could have reached up to do it, but the natural way to graffiti is at your own height.

Could this have been done by one of the counselors or CITs? But who, and why?

The person in the forest watching us hike and removing flags?

Or maybe . . . *Nope, not going there.*

Andy takes his phone out. "I'll get a photo and then we'll clean it off."

He snaps a picture and slides his phone back into his pocket.

"The campers will be outside soon; I need to get the canoes ready. Esme and Rebekah, do you think you could take care of this? Cora and I will need to be on the lake with the campers."

I nod and Rebekah says, "Sure."

As soon as Andy and Cora leave, muttering about what's happened and who could have done it, I dunk a sponge into the water.

"This is insane," I say, dragging the soggy sponge across the first letter. The metallic taste in my mouth makes me gag. I drop my head so Rebekah can't see my reaction. I'll look like a crazy person if I panic over a little graffiti. Or a guilty one.

"Yeah. I know we're all in for the pranks now, but I don't know, maybe this is too far. Do ya think?" she says.

"I *really* do. Why do you think that it would be written *here*?" I ask. "It's not like it's out in the open for all to see." I want someone else's thoughts on this, someone who will give me all the reasonable explanations for why a camper had done this.

Rebekah shrugs, scrubbing with all her force at the letter *R* at the other end. It doesn't come off. "Maybe they don't need it on display. They're pranking us and we're pranking them. No reason for them to need all the other campers to see."

"Yeah, that makes sense." It actually does. Campers are pranking us, not each other. "Why say 'the lake never forgets'? What does that even mean?"

Her pale eyes cut sideways at me. "Why do you think it means somethin', Esme?"

Um . . .

I scrub harder, the sponge almost shredding against some of the rougher parts of wood. "I don't know, it just seems like an odd thing to say."

"We're at a lake."

"Right," I reply. I haven't forgotten about the massive oval of water I walk around every day.

Rebekah glances at me and then back at the writing. Then back at me again.

"What?" I ask, my stomach lurching.

"Huh?"

"I can tell you want to say something."

She sighs. "Are you okay? Your reaction . . . Esme, are you worried about this? Do ya think it's more than a prank?"

"I don't know," I whisper.

There are a lot of dots here and I'm not sure whether I'm trying to force them to connect.

I dunk the useless sponge. "What do you think about this?"

"I think one of the campers likes horror."

"What about the fact that this is written at adult height?" I ask.

Rebekah stills. "What?"

"The writing is at our height. The campers are shorter, so wouldn't this be a little lower down if it was one of them?"

"Hey, maybe that's how we find out who did it. Maybe it's one of the taller ones?"

I shrug one shoulder. "Could be."

"What's your theory?"

"I don't have one," I lie.

"I know we're not really close yet, but I would like to change that. You can talk to me, Esme."

Rebekah said that she doesn't have friends. No one to talk to and here I am closing up on her. That can't feel good after years of being bullied.

"Totally. I'd like that. Hey, I think it was someone else who wrote this," I tell her.

"Someone else?"

"Yeah, like someone from town. It just doesn't add up. Why

would someone working for the camp want to remove flags and get us lost? Ava thought she saw someone in the woods when we were hiking."

"Really?"

"There was no one there when Cora and I looked. Cora said it was just the trees."

"But you don't think it was a tree?"

I dunk the sponge again, getting frustrated. "I mean, it could have been, but then the trail was tampered with, and now this."

"Who else have you told?" Rebekah asks.

"No one," I say, not wanting to drag Kayla into it. "They will probably think I'm crazy. I have the tendency to overthink. My mom is the same; anytime I'm late she calls, worried something has happened to me."

"At least she cares."

"I'm lucky. So . . . do you think I'm crazy?" I bite my lip in anticipation of her reply. Sometimes *I* think I'm crazy.

"I don't think you're crazy at all. I can see how you got there."

"Do you think I could be right?"

"It's not impossible."

"But?" I prompt, wanting the rest.

"But *why* would someone do all of that?"

I shrug. "Good question."

That I can answer.

"I don't think this is going to come off," I say, exasperated. We decide to cover it with three thick coats of paint and that does the trick. It's not perfect, but at least the words aren't visible. I wish they would just disappear.

As we walk away, Rebekah turns to me. "Hey, maybe Andy has annoyed someone. He comes to camp early from what I overheard. He spends a lot of time in town."

"Really?"

Her eyes glow. "Uh-huh. Maybe he slept with someone's wife."

"Nasty."

She guesses again. "Maybe he offended the whole town, called them hicks or somethin'."

Or maybe this has nothing to do with Andy and everything to do with Kayla and me.

15

"I can't believe anyone would do that," Mary says. Her dark eyes narrow under her fringe.

I look away from her, but I feel her gaze long after she's turned away.

Jake shrugs. "It's extreme but a good prank, to be fair."

I've heard enough.

It took a lot of scrubbing to make the words fade even a little. Then we had to paint over them.

I get up, walk away from the table and dump my plate and cup on the trolley. The counselor tables have one topic tonight: our not-so-friendly graffiti artist. Some think it's a bad joke; others are horrified. One thing we all agree on is that they went too far.

With a prank you should be able to laugh. No one is laughing at a creepy message smeared on a wall in blood-red paint.

"Esme, wait up," Kayla says. She runs after me as I head to our cabin. I wanted a few minutes to myself before the guitar lessons by the campfire tonight.

"Yeah?" I say, folding my arms.

Sighing, she tilts her head. "Are you okay?"

Oh, now she's concerned for me.

"Yep. You?"

"I know what you're thinking. That the message was for us."

I look over her shoulder to check that no one else is coming outside and duck into our cabin. Kayla is hot on my heels.

"How can you not?" I ask.

"It's a weird message to leave."

"That's not what I asked, Kayla."

"Okay." She throws her hands up. "Okay, I'll admit it. Maybe you were right and it was for us. Bad girls and the lake never forgets." She shudders. "Who could it be? Lillian? No one else knows."

I arch one eyebrow. "We can't be sure. Lillian could have told someone what happened that night. Or maybe someone saw."

"What about the man Ava thought she saw in the forest? Maybe it was him."

I bite my lip and sit on the bottom bunk. "The man in the forest could have easily been a woman. Ava only assumed it was a man. Lillian could be out there watching the same way she was ten years ago." A shiver rips through my body. "She likes to keep to the shadows, remember?"

"I can't forget," Kayla replies. "But why would she say the lake never forgets instead of '*I* will never forget'?"

"I don't understand her shady mind! She's obviously trying to freak us out without advertising what happened."

"Why?"

I shake my head, then stop dead as a realization slams into my mind.

Oh no.

My hands shake. "Because she isn't finished. This is just the start. Think about it, if she wants revenge it would be dissatisfying to come out and tell everyone what happened straightaway. Proper revenge is messing with someone's head, ruining their life *before* the big reveal."

"I think you need to get some sleep."

I grit my teeth. "Kayla, don't play dumb. You want to pretend, but we both know you can't, so let's move past that. Okay? This is happening and we need to figure out what Lillian wants."

Kayla sighs and slumps onto the bed. Her glossy blond hair falls in her face. "Esme, I don't want this to take over our experience here if it doesn't have to. You can't be *sure,* and you're going to let it become an obsession."

My obsessions used to be fun. There were my One Direction, piano, *Riverdale* and, most recently, adult coloring book phases. I should have brought some coloring books with me. I'm not even sure my mom's Valium would help at this point.

"If someone is out there and they're trying to mess with us, we need to deal with that. Lillian has every right to be angry with us," I say.

"Unless she *did* run and you're freaking out over nothing!"

I want to curl up inside myself. "After . . . what happened, I tried to look back once the fire spread, but I couldn't see through the flames. I wanted to be sure, but we ran back to camp. I don't know what happened to Lillian next."

"Do you even understand what you're implying?"

"Yes. Maybe . . . she was *really* hurt."

Kayla's eyes are big and full of concern. "I think you should have an early night, Esme. You're pale and you have dark circles under your eyes. I'll tell everyone that you have a headache."

I tap my fingers under my eyes. "No, I'm fine."

"You're not! I can see this on your mind all of the time! Sleep!"

"I get eight hours a night, Kayla. I don't need more rest."

Okay, it's more like six hours, but that's still enough. It's more than I used to get around exam time when I'd cram in last-minute studying until midnight.

"Maybe we can arrange for you to see one of the counselors?"

My jaw drops. "Are you serious? You don't believe me?"

"I'm not saying that. I think you're right and someone *is* pranking us, but I don't think there's anything more to it than that."

"But what if there *is* more to it?"

Kayla tilts her head the way you do when you think someone is ridiculous. "Like what?"

"Like it's Lillian and she wants us to pay!"

"For what? We didn't do anything to her. If anything, it was *her* fault."

Her words chip away at my sanity. Kayla is mostly right, I suppose.

"Hey, it's okay. I understand why you think all this stuff, Esme. You just want to protect us."

"I want to come into town with you guys tonight."

Kayla stands up and sighs. "If you promise to rest now, I'll wake you before we go."

"Thanks."

She leaves the room, and I climb up to my bunk and settle in.

I close my eyes, listening to the faint sound of terrible guitar playing and laughter.

They all sound so happy out there, without a care in the world.

Sighing, I turn onto my side and take my cell from under my pillow. Maybe I can find Lillian on social media. All I know is her name and that she lives around here. That might not be enough, especially if she doesn't state exactly where she lives, but it's worth a try. If I can get in contact with her, then maybe I can fix whatever she's angry about.

If there even is anything.

This still could all be random, just bored kids from town looking to get their kicks by spooking the campers.

I commit each face of a girl named Lillian who lives in this area to memory. None of them look like the girl who Kayla and I saw ten years ago, but yeah, ten years is a long time. She could have changed a lot, dyed her hair, gained or lost weight.

Kayla will worry if she knows I'm still obsessing, but I hate that we've potentially hurt someone. Whatever really happened that night, I want to make it right.

An hour later, the cabin fills with girls. I listen as they chat excitedly about the guitar lesson. I didn't hear anyone playing well, but that's the point of learning, right? You're terrible until you're not.

Kayla creeps into our room and whispers, "You awake, Esme?"

I sit up. "Yep."

"You feeling better?"

She asks that as if I've been ill. There is nothing wrong with me. "Much better," I say to appease her. "Is Andy in his cabin?"

"Yeah, and the counselors with the night off are all in the staff cabin playing cards. They invited us, but Tia said we wanted to take a walk and then use the multiuse cabin for dodgeball. I was sure they were going to bust us then. Who *wants* to play dodgeball?"

"It's good for aggression," I say, and climb down the ladder.

"Are you feeling aggressive?"

"What? No. I was just saying. I don't want to play dodgeball. I want to kick your ass at air hockey."

"As if."

I grab my jacket and pop my cell in my pocket. "Let's go."

I'd be lying if I said I wasn't slightly nervous that we're finally doing this, but a rush of adrenaline keeps telling me it's a good idea.

Even if I don't find Lillian maybe I'll experience this little thing called fun. I'm in dire need of getting away from camp for a while. The isolation could be the reason for my latest stretch of paranoia.

Everything is worse when you're trapped.

16

Olly, Jake, Tia and Rebekah are waiting by the multiuse cabin, which is the closest to the man-made path between town and camp. It isn't really a path, but instead a thin strip of mud that's been trampled down.

We're all assuming it was made by CITs wanting to get out for the night. No one but me—*hello*—seems to think it could also be used by people from town coming in.

"Your headache gone?" Olly asks. He steps close to me.

"Yep, I feel great."

"Let's go then!" Tia cheers quietly.

"We're doing a lap of the lake first, right?" I ask. "The counselors think we're going for a walk."

Rebekah nods. "Good idea, Esme. Let's make it look like we're good little CITs."

She looks happier now than I've seen her since we arrived.

I link arms with her as we walk, despite wanting to be near Olly.

"How are you doing?" I ask.

She smiles tightly. "Me? Oh, I'm fine. This is cool and scary. Should I be scared? Are you?"

Laughing, I nudge her with my shoulder. "Breathe. No one has ever come checking on us before. There's no reason why they would now."

"That's true. I still feel like a criminal, though."

"Actually, it's not a crime what we're doing," I inform her.

We do one lap and stop by the shrubs that are doing a poor job of hiding the sneaky little trail. Kayla and Tia are animated, talking loud and fast.

I look over my shoulder. The camp looks deserted, like one of those creepy abandoned theme parks, but without the roller coasters. Above the lake a large bird glides in a circle and crows.

"Let's get out of here," Jake says. "Coast is clear."

He ducks between the bushes and Kayla follows straightaway. Rebekah takes a breath, but she doesn't have time to chicken out: Tia grabs her hand and pulls her along.

"Shall we?" Olly asks, nodding to the trail.

Biting my lip, I grab his hand and we disappear into the bushes.

He doesn't let go of me, and I'm not about to complain. His hand is warm; his grip firm yet gentle. He feels safe, which is nice since I haven't felt that today.

We walk quickly through the forest. Jake has a flashlight, but he's keeping it low to the ground in case anyone sees us. It's not that dark, but as we go deeper, we lose a lot of light.

The temperature has dropped to a comfortable heat, and I find myself smiling in the darkness.

This is what I'd hoped camp would be: hanging out with new friends and doing something fun. Olly squeezes my hand as we come out the other side of the forest. Across the quiet road is the teeny town. It's quaint and cute. From here, the streetlights make it look prettier, like the town is dotted with fairy lights.

"Okay, there's a little arcade on the outskirts. They have Rollerblading too, if anyone wants to break an ankle," Tia says.

"I'll pass," I reply as we cross the deserted road.

Kayla's eyes dart from my and Olly's joined hands to my eyes.

Don't say anything!

She presses her lips together, stifling a smile. Tia nudges Rebekah.

Great, everyone has seen.

Olly either doesn't notice or doesn't care that we're being watched.

"Lead us to the arcade then, Tia," Jake says. "I'm dying for a drink."

I want to ask how he's going to get a drink, but my filter kicks in before I open my mouth. Yay for that. There might not even be a bar or restaurant nearby.

Fake IDs are a thing and Jake, being one of the popular kids at his school, is likely to have one. Kayla and I thought about it once, but we were both too scared to buy one from Mason, the dude at school with a supersketchy private life.

"Easy, Esme," Olly says, shaking our joined hands.

I release my death grip a smidge. "Sorry, didn't realize I was squeezing."

I'm not sure what I expected, but a run-down arcade on the very edge of town was not it. The place is huge, but the games are old, and the patterned red carpet is so worn in areas there are bald patches.

"Right," Tia says. "It's . . . nice."

Jake laughs. "It's not Vegas, but it'll do."

"Come on, Esme, I'm challenging you to a game of table hockey," Olly says.

"Does anyone even have cash?" Rebekah asks, looking around as if we could be busted at any moment.

She and Tia follow closely behind us. Jake and Kayla stop by a claw machine to try to win a stuffed animal.

"I do, but I need change," Olly replies.

Tia grabs Rebekah's hand. "I already have change. Come on, Rebekah, I see Pac-Man and I'm awesome!"

Rebekah follows without a word.

"This has always been my favorite game," Olly tells me as he picks up a puck.

"Mine is the claw."

He looks up from across the table. "You know they're rigged, right?"

"Yes, but it's so satisfying when you finally win."

"After twenty dollars."

I roll my eyes. "Okay, so once my dad did spend twenty-three dollars before we got a prize, but I still have that little stuffed pony."

"Your dad rich or just enjoy burning money?"

Laughing, I grab the other puck and send it flying to his side.

"He's never been very good at saying no to me, and I wanted that pony more than anything," I say.

I glance up quickly as Olly positions himself to hit the puck back to me.

The chances of Lillian being in here are small. What is she doing, messing with camp by day and hitting the dance mat by night? There is a chance, though. In this small town, there isn't a lot to do.

Olly and I play two games, each winning one, and then we move on.

"Olly," Jake calls, "basketball!"

He's standing with Tia and Kayla.

"I'm going to see if Rebekah is okay," I tell Olly. "I'll meet you over there."

He walks off to the basketball hoops and I split, heading to Rebekah. She's in a corner with her back to the room and her hands up to her face.

"No, they don't know . . . ," she mutters.

Is she talking to herself?

"Rebekah?" I ask.

Startled, she jolts and spins in my direction. One hand clutches tightly around her cell phone.

"Sorry, I didn't know you were on a call," I say.

"Esme." She smiles and her finger hits a button on the screen. "It's okay, I was just speakin' to my mom. She worries if she doesn't hear from me."

What did she say? *They don't know.* Who doesn't know what?

"Shouldn't you call her back? My mom would go crazy if I hung up on her."

Shrugging, Rebekah tilts the screen so I can't see. "I'll send her a message. We were almost done anyway."

I watch her tap away and then she slides the phone in her pocket. "Okay. Hey, you want to play Whac-A-Mole?" she asks.

"Sure."

"So, are you havin' fun?" she asks, glancing behind us.

I follow her line of sight and there is no one there. "Yeah. You?"

"Yep. Tia and I played a couple games and then she wanted to find Jake and Kayla. I don't think she enjoys my company that much."

I start the game and pick up the giant spongy hammer. "Of course she does. She probably saw some girl she likes and went to talk to her."

"Thanks, Esme, but I saw her with Jake and Kayla two seconds later. I'm not the most fun person, I know that."

We whack moles, Rebekah as if she's actually trying to kill them, teeth bared and eyes narrowed. I wouldn't like to be on the end of her anger.

Her phone buzzes in her pocket, but she continues hitting moles.

"Don't say that," I tell her. "I thought we were all having fun together. It wouldn't be the same without you."

"Thank you," she says quietly. With a frown, she adds, "You're so *nice*."

We spend an hour at the arcade, and I have the face of every person in here memorized. I age them, or rather de-age them ten years and none look like Lillian.

She isn't here unless she's had facial reconstruction.

"We should get back," Jake says. "It's been almost two hours."

When we get closer to the entrance, my heart stutters. On the sidewalk, right outside the open door, is a blond girl, around twenty. Suddenly, she whips around and runs.

I do a double take, my pulse racing.

Lillian?

"Let's go now," I say, jogging outside.

"Esme!" Kayla calls after me.

I hear their footsteps close behind.

The slightly cooler dry air hits my face. I whip my head in both directions.

Rebekah steps in front of me. "Esme, are you okay?"

"I'm fine. I needed air."

"All good?" Olly asks.

I take one more look around, but there's nothing in the empty parking lot. "Yep, let's get back to camp."

Was that her waiting outside the arcade. Watching us?

17

Rebekah dashes across the road, calling, "Let's go before Andy realizes we're gone!"

"Where's the fire, Rebekah?" Tia says, running after her.

We cross the road and race into the forest.

They're running so Andy won't realize we're gone. I'm running from Lillian.

Dry grass and sticks crunch beneath our feet.

"How much further?" Rebekah asks.

"We've only been in the forest for five minutes," Tia replies.

It took us about twenty minutes to reach the road from camp. It's darker now because we're not using the flashlight, and we're slower. The last thing we need is someone noticing us.

"I hate this part. What if we make too much noise gettin' back into the cabins?" Rebekah says.

"Don't," Olly replies.

I nudge his side. "Unhelpful. Just say you were going to the bathroom and heard a noise outside."

Olly grins. "Ooh, I like it, Esme. You're good at being sneaky."

"Is that a compliment?"

I can just about make out Kayla looking over her shoulder at me.

"It is," he replies.

To the left of us something flashes, lighting up the forest like freaking fireworks. I blink and a dot of white dances in front of my eyes.

"What the hell was that?" Jake says, whipping the flashlight from his pocket and turning it on. He shines it in the direction of the flash.

I gasp, my free hand flying to my throat. "Was that a *camera*?"

Another flash.

"Shit, it is!" Olly hisses.

"Who's there?" Jake calls.

I push against Olly, my hands shaking. "We need to go *now*!"

"Shh, Esme."

"Someone is taking our picture!"

Another blinding flash.

"Go!" Jake snaps, turning around and running in the direction of camp. He's holding Kayla's hand and practically dragging her. We all take off after him.

We sprint single file, and I wince every time another flash of light hits the forest and casts long shadows between the trees.

My stomach churns.

I push my legs to go faster and faster to keep up with the others.

The forest lights up again. My pulse is thudding loudly in my ears.

Someone is taking photos of us.

Another light makes me gasp again and turns my blood to ice. What if the next flash reveals the person behind it? If they're standing between the trees we'd only see them when the flash went off.

I want to know who it is, but I'm also scared to know.

"Almost there!" Jake snaps in something between a shout and a whisper.

If I fall over now, I'm going to kick myself.

I dart between two trees behind Rebekah. Olly's footsteps are thundering right behind me. My thighs scream in protest of the pace I'm keeping.

I ignore the pain and press on, gulping air and trying to remember if you should breathe in through your nose and out through your mouth when you're running or the other way around.

"Go, go!" Olly says, putting one hand on my lower back.

I push harder, gritting my teeth. My legs feel like they're going to snap off. We burst from between the shrubs and run along the forest, toward the cabins.

The flashes stop abruptly.

Jake slows and turns. I almost run into Tia as everyone else slows down too.

"What?" I ask, bending over to catch my breath.

Olly and Jake exchange a look, one that turns their faces red with anger and makes me flinch.

"Oh no. You cannot go back," I tell them. Are they crazy?

Their male pride has been hurt. We were chased out of the

woods by someone with a camera. But it's not like we can afford to be caught. Andy wouldn't be too happy that we went to town in the middle of the night.

He's big on responsibilities, and he has one to keep us safe, too.

Olly's jaw clenches in the dim light of the wood lamppost. "We can't let whoever that was get away with it."

"Why would they want photos of us anyway?" Rebekah asks. "What were they trying to do?"

"I intend to find out," Jake replies.

Kayla puts her palms on Jake's chest. "Wait up a second. We don't know who it is or what they're capable of. They might be dangerous."

"Me and Olly can take him."

I throw my hands up, annoyed with all the testosterone flying around. "And if he has a gun? You stronger than a bullet, Jake? Let's go inside and pretend this never happened."

She could have just been trying to scare us.

It was a success.

"It's probably just someone trying to freak us out," I say.

"Esme is right," says Tia, backing me up. She points toward the forest. "We don't know what that person is capable of. It's most likely that he was there to freak us out, but I don't want to take that chance. Do you?"

Jake growls a no that sounds like it wounds his ego, while Olly grits his teeth.

Tia shakes her head. "What if they send the pictures to Andy?"

"Even if they do, all they got is us running through the forest and we told everyone we were going for a walk."

"That's true," Kayla says.

"Let's just go to bed, I'm over it," Jake mutters.

I take Olly's hand and he grips mine tight. I'm just happy to help calm him down. "Hey," I say, leaning against him. "It was just some crazy guy in the woods. We don't need to get mixed up in whatever he was doing."

Olly's green-and-blue eyes slide very slowly to mine as if he needs a second before dealing with me. My mom did the same thing when I was nine and I accidentally smashed her very expensive eye shadow palette.

"If he comes back . . ."

I nod. "Then you can kick his ass."

Rebekah peers over her shoulder and into the forest. "Can we please get to bed before someone hears us out here?"

We split up and head to our cabins. The boys' cabin is closest, but Olly and Jake stand on the porch, watching us get inside safely before they go inside. *That is so cute!*

Rebekah and Tia tiptoe into their cabin and close the door.

I can hear my ragged breathing as we walk up to our door. Kayla and I walk up the two steps at the same time, carefully placing our feet in case the wood creaks. I look back at Olly and Jake as Kayla slowly turns the door handle.

With a quick wave to the boys, I turn and slide through the small opening. Kayla didn't open the door wide; I'm guessing so the light from outside wouldn't creep in.

The room is filled with heavy breathing and soft snoring. I glance at each of the bunk beds in the large room. The girls are all very still. It's sometime after one in the morning.

Kayla and I pad into our room. We undress in silence; I clumsily pull my pajamas on and climb up to my bunk quickly and quietly. Neither of us speak. We usually say good night, but tonight we're too scared.

Lying on my back, I replay the events of the forest in my head. I can't remember exactly how many flashes—photos—there were, but it was a lot.

Somebody wants evidence that we snuck out.

Evidence that Kayla and I snuck out.

Like we did ten years ago.

18

Edge, meet Esme. Yep, I'm on it, the edge, in a major way.

It's morning and no one but me is acting strange. Andy is his usual self, which tells us he has no idea what we were up to last night. But still, I can't calm down.

Every time a noise comes from the woods, I jump. Which is freaking often since the kids are collecting sticks and branches to make dens.

Olly and Jake are with some of the other guys, lugging larger branches for the structural parts of the dens. Once each group has four large branches and a bunch of medium and small ones, they have to make their own den and it needs to stay upright.

It's a little challenge that Andy told the campers about over breakfast, and it's caused a lot of excitement.

I haven't spoken to anyone about last night yet, not even Kayla. We haven't had any time alone, and to be honest, I don't think anyone wants to relive it.

In the cold light of day, we seem a bit dramatic, not even asking whoever it was to show themselves. We all ran as if we were being chased by zombies. Not that I was ever going to ask the cameraman if he wanted to chat over an iced tea.

My little group of four are piling up medium sticks on the beach.

Andy stops beside me with his clipboard. "Good haul," he says. "Looks almost there."

"Yeah, I sent them on one last trip."

"Excellent. How are you today?" he asks.

My heart misses a beat. I blink heavily. What does he know? "I'm fine, thanks," I croak. "How are you?"

He smiles. "I'm well. Are you ready for a day of camp building and fire lighting?"

"I am."

Dipping his chin in a curt nod, he says, "Well, shout if you need anything."

I watch him walk off and my tense shoulders relax a fraction. If Andy knew we had snuck out he would definitely say something. I don't know why I'm so jumpy around him. He's the kind of guy who sorts things out right away, not someone who waits and sees how it goes. We would have all been in the staff cabin first thing. Hell, he would have had us in there the second we got back in the very early hours.

Inhale, exhale, act normal.

Guilt doesn't feel good on me. It's a shame I can't remember a time before it.

I watch my girls carry back armfuls of sticks that are about as long as their legs. "Well done, girls. I think we're ready."

They wait with me. I'm not allowed to leave the beach because I'm in charge of making sure all the groups have enough sticks and that the campers who dump them here don't wander off.

A little bit ironic that I'm in charge of keeping them out of trouble when I can't even manage to do that myself. Still, what Andy doesn't know . . .

When everyone else gets back from gathering wood, Andy instructs the groups about what they will need and sends each merged group of eight to different parts of the forest.

Cora and I follow eight massively hyper girls who are bouncing, dropping sticks and talking a million miles an hour. I bend down and pick up another dropped stick.

"What did you do with your night off?" Cora asks, brushing one hand over her smooth ponytail.

It's an innocent enough question, but my mouth goes dry in a nanosecond.

"We just went for a walk."

"Yeah, there isn't much to do. When I was a CIT, I think I played Go Fish about a thousand times. I was so jealous of counselors who could get dressed up and go out for the evening."

My hand tightens around the stick. "Maybe next year I'll get to go out."

"Oh, you think you'll come back next year, then? To here or somewhere else?"

"I like it here," I tell Cora, even though I'm almost positive I will never return. I love camps, but this one has way too much baggage.

"That's great, Esme. I love it when I hear that people want to return. You're so good with the girls and they all love you."

We're halfway to our designated den area, the furthest from camp.

"Okay, girls," Cora says, and launches into instructions.

We can use whichever trees we want in our area and the den has to be big enough for all the girls to sit under.

Cora and I help them with the large logs since it took four girls on each end to carry them up here. Why we weren't just sent to our zone to collect sticks there, I do not know. Andy might have some control issues, wanting to see each freaking stick before we took them away to use. Or maybe he was promoting teamwork, getting everyone together to gather the most suitable materials for everyone to use.

"Ew, look," Alana says, pointing to a collection of cigarette butts on the ground.

I bend down and count five of them. "No one here smokes, right?"

Cora folds her arms. "They're not supposed to."

Alarm bells chime a very loud song in my head: It's the creepy cameraperson!

This was the direction that we came last night. Did they stick around and watch us? But who hangs around long enough to smoke five cigarettes when everyone has already gone inside?

Unless this isn't the first time they've watched.

"That's not safe," Isabel says.

"You're right," I tell her, collecting the butts and trying not to gag. Someone's mouth has touched them. "I'm going to throw them in the trash and disinfect my hands."

"Will you let Andy know too, please?" Cora asks.

"Sure thing."

The second I turn around, the girls have forgotten. Cora gets them on task and they fuss over which sticks to use first.

At least our phantom smoker had the good sense to properly extinguish the cigarettes. They're almost flat they've been stomped into the ground so hard.

I walk back toward the cabins in the thick heat.

"Found these by our den," I tell Andy, opening my hand so he can see what I'm holding. Then I dump them in a trash can near the multiuse cabin where he's scribbling something on his clipboard.

His frown makes his whole forehead crumble. "Who's been smoking?"

I shrug. "I'm not sure. Us CITs walked around last night, but no one smoked, and we didn't see any counselors doing it either."

Sighing, Andy nods. "Okay, I'll have to make sure I speak with each staff member today and remind them that it's forbidden to smoke on campgrounds. And in the forest too," he grumbles, tutting. "Thanks for cleaning them up, Esme."

"No problem."

"There's someone there! There's someone there!" Isabel screams.

My head whips in her direction. She's pointing into the forest.

Cora steps in front of the girls, her head bent forward as she tries to get a better look.

Jake and Olly are running toward them. Andy and I take off too, with him shouting at everyone else to stay where they are.

"Mary, watch the campers," he says as we pass her.

"Where?" I ask when we reach Cora. I've got a stitch in my side and ice in my heart.

There has to be someone out there watching us. Ava's sighting in the woods, the creepy message, the pictures that were taken.

Kayla can't explain it away with coincidences. Lillian is trying to mess with us.

Olly and Jake are in the forest, and spread a little too far apart for my liking. Does safety in numbers mean nothing to them?

Andy follows them as Mary looks at us from the other side of the lake.

I put my arm around Isabel. Her slender frame is shaking. "Hey, it's okay," I tell her. "Remember, we don't own all of this forest."

She looks up at me with fear in her eyes. "He was walking."

"Toward us?"

"Um, kind of, I think. I saw the side of his face."

Cora turns. "It was definitely a man?"

Isabel nods. "I think so. I couldn't see his face very well."

Translation: It could have been a woman or a man.

"Okay." I look at the twelve girls huddled together. "Look, there is no reason to be alarmed. I'm sure people go on hikes all the time out here and not everyone pays as much attention as they should. Sometimes they miss the sign saying this is private property. I'm sure Jake and Olly will find him and remind him that he shouldn't be here."

Biting my lip, I watch the spot in the forest where the boys disappeared.

Five tense minutes later and my arm is still around Isabel. No one is building anything, and I can't take my eyes off the last place I saw Olly.

"All right," Cora says. "I think we should all get back to camp and wait."

She takes out her walkie-talkie and speaks to the other counselors, who are dotted around the forest.

"We all agree," she says, finally putting the device away. "We're going to go into the food hall and grab a snack until the guys get back."

"Good idea," I say. "Come on, girls, who needs some sugar?"

They cheer, but their hearts aren't quite in it.

Cora and I walk behind them, slowly joining the other groups as we all trudge back.

My heart flutters wildly and my stomach sinks. Am I going to have to tell everyone what happened? Maybe Kayla and I should leave.

I should have thrown that damn pamphlet in the trash.

"It's okay, Esme," Cora says. "This happens sometimes. I swear some people think they're above the rules. If a sign says private property, keep off, you damn well keep off!" She shakes her head.

"Now our activity has been interrupted, and I don't think the girls are going to want to go back out there today."

I can't blame them. I don't want to go back out there either.

We enter the food hall and gossip flies as quickly as the candy wrappers. At least the campers are all happy with a midmorning treat.

I wash my hands and then sit at a table with Kayla, Rebekah and Tia.

"This is crazy!" Tia says. "So much drama over a dude getting lost on a trail."

Rebekah's mouth pops open. "After last night you're seriously trying to make this sound random?"

"Oh, come on, you're not telling me you think that guy was here to pick us off one by one?"

"Okay, I wasn't thinking we're in danger like *that*," Rebekah says.

"What are you thinking?" I ask, desperate for other options that don't involve Kayla and me.

"He's a weird dude who gets his kicks from people watching," she says.

"He's watching a camp full of *children*!" Kayla squeals.

"No, he was watching *us*. Same as last night, and he wrote on the *staff* cabin. The dude is here to freak *us* out, not them. What's scarier than having to deal with something like that all while making sure the children don't worry?" I say.

"Esme's right," Rebekah says. "This is about the counselors. Do you think he could have been one?"

"A disgruntled counselor from the past. Maybe he did something and was made to leave," I say. "He might think that he was treated unfairly."

Rebekah nods. "Kayla and Esme, you've been here before. Anyone you can think of?"

I can't be sure, but I think I sense an edge to her voice.

"No," we reply in unison.

I swallow and add, "We wouldn't have known about any issues with the counselors. You know how well we hide that from the campers. This guy saw us out there doing a job he thinks he should still be allowed to do."

"You two are getting ahead of yourself," Tia says. "It might not be that."

"Maybe, but it's possible," I reply. "Cora?"

She looks over from where she's sitting with a few other counselors and immediately gets up.

"What's up?" she asks.

I tell her our theory and she sits down at our table. "Okay. That's a possibility. I don't like that we've had two sightings of someone in the woods, trails tampered with, and cigarette butts left. Andy radioed a moment ago; he and the guys haven't found anything, so they're coming back. Andy is going to head into town and talk to the cops to see where we stand."

"Whoa, you think we need to involve the cops?" Rebekah asks.

"We're responsible for the safety of children, so we have to. Even if Andy just files a report. Sometimes the police will ask him to put a post on the camp's Facebook page about the land being private and they share it. I'll speak with him when he gets back and see if he can think of any counselors or CITs who left on bad terms. I know I don't need to say this . . . but not a word of this in front of the kids, okay?"

She gets up and goes back to her table, leaning in and whispering to the rest of the counselors, telling them our theory.

So, we're running with this one. Going for the angry ex-staff member. I like it, and I want it to be true.

It certainly fits better than the Lillian thing. I mean, she isn't a dude and the motive is weak.

This isn't Lillian and it's not about what Kayla and I did ten years ago.

It can't be.

19

Olly and Jake walk into the food hall as Cora walks out to meet Andy.

I sit taller when they reach us. "What happened?"

Jake turns to address the room.

"Everything is okay. We caught up with the guy; he'd taken a wrong turn on a trail from the other side of town. He was apologetic, and we helped him get back to where he needs to be."

"He's gone?" one of the boys asks from across the room.

"Yeah, he didn't mean to be here in the first place."

The room erupts with chatter again, this time voices are higher and filled with laughter and about Olly and Jake chasing away the "stalker man."

Olly sits close to me, his arm pressing against mine.

"That's great," I say.

Olly subtly shakes his head.

"It's not?" Rebekah asks.

I sink into my seat, understanding. "You were just saying that so they wouldn't worry."

Jake rubs his jaw. "It was Andy's idea. I'm going to go and tell the other counselors."

He walks away, heading to Mary's packed table first.

I place my clammy palms on my knees. "What happened?"

Olly clears his throat. "We couldn't find anyone. But we did find a box of matches that he must have dropped."

"Esme has a theory that it's someone who worked here and was fired or whatever, since this guy seems to only be messing with the counselors," Rebekah says.

Olly glances at me, smiling. "Good one, Esme."

"Cora is telling Andy."

"This jackass is going to get hurt if he comes back here again. Did Isabel mention anything about a weapon?" Olly asks.

"What?" Kayla hisses.

"Last night you didn't want me and Jake to go after him because we couldn't be sure he wasn't armed," Olly says.

"She didn't say anything about a gun, but that doesn't mean he didn't have one. It could be concealed," I tell them.

Olly leans back, effectively ending our little arm cuddle. I do my best not to pout.

"This is insane. I came here to help kids have an awesome summer," he says, shaking his head. "I didn't sign up for some freak in the woods."

"I'm sure the cops will do something now," Kayla says.

Tia huffs. "What can they do? We don't know who it is or why he's doing this."

"Andy will have records of who's worked here and how they left. They'll start there," I say, backing Kayla up, although I'm not at all convinced there is anything the cops can do.

We have two sightings of a man, one of which was uncertain and possibly a tree. We can hardly say we were chased through the forest at one a.m. by someone taking our picture.

Still, the police might take it seriously because there are children here.

"What's the relationship like between camp and town?" I ask.

Tia shrugs. "I don't know, why?"

"Well, my cousin was a counselor at a camp in Michigan and said that the camp and local community hated each other," I say. "The town was mad because of the noise or something stupid like that. There were arguments and a lot of bad blood between staff and residents."

"Where are you going with this?" Olly asks.

I shrug. "I just wondered if it could be someone from town. Andy visits, so they know him and maybe someone there is tired of staff getting wild in their town. Did you hear that Cora and the others go drinking there?"

Tia ties her hair into a bun on top of her head. "Ugh, I wish we could go drinking."

I ignore her. "Maybe someone has a grudge against Andy?"

Olly leans forward. "Maybe."

He doesn't sound like he believes me. But it's a totally plausible explanation for the strange things happening around here.

So is Lillian.

"What do you think?" I ask him.

"I have no idea, Esme." Olly looks away, toward the table of food. "I need something to eat."

I watch him with narrowed eyes as he gets up and walks away.

Rebekah's eyes slide from Olly's vacant chair to me. "That was odd."

I turn to her. "What do you think?"

"Well, I think the same as you. Maybe someone in town is annoyed with the camp. We're close to town. They can probably hear us sometimes, smell smoke from our campfires if the wind is in the right direction."

"We should find out if there is a grudge. Maybe Andy has been invited to town meetings or something," I say.

"How would we find that out?" she asks.

Tia rolls her eyes. "We ask him."

Such a simple response.

"I vote Esme has that discussion with him," Kayla says.

"Why me?"

She arches a plucked brow. "You're the one who's going full Sherlock."

"I'm not," I defend weakly. "Don't you want to know who's behind the graffiti?"

"I can sleep without knowing who's been turning innocent pranks creepy. Now, if I wake up to find a bloody deer head on my pillow, I want to know."

How can Kayla say that?

Has she forgotten all about the note we found in her jacket pocket?

Despite my best attempts at distracting myself with theories, the more I think about it, the more I think Lillian *is* behind this.

Why else would this all be happening now?

20

Andy wanted a full staff meeting. It turns out that's no simple task.

So here we are, hours later, *finally* sitting outside the cabins at ten-thirty at night. The children are tucked up in bed and snoring.

We're in a circle. I'd like to think that's because we all want to be involved, but really, it has more to do with the fact that we have eyes in every direction around camp this way.

Let's say hello to pessimistic Esme.

As the meeting starts, I plan how to catch Andy after and ask about the camp's relationship with town.

Andy speaks in a low voice so we can hear but not be overheard.

"What are the cops doing?" Cora asks as he finishes explaining that they didn't find anyone in the woods.

"They're going to look into some names I've given them."

"Who are they?"

He dips his head. "I can't say. Both worked as counselors before any of you started. Both left on unhappy terms."

"Can you tell us what those terms were?" Jake asks. He and Kayla are sitting side by side, holding hands. She hasn't told me that anything happened between them, but it sure looks *on* now.

Andy presses his mouth into a thin line before he looks at Jake. "I'm sorry, I can't. But rest assured that the police will speak with both of them in person. For now, we're going to make sure that groups are doubled up. CITs *must* be with their counselor when doing any activity with the campers. We're cancelling our hike this week, unless the police have good news, so we'll have kayak races, extra swimming time and cooking lessons instead."

"Should we inform parents?" Mary asks.

"The police didn't seem to think the campers are in danger and neither do I, but we have to take it seriously. We will inform parents if there is another sighting or any evidence that he's been back. Security will be upped, no campers will be allowed to go into the cabins alone, and we'll remain vigilant at all times. For now, we just need to carry on as we are and make their summer the best it can be."

My stomach twists with unease.

"I'm glad the cops don't think the campers are in danger," Rebekah says.

"But are *we*?" Tia asks.

I hold my breath.

"I really don't think so. There's a big leap between wanting to frighten people and wanting to harm them. The two suspects never showed any signs of violence and were let go for a number of minor grievances," Andy replies.

But let's face it, it's not the two former staff members who are doing this.

Rebekah curls her arms around her body and nods.

"Everyone stays in their cabins tonight. Does anyone have any other questions?" Andy asks. No one says a word. "Right, let's all get some sleep."

I stand and turn to Olly. "Are you okay?" he asks, brushing his knuckles along my jaw. His fingers leave a warm trail behind them.

Don't faint!

"I'm all right. This is all a bit scary, though."

"You'll be fine, Esme. I'll watch you go into your cabin."

"Thanks. Night."

He smiles. "Night."

I link Rebekah's arm with mine as we walk toward the girls' cabins. "You okay?"

She looks straight ahead, nibbling her lip. "Yeah, I guess. I'll see ya in the mornin'."

"Yeah."

"You doing this?" Kayla whispers to me as we walk on to our cabin.

I look back and locate Andy. What choice do I have? Everyone has volunteered me. "Yeah, I'll be there in a minute."

"Esme?" Cora asks when I stop following her.

"Oh, I just need to speak to Andy real quick, then I'll be right in."

She nods and follows Kayla into our cabin.

"Esme, is there a problem?" Andy asks.

"I just wondered about the graffiti and the guy in the woods. Could it be someone from town? I know a lot of camps don't have the warmest and fuzziest relationship with nearby towns."

He frowns. "We've had a few small issues, but nothing too bad. I can't see why a local would want to do this."

"How small were the issues? Maybe a local thinks they're major?"

"Yes, perhaps they might. I'll mention it to the police," Andy says.

Wow, he really isn't going to tell me what these "issues" are.

"Are you going into town now?" I ask.

It's a small town; there is no way the police station will still be open.

"No, I have a contact I can call," Andy says.

"Good."

He smiles and his thin lips disappear. "Great thinking, Esme. You're smart."

"Er, thanks," I reply.

"Get some sleep. And don't worry—I'll sort this out."

He turns and walks away. *Don't worry?* Sounds like Andy *really* doesn't know me at all. My nan, my mom and I are Olympic-level worriers.

I sneak into the cabin, tiptoe through the main room and climb up to my bunk. My body is heavy and aches. I sink into the mattress and sigh. Every part of me is tired.

"You all right?" Kayla whispers in the darkness.

I left our door wide open so we can see and hear the campers.

"I am, but I don't think Rebekah is," I say, keeping my voice quiet. "We should check on her first thing."

"What's wrong with her?" Kayla asks.

"I don't know, but she seems really scared. During the meeting she looked like she wanted to hide, and she was chewing on her lip and staring when we walked back to the cabins. I know that she was bullied in school, and I've noticed that when someone disagrees with her, even nicely, she tends to go inside herself."

"You notice everything, Esme."

I turn onto my side and am confronted with something that steals my breath.

I stare, unblinking, until my eyes sting and water leaks from the corners.

No.

I suck in air as fear clutches my stomach in a vise-like grip.

Carved into the wall by my pillow are the letters *LC.*

They were not there before.

I freeze, staring at the letters while anxiety curls in my stomach.

Lillian Campbell.

I lick my dry lips and force my breath to slow down. In for five, out for five.

God no.

She has been in our room, in my *bed.* I want to jump out of the bunk, run away and never look back.

She was right here.

Nausea rolls my stomach.

Kayla is in bed. Do not freak out.

I reach out, my hand trembling as it gets closer to the wall. My index finger pokes into the rough scratches and loose shavings drop to the floor.

No.

Retracting my hand, I ball it into a fist.

My shoulders hunch.

What do I do now? Someone here besides me and Kayla knows what happened ten years ago. Maybe it's Lillian, or maybe it's someone else—someone she told or a witness we didn't know existed.

Ten years. That's a long time to carry anger.

"Esme?"

I clear my throat, but I'm unable to look away from Lillian's initials. It takes everything I have to keep my cool. "Yes, I notice things. And you only notice when cute guys are around."

"It's a talent, I have a cute-guy radar. Night, babe," Kayla says.

Her voice is barely audible over the shrill ringing in my ears.

"Night," I whisper as my shaking finger curls around the *C*.

Why am I not telling Kayla about this?

21

In the morning, we're in the lake. The sun shines brightly through a thin smattering of fluffy clouds. Andy thinks it's a good idea to keep the campers' minds off the person in the woods by switching our hike today with the water sports that were scheduled for later in the week.

My fingertips graze the lake's surface of the water. I know the water is smooth, but all I feel is the rough texture of the carved initials. Lillian has been in our room.

I'm in up to my knees watching my and Cora's group swim the length of the lake.

On the other side of the lake, four merged groups of boys are having a kayak-racing mini tournament. Andy said the winners will get extra s'mores, but we all know he'll let everyone have extra.

The inflatable water course is coming out soon. Some of the guys are setting it up.

The atmosphere is somewhat tense. The staff have information that the campers don't and it's making us slightly paranoid. Well, it's certainly making *me* paranoid.

If I had a dollar for everyone I witnessed looking at the forest, I could buy a beach house in Malibu.

"Keep going, girls, you're doing great," I call as they swim back to me. The trained instructors and lifeguards watch closely and occasionally tell one of the girls how to improve their stroke. Bless, some of them still look like they're drowning.

"Did you manage to speak to Rebekah?" Cora asks, staring ahead at the girls. Or maybe she's staring beyond them, into the trees. "Kayla mentioned at breakfast that you were worried about her last night."

"Not yet. She got up late. She seems okay now, though, cheering her girls on in the race," I say, blinking my heavy eyelids. I'm tired after last night and can barely focus on anything.

I remember how weird Rebekah was at the arcade. And the possible sighting of Lillian outside.

"Good," Cora says.

"Is it always like this? Not the 'someone's watching' thing, but are there always issues coming from all directions?"

She laughs. "Pretty much. How are you handling it?"

"It's slightly exhausting, but I'm much better at helping other people with their problems than I am with my own."

"You can talk about yours with me, if you want."

"Thanks, I'll keep that in mind."

Yeah, no. I don't think I'll be doing that. Talking to Kayla right now feels weird and we share everything. How would she react to the initials on the wall?

Not great.

I shiver at the thought of Lillian creeping up onto my bed and carving those letters. Was she snarling as she dug into the wood? Did she pretend she was cutting into me?

"It's good to talk, Esme," Cora tells me.

I clench my jaw. "I agree. I'm fine for now."

"You're a fixer."

"Sorry?"

Laughing, she turns to me. "You fix things for other people, you're good at it. Unfortunately, that usually ends with neglecting yourself."

Ugh, really? We're going there. I can't have her worrying about me or telling anyone that she has Esme concerns.

"I overthink," I tell her. "So right now I'm convinced that something bad is going on. Like, more than pranks."

"Ah. My sister is just the same. If I don't check in, she thinks I've drowned in the lake or something."

"That sounds like me."

"You care, that's not a bad thing. And bad stuff does happen at camps."

"What?"

"Accidents, I mean. We're doing games and sports in the water and in the woods, and that brings more dangers."

I gulp. "Has anything really bad happened here?"

"We've had a few near misses. Last year a kid got into trouble in the water and almost drowned. That's why we test their swimming ability before they get in and have the waist-high rule for non-swimmers. Another camper tripped over a branch when she wasn't looking and broke her ankle."

I'm looking for something more sinister. Besides, I don't think a camper is behind what's going on.

Lillian. Obviously. Hello, you have her initials carved into your wall!

"There's a shoe! Gross!" Ava shouts.

Cora and I look up.

Ava drops the shoe that she's holding back into the water. She and Addison back up.

"What?" I ask, wading over to her. The water hits my shorts. "A shoe?"

"Ugh," she mutters, and bends down, keeping her head above water as she reaches into the water. "Here."

I take the tennis shoe that was probably white once but is now green.

"Wonderful."

"You think someone threw that in?" Ava asks.

I nod. "Yep."

Addison's eyes widen. "I would be so mad if someone threw mine in the lake."

"Me too," I tell her. "Looks like it's been here a while, though, so it was probably from years ago." The shoe is slimy. "I'll chuck this. You two go catch up with the others. You're both doing so well."

"Thanks, Esme," they chime in unison.

They dive back into the water belly-first.

I manage to turn before I get a face full of water.

Holding the shoe by the heel with two fingers, I take it out of the lake and dump it in the trash.

Andy shakes his head. "I once found a T-shirt and a hairbrush in the lake."

"I guess it's not one big happy family all the time," I say.

"We have our fair share of arguments among the campers," he confirms. "It usually happens week three, when they really feel like they're family."

"A week of peace left."

"Enjoy it while it lasts," Andy replies.

"Have the cops got in contact yet?"

"Not yet. I called last night, and they said they'll keep me informed. I'll let you all know when I hear from them. No one has noticed anything so far today."

"The forest seems quiet," I say. Since I've been out here this morning not once has the hair on the back of my neck stood up.

"Let's hope it stays that way. The last thing the camp needs is a reputation for having a stalker lurking around. We're the best youth camp in the area and I intend to keep it that way."

"Are you worried?"

His red eyebrows meet in the middle. "No. Are you, Esme?"

Yes, I'm worried. I'm scared for the campers, I'm scared for Kayla and I'm scared for myself. Mostly, though, I feel guilty. If I weren't here, would any of this be happening?

"A little." He can tell that I am, so lying isn't going to help me. "I don't want the campers to be frightened."

"It's okay to worry. In fact, it's normal. This isn't the first time I've had to deal with the public wandering onto camp land. It just takes a conversation. Plus, we have cleaning staff, cooks and delivery people coming and going, the campers rarely notice who's supposed to be here or not."

Isn't that *more* dangerous? If the campers assume everyone here is part of the camp, they could trust someone they shouldn't.

"Don't look so concerned," Andy says. "It really is fine. You'll come to realize that in time, especially if you come back next year. There are things that are part of being a counselor that the campers have no clue about." He smiles. "I bet there were people closer to camp than you think when you were last here."

I know there were.

22

Jake and Olly help the guys set up the inflatable obstacle course on the lake.

All of the campers are standing on the edge of the water, bouncing.

After anchoring the course, the guys test it, climbing up, running through and around obstacles and sliding down the slide into the water at the end.

Andy laughs. "Okay, looks like it's ready to go. Four at a time."

Two counselors stand by the start and two by the finish.

Kayla and I wade into the lake and stop about halfway along the giant orange inflatable. The water is almost up to my shoulders, but I love being in the lake, so I don't care.

I watch as camper after camper runs along the obstacle course, some making it and others falling in.

When they get off, I'm getting on it.

Kayla moves along the inflatable, a little further from me, getting a better look as the campers go by.

My eyes drift to the forest, to the entrance of the trail that leads to the green flag route. It also leads to the site of the fire.

I blink, my eyes flitting past and then shooting back. Was that a flash?

I turn to face the forest, and through the pine trees, I see it again. A glint, like light bouncing off glass.

Lillian is watching.

I'm about to call to Kayla when the inflatable suddenly dips toward me. I gasp and hold my hands out as if I can single-handedly stop it from tipping over. The four campers on it scream as they're thrown into the lake. It's too deep here for some of them.

I grab Ava as she kicks to the surface. The other counselors rush over, and Andy shouts orders to the rest of the children to get out of the lake. Kayla has two of the campers who fell in, and Isabel is tall enough that she can walk on tiptoes back to land.

"Are you okay?" I ask Ava.

"That was so cool!"

That's great, they loved it.

The inflatable shrinks as it loses air.

All of the campers are standing on the beach, laughing and chatting about the "inflata-fail." At least they're not scared.

Cora takes over from me and Kayla. She sits the girls who fell into the water down with a towel and asks them what happened.

"What the hell was that?" Olly asks me.

I shrug. "I have no idea. One minute I'm watching them and the next minute the thing is falling toward me."

"There must be a hole in it," Kayla says.

Andy shuffles over, face ashen. "Are you two okay?" he asks me and Kayla.

Kayla nods, linking arms with Jake.

"Do you know what was wrong with it?" Jake asks.

"I had a look and found a small hole." Jake shakes his head. "I must have missed it when doing my checks."

Or Lillian did it after his checks. Then she watched from the forest as the thing went down.

I shiver and wrap a towel around myself, though I'm not actually cold.

"It might have torn on the way out there. These things happen, Andy," Mary says, joining our group.

They don't, actually.

Are none of them concerned that this could be more than an accident?

How did it stay up for so long, though?

The guys tug the inflatable to the beach and pull it up onto the grass.

"All right, campers," Cora says. "Let's get changed and head back out for lunch. Hot dogs and s'mores!"

There's a collective cheer before the campers bundle into their cabins.

I walk away from the group, my hands in fists, and head over to the inflatable.

Marcus and Lorenzo are frowning at something.

"What is it?" I ask, crouching down next to them.

The inflatable material is slit.

I take a deep breath through my nose. "What could have done this?" I ask.

Lorenzo shakes his head. "I dunno. It looks like a neat cut but could have been a rock."

There are a few rocks on the beach, but none of them look particularly sharp. Something near the slit catches my eye.

"Let's leave this here until it's dry, then see if Andy wants to get a new one or have this one repaired," Marcus says.

He and Lorenzo walk away.

I run my finger over a sticky residue around the slit. It looks like the material was cut and then shoddily fixed. Someone taped it so it would stay inflated temporarily, until the water ruined the tape. It was probably masking tape, which wouldn't hold for too long in water.

"Esme, come on, we need to get changed," Kayla calls.

I stand and nod. "Okay."

What should I say to them all?

I'll tell Kayla while we're getting ready and see what she thinks.

I jog to our cabin and Kayla closes the bedroom door behind us.

"That was insane," she says, stripping off her soggy swimsuit.

"Uh-huh," I say, pulling clean underwear, a pair of shorts and a T-shirt from the tiny dresser. "It's actually more insane than you think. . . ."

"Oh no," she says, rolling her eyes. "I don't want to hear any more conspiracy theories, Esme."

"It's not a conspiracy theory. The cut looks like it was done with a blade and there was this residue on it, the kind you get when you try to wash off a sticker. It was taped, badly."

Kayla shakes her head. "You need to stop with this."

"Can you please listen to what I'm telling you? Right before it went down, I saw a flash in the woods."

"It's daylight, a flash wouldn't be visible."

"No, not like the camera the other night. This was like the sun bouncing off a lens. I'm telling you Lillian did this. She watched and took photos too."

"Okay, stop!" Kayla pulls on a T-shirt and scowls at me. "If *we* stop talking about this, then it didn't happen. You're playing with fire, Esme, and it has to freaking *stop*! Forget this and forget Lillian. The whole thing was her fault anyway. I'm not risking my time here or my relationship with Jake over that crazy freak."

I stand there, speechless, as she whips the door open and slams it behind her.

Kayla has checked out. The games are getting more sinister.

And I'm alone.

23

I spend the rest of the day avoiding Kayla, and she does the same.

Andy sees no reason why we can't have the night off as planned. The inflatable was an accident and the campers are all fine. He said the cops are looking into the ex-counselors.

But I know they won't find anything.

I'm by the campfire with Tia, Rebekah, Olly and Jake.

Kayla is getting changed into sweats and meeting us out here.

The flames crackle gently as the last of the fire struggles to stay alight.

I watch the embers float before disappearing into the air.

Olly nudges my side with his. "What's going on?"

"Huh? Nothing."

"We can tell it's not nothing, you know," Tia says, scooping her long hair over one shoulder.

I raise my eyes to hers. "I've been distracted, but I'm fine."

I'm on my own and have no one to talk to. Kayla has made it clear that she's done with the whole thing, and I can't bring anyone else in on this.

Mostly I feel horrible for keeping the inflatable tampering a secret.

Rebekah twists her hands together like she's trying really damn hard not to voice her opinion.

I'm not sure I want to hear it right now.

There are more important things I need to worry about. Like Kayla.

"What's happening?" Olly asks. "Please tell us."

"We . . . I thought we were closer than this, Esme," Rebekah says. "Whatever is goin' on, we can help. Are you homesick?"

That sounds much better than the truth. "I'm close to my parents," I say. "I've missed my nan's birthday. It was last week."

Actually, it was two months ago and I was there, at her place. We ordered Mexican food. She drank a lot of tequila and sang sixties songs on her karaoke machine until three a.m.

"I'm sure she won't be angry with you," Tia says. "You can always celebrate when you get home."

"Yeah, I will. Thanks. What do you guys want to do tonight? No walks in the forest!"

Please go with the subject change.

Jake laughs. "The next time we go into the forest, I'll find that creep."

"We don't need to go search for anyone," Tia says. "Town is a bad idea after last time."

"Does that mean we're not goin' back?" Rebekah asks.

Tia's smile widens. "Not at all."

I'm not going back.

"Are you sure that's it?" Olly asks me while the other three argue about whether we would be crazy to go back to town.

"Uh-huh," I reply, looking at the dimple in his cheek because I can't meet his eyes.

He nods. "There's something you're not telling me."

There's a lot I'm not telling you, to be honest.

"No, it's just . . . Some things are complicated."

"I understand that we haven't known each other for long, but you can talk to me."

It's kind of weird, being secluded with these people twenty-four seven. It feels like I've known them for years. It's the oddest feeling ever.

"I can talk to you, and I'm grateful for that," I say.

"You want to start doing that now?" Olly asks.

I really don't.

Olly thinks I'm a good person, and I'd like to keep it that way. He would hate me if he found out what I had been involved in. Maybe he could look past the accident, but his opinion would change if he knew I lied about it for *ten years.*

"I'm freaking out that we were chased and watched. Okay, there you have it. I'm a massive baby."

Chuckling, he lowers his voice. "We're all a little freaked out. Even Jake, but he will never admit it."

"What the hell is this?" Cora's voice isn't particularly loud, but it's heard clearly by us and by a group of counselors on the dock.

She comes running down the porch of the staff cabin holding a piece of paper in one hand and a kitchen knife in the other.

I push myself to my feet, feeling gritty sand embedded under my nails.

"What's wrong?" I ask.

"This was *stabbed* into the door!"

The counselors run toward us and we all meet a pale Cora.

She turns the paper around with shaking hands. It reads:

We're going to have some fun
Alert the cops and you'll be done

My heart thuds.

I try to take a breath, but it's like breathing through a blanket.

"That's creepy as hell," Jake says, snatching the paper from Cora. "Who do you think wrote it?"

"What do you think it means?"

"Could it be one of the kids?"

"Why would kids write that?"

"Is it the stalker in the woods?"

"What do they want?"

"You guys need to calm down."

I stand back and listen to the comments flying all around me.

My head is spinning so fast, I'm dizzy.

Lillian wants us alone out here.

24

We're outside in the middle of the night with the campers fast asleep in their cabins because Andy has called *another* emergency meeting. I think he actually likes calling them.

He's holding the note in one tightly clenched fist like it's a prize he never wants to let go of.

I'm still sitting on the tampered-with-inflatable information.

I've left it too long and now I don't know how to speak up or what I would say.

What a nightmare.

"All right," Andy says, clearing his throat noisily. "We received this note this evening, and I find it completely unacceptable. Pranks are fine. I started them and encourage everyone to have silly fun." He holds the note up. "This is going too far, though. We need to find out who's responsible for it."

Why does he think it's a camper or a counselor?

"What will happen to the person responsible?" Jake asks. "Do they get booted?"

Andy shakes his head. "No, we will speak to them. *I* will speak to them. We're not about punishment, but the young person responsible has to understand that a prank like this won't be tolerated."

The prank angle seems to be the only one he's willing to accept.

Kayla hasn't said a word since she walked out of the cabin and into the middle of this mess.

I can see in the tightness of her eyes and her hard jaw that she's thinking. Maybe she's finally accepting that this is about Lillian. That this, quite possibly, *is* Lillian.

So many scenarios run through my mind about what happened after we left, what Lillian wants to happen now and what could happen if I react in different ways. Does she want to talk?

"Esme?" Olly says.

"Huh?" I look around. Everyone is gone. Well, they're standing up and chatting in smaller groups.

Tia, Rebekah, Jake, Olly and Kayla are still sitting with me.

"You haven't blinked in five minutes," Rebekah says.

"Sorry, this is all a bit crazy."

Kayla shakes her head. "This isn't happening."

"What isn't happening?" Jake asks.

I widen my eyes at Kayla, telling her to shut up.

Of the two of us, the most likely to crack is me. *What is she doing?*

"Can't you see? All of this is connected. Someone is trying to hurt us," Kayla says.

Tia laughs. "Don't you think that's a bit dramatic?"

"How? The missing tags, the photographer in the woods and now this note."

And the inflatable. And the initials on our cabin wall. And the note in Kayla's pocket. I swallow all the secrets I'm keeping.

Rolling her eyes, Tia tilts her head like she thinks Kayla has lost it. "I'm not denying that someone is messing with us, but that doesn't mean they're an ax-wielding murderer."

I hold my hands up. "Calm down. No one said anything about a murderer or axes!"

"All right, let's stop with the wild theories," Olly says. "No one is talking about anything as crazy as that. Let's think rationally."

"I am!" Kayla snaps.

Her hands curl into fists and she takes deep breaths, like she's trying to calm herself down. She is getting more and more agitated.

"What do you think Andy is going to do?" I ask. "Do we believe the threat?"

Jake snorts. "Why would we believe this? It's clearly someone screwing around, just like the graffiti."

"Well, I think the fact that Andy called *another* meeting shows that he believes there is some threat," I tell the group. "I don't know that this creep will do anything to us, games or whatever, but I do think they want something."

"We should find out what and give it to them," Rebekah says, looking between Tia and me. "Right?"

I shrug and look away.

"What do we do?" Jake asks. "Leave a reply stabbed to a tree?"

"You're not helping," I tell him.

"No one is helping because there is nothing to help. We ignore the note and burn it, like we hid the writing on the staff cabin."

Rebekah shakes her head. "You want to pretend nothing is wrong?"

"I don't want some idiot who thinks they're freaking Jason Voorhees getting in the way of our summer."

"Jason Voorhees, really?" Tia scoffs.

Jake's eyes turn black and he grits his teeth.

"All right, everyone get some rest!" Andy shouts. "We'll do the same as when we saw someone in the forest. Always double up with teams, CITs with counselors."

"We're not going to the police?" Mary asks, her piercing eyes wide below her bangs.

Catalina puts an arm around her and stares at Andy.

"Not tonight. I'll go tomorrow if anything else happens," Andy replies.

He walks off and half the counselors follow.

Mary doesn't move.

"Are you okay?" I ask.

"We should go to the police now! They can protect us better than Andy. Why would he want us to keep this quiet?" she says.

"He's scared for the camp and its reputation. *His* reputation," I say.

She grinds her teeth so hard I hear them creak together. My stomach lurches.

"Mary," I say, shuddering. "Stop. You can talk to me, but I really need you to stop doing that."

Snapping her lips together, she looks away, her cheeks turning pink. "Sorry. I do it when I'm stressed."

"What are you going to do?" I ask.

"I think we should all agree to go to the cops," she says.

"That might not be a good idea."

"Or it might be the only thing we can do to stop this weirdo from hurting us."

Rebekah and Jake stop dead in front of us. Jake tilts his head. "Are you seriously thinking this crap is real? This dude wants us to panic. He wants to watch us run around, paranoid and worried about what he'll do next. Mary, he's just going to play games. We can beat him at that."

In my mind, I substitute *he* for *she*.

"Beat him at his games?" Mary says. "What does that even mean? Do we play along? Pretend that we don't see whatever he does? That doesn't work for me. I won't stay here in fear and allow someone to *threaten* us."

"You're right," I tell her. "We shouldn't allow anyone to make us live in fear. But we have to be sure of what's going on. If we go to the cops, tell them there's a new crazy development, cause panic and this turns out to be a hoax, someone with a sick idea of fun, then who will trust us with their kids again? This is bigger than us, Mary."

I'm so scared that Lillian will follow through with her threat. Before we do anything, I have to know how far she will go for revenge. I'm also totally not on board with the cops finding Lillian. Once they do, she'll talk, and then it's all over for me and Kayla.

We could end up with a criminal record.

My parents preach honesty and truth about every five minutes. If I lie, like *ever,* they are right there to set things straight. Which usually means I'm guilted into telling the truth and then chastised for not doing it earlier. They make their disappointment clear.

It's no fun.

I can only imagine what they'd do if they found out I've been lying for *ten years.*

"Not yet. Andy wants to wait," Mary sneers. "All the while this freak is watching us." She looks at the forest again. "He's probably watching right now."

"Okay, let's not get too ahead of ourselves," I say. Her words send a shiver right down the center of my spine.

"Someone has left a goddamn threat at a kid's camp!" Kayla snaps. She throws her hands into the air. "We are in danger and we're sitting here having a chat about it?"

"Okay, Kayla," I say, grabbing her hand. I tug her closer and she doesn't resist. Suddenly, I feel like our roles have switched. "I'll take her to bed," I tell the others. "She's tired."

Cora nods. "That's a good idea. Get some rest."

Kayla doesn't need a good night's sleep, she needs to see clearly. We can't go telling people about any of this stuff.

No one can ever know what we did.

25

"Kayla?" I say once we close the door of our small room.

She completely ignores me and changes into her pajamas, punching her legs through the leg holes as if she's angry with them. She rams both arms through the sleeves and tugs the top over her head.

"This is too much, Esme!"

"I know, but we *have* to keep it together."

She swings around to face me. "What's going to happen?"

"We'll be okay if we stick together and *stay calm.*"

"They're going to find out what happened that night."

My heart misses a beat. "No, they won't."

I don't believe my own words, but I want to calm her down.

"Of course they will! How can they not?"

"If Lillian wanted everyone to know, she would have said something by now. She isn't trying to out us; she's trying to scare us. She wants payback. If they find out and Andy kicks us out, her game is over."

"You think so?"

Maybe.

"I do."

"She was the crazy one that night, Esme."

I take a deep breath as I change into my pajamas. "I remember. That doesn't mean we're innocent. We did something wrong as well."

"We didn't mean to . . . ," she whispers as she slips under the covers.

"I know that, too," I reply. "We need to get some sleep. We're not going to figure anything out tonight."

Kayla rolls over and faces the wall, away from me. "Night, Esme."

"Night," I reply, climbing up the ladder.

The last thing I see before I close my eyes is Lillian's carved initials.

≈

I jump, awake and gasping and clutching my blanket as a loud thud seems to echo outside.

"What the hell was that?" Kayla asks.

I chuck the blanket off and scramble down the ladder.

She's already out of her bunk, waiting for me, and we run into the main room.

"What's happening?" Alana asks.

All of the girls are awake and sitting up in bed.

Cora comes out of her room sliding shoes onto her feet.

"Stay in bed," I tell the campers. "We'll go and see."

Kayla, Cora and I go outside. It's beginning to get light out. The sun is peeking through the trees.

What was it? I look around, scanning the area. The lake is fine, the beach, the outdoor equipment. What . . .

"Oh my God," I breathe, finally locating the cause of the noise.

Wedged into the door of the shed by the road is an ax.

Cora turns around and says into the cabin, "It's all right, girls. It was just some equipment that has fallen over." She glances back at Kayla and me with a look that means "sort this out *now.*"

By the time we reach the bottom step, counselors from every cabin are outside. So is Andy.

The air is warming.

"What on earth . . . ?" Andy says.

The staff cabin is next to the shed, so he gets there first.

Written on the door just above the ax in red paint:

I SAID NO COPS

"I don't like this at all," Mary says, pressing one hand to her mouth. She turns in a circle, looking into the forest. "Last night I said I wanted to go to the cops. He was out there. He's out there now. Watching."

Paranoia will drown you, and Mary is starting to sink.

"Hey," I say, laying my hand on her tense back.

She flinches away from me, spinning around as if she's afraid I'm the one stalking the camp.

Jake steps forward, places one foot on the door and pulls the ax from the wood.

Andy nods at him. "Marcus, Lorenzo, can you deal with the door quickly? The campers will be up soon."

Olly isn't here. I guess he's the one staying with the boys in the cabin.

Mary shakes her head, cowering.

"It's going to be fine," Catalina says, but her quavering voice suggests otherwise. "I'm going to check on Tia and the girls."

"Are you okay, Mary?" I ask.

"An *ax*."

The other counselors disperse, either going to tell the campers nothing has happened or to conceal the evidence.

Andy takes the ax from Jake and heads into the staff cabin.

Jake shakes his head and touches my shoulder as he walks past.

It's just me and Mary now. Kayla walks off with Jake.

Mary hugs her arms around her stomach. "This isn't right. What if the man in the woods comes with a gun next time?"

"Mary, he won't. Okay? We'll figure this out, find whoever it is and stop them without putting the kids in danger. We have to stay strong for them."

Lorenzo and Marcus come running back with a bucket of soapy water and two sponges. They dunk the sponges and start scrubbing immediately.

Mary takes two deep breaths and closes her eyes. "Okay," she says, opening them again. "I'm giving this a couple of days and then I'm taking things into my own hands."

"Let's talk about it again later. Right now we need to make sure the campers are getting dressed and then feed them. It'll be breakfast time soon."

Mary's worried eyes look straight through me. She glances toward the forest once again and then walks away.

If she's not careful, she's going to push Lillian even further.

26

Tonight is . . . what's the best way to describe something that's on a downward spiral? We're in a tornado about to touch down.

The day was fine, after the door was scrubbed. We hiked close to the forest's edge, made campfires, built dens and ate bowls of chili with nachos.

The campers are happy.

The counselors, behind fake smiles, are not.

We seem to be divided, too, figuratively and literally. On one side of the campfire are the counselors and CITs who are pro-cops, and the other side—hello, my side—are those of us who think cops are a bad idea. You could also divide the no-cop camp into two groups. There are the no-cops basing their opinion on this being some dumb, harmless joke, and the no-cops who think it's more than that.

How can anyone think this is nothing more than a silly prank?

I don't know how to handle this. Maybe if Kayla and I tell

everyone what happened with Lillian this will be over. Or maybe it will anger her and she'll hurt someone.

It's a huge gamble.

Lillian is messing with us, and I don't know how far she will take it. I still haven't told Kayla, or anyone, about the LC carved in the wall. She was *in* our room. Kayla wouldn't be able to relax if she knew that; she would be petrified that Lillian would smother her in her sleep.

It would set off the anxiety in Kayla that she's fought so hard to get under control. She was in a bad car accident as a kid, one that killed her nana. It took years of therapy for her to get to where she is now. That could all be undone if I'm not careful.

Never again do I want to see her sobbing hysterically on the floor because she can't deal with the possibility that something bad might happen.

Kayla and I should leave. What would Lillian do if we tried? I think back to the CIT pamphlet both Kayla and I got. It said we'd regret it if we didn't come back. What if that *was* Lillian making a threat? Would she make our lives even worse if we left?

Besides, how would we explain coming home *weeks* early to our parents?

They would call camp and boom, suddenly we're having a lot of talks. Or rather an interrogation. Mom and Dad would not let it go lightly and they would absolutely not believe I was just homesick.

My dad is quite literally a human lie detector. He's a polygraph examiner and conducts the test for hopefuls applying for a job with the FBI. That makes him sound a lot cooler than he is, like he's *in* the FBI and could be an extra on *Criminal Minds.* It's not like that at all.

He conducts the test and sends the results off.

"What are we going to do about this?" Jake asks.

"We?" Tia curls her top lip.

He scowls. "I'm not sitting here waiting for some creep in the forest to take another picture or stroke my hair while I sleep!"

"Let's not go there," I say.

"Whoever it is, they can't get into the cabins," Rebekah adds.

Untrue. Lillian carved her damn initials into the wall by my freaking pillow.

I bite my tongue. Rebekah doesn't need to be worrying about the very real fact that our resident stalker can get inside the buildings we sleep in.

"You sure about that?" Olly says. "I don't think it would take much."

My jaw drops as I twist my head toward him. "Can we not? How would someone sneak into a cabin of twenty people? Also, the doors are locked at night."

"If it was an ex-counselor, they might have a key," he replies.

Groaning, I close my eyes. But then I'm hit with a thought . . . how did *Lillian* get a key?

Was she a CIT?

She must have been about a year or two older than us. She might have worked here last year in order to get a key, to learn the layout and routines of the camp.

My rapidly thudding heart is making my head spin.

Andy has staff files in his office. Which is a locked filing cabinet inside the staff cabin.

I have to get into the files and find out if Lillian was here in the past couple of years.

"Andy!" Tia calls, standing up.

Silence falls. A sea of heads whip her way, mine included.

Andy, frowning, says, "Yes?"

"Your theory about it being someone who worked here is right. Only, they might not have been a 'bad' one. Which means they could have a key to the cabins."

"CITs aren't given keys, Tia," Andy says.

"That doesn't mean he couldn't have gotten one when he was working here!"

Andy chews his lip.

I glance at every member of cops and no-cops. They're all thinking the same thing, that this person might be able to get to us. Even the doubters have frown lines.

"I think we should go to the police *now*!" Mary says. She stands and folds her arms, her pursed lips and darkening eyes a warning to Andy: *You go, or I will.*

"Shh! We don't actually know anything for sure," I say. "All we have is a lot of speculation."

"And we should let the cops find out if there's anything behind this threat!" Mary throws her hands up in the air, exasperated with all of us. "What's wrong with you people?"

"Mary," Andy says softly, "let's calm down so we don't wake the campers. I understand you're worried, but there is nothing to suggest that we're in danger."

"This guy tried to get a group lost, graffitied a cabin, watched us from the forest and left threatening notes stabbed and axed into doors. What more do you need, Andy?"

Well, when you put it that way . . .

No one actually moves, but a few on the no-cops side nod. The balance is shifting. We were about even, but Mary's little speech has them spooked.

"There has been nothing that's an actual threat to our safety," Andy says.

"All right," Jake says. "What if a few of us go into the forest and check it out, see if there's anything suspicious? Would that make you feel better, Mary?"

"Are you crazy?" Kayla snaps. "You can't go out there in the dark."

"I'll take a flashlight," he says. "A group of us guys will have a look."

"I'll go," Olly says. Marcus and Lorenzo offer too.

"In a world of evolving equality, I'll be going with you," I tell them.

Olly shakes his head, but I raise my hand.

"I'm not a damsel in distress. I'm going. We have kids here and I won't figure anything out just sitting around." And if Lillian is out there, I need to get to her before they do.

Andy nods. "All right. I want you to have radios . . . and pepper spray. Actually, I'm going to come; I should be with you. Cora, I need you in charge here. Have your radio on and we'll keep in constant contact."

"What about weapons?" Mary asks.

I side-eye her. "We're not taking weapons!"

"We don't need any," Jake says.

"Pepper spray is all we'll take," Andy says sternly. "All right, everyone who is coming wait by the staff cabin. I'll get the supplies."

Cora walks with Andy and they chat in hushed tones.

I start to follow Olly, Jake, Marcus and Lorenzo, when Kayla catches my wrist.

Her eyes are wild, freaked. "You can't go out there, Esme."

"Yes, I can. I'll be fine."

"What if she's out there?" Kayla whispers, her eyes wide.

"Maybe that's a good thing. If I can talk to her, find out what she wants and apologize for not making sure she was okay that night, maybe this will all be over," I reply in a hushed voice.

"I don't like it."

"Not exactly wanting to sing from the rooftops either, Kayla, but I have to try *something*."

"You're absolutely, one hundred percent sure it's her?"

"Yes. *Absolutely*," I say. "I'll be with the others. It's fine."

She drops her arm. "Please, *please* stay safe."

Kayla would never come. She won't do anything remotely dangerous.

"You sure you're coming?" Olly asks.

I turn to him and smile. I probably look like that cringing emoji. "I'm sure."

"All right, let's head out," Andy says. "We stick close together.

Cora, stay with Tia and Rebekah, watch the cabins, make sure no one gets near the campers. Mary and Catalina, watch the forest but don't go into it."

Olly holds my hand tight and we follow Andy.

I take a breath as we step into the dark woods.

The temperature drops.

Goose bumps raise along my arms.

27

A thick white blanket coats the ground ahead of us.

"Mist," I say, swallowing a lump of fear. Well, that's not at all ominous.

I wrap my free arm around my tummy and squeeze Olly's hand.

"Do you want to go back, Esme?" Andy asks.

"No, I want to keep going."

Want isn't quite the right word.

You are fine.

"Where are we going?" I ask.

"We'll check this area and see if there's anything suspicious. I don't think we'll find anything, but it will make everyone back at camp sleep much easier."

Does he think that the stalker dropped their driver's license in the forest?

Our feet disappear as we walk into the mist.

"If I was terrorizing a camp, I'd be very careful about leaving Scooby-Doo clues everywhere," Olly says.

I smile at his Scooby reference.

"If this asshole has left anything, we're going to find it and catch him," Jake says.

"I'd like to get my hands on him," Olly agrees.

Andy looks over his shoulder. "I'd like that too, but we have to be careful with this."

I can't imagine Andy in a fight. Not winning one, anyway.

Snap.

We all turn to the left at the sound. My long hair whips against my face.

"What was that?" Olly mutters.

I blink as a sudden flash of light blinds me.

Pictures.

This time the flash is brighter, like our stalker is much closer.

Flash.

Not again.

I spin around. This one came from the opposite direction.

Flash, flash, flash.

I slap my hand over my eyes. The onslaught of light from both directions makes it almost impossible to see. The fraction of a second between each one isn't enough for my eyes to adjust.

There are orbs of red behind my eyelids.

"Back to camp!" Andy shouts.

I let go of Olly's hand and we all turn around.

I blink again, wincing at the light. How is it possible that it's this bright? The flashes are constant.

Without thinking, I take off. My feet thud against the ground as I sprint, the wind whipping at my face.

I can't see, and I don't know where the others are.

My stomach coils around and around.

What is she doing?

Does she want to get to me?

The air is cold, and I can barely see between each painfully bright flash of light.

Flash, flash.

Flash, flash, flash.

They're nonstop now, one after the other, like a rave without music or fun.

"Olly!"

Where is everyone?

"Olly! Andy!"

I cover my eyes with one hand, leaving a small gap at the bottom so I can see the ground a little. My other hand is stretched out in case I hit a tree.

"Where are you?" I call.

Whimpering, I push forward and shout, "Answer me! Olly! Jake!"

Flash, flash, flash, flash, flash.

My head hurts from the bright light, and I cry out.

Biting my lip, I stumble forward.

I can't hear anything but my own heavy breathing and my own heavy footsteps.

"Andy?"

Where are they?

The light stops.

I gasp and squeeze my eyes shut. When I open them again, all I can make out is the outline of trees and dancing circles of light.

Turning around, I look for the others.

But no one is here.

A chill travels down my back.

Where am I?

I turn my head and crouch on the ground. Fear claws my throat.

Where is everyone?

Where is camp?

I'm lost.

Digging my fingernails into a tree, I say a silent prayer. I've never thought much about whether I believe in God, but I will start if I can just get out of here.

In the distance, a sharp *crack* sends goose bumps up my arms. I turn my head and strain to see into the forest.

My heart stutters.

I don't know which direction the noise came from.

Whoever is out there, they could be anywhere.

I want to go home.

I flatten myself against the tree when another crack comes closer. Pressing my palm against my mouth to stifle a scream, I slowly lean my head to one side to look around the tree. I stay close to it, my forehead touching the rough bark.

In front of me is someone dressed head to toe in black, with a hood pulled over their head.

I press my lips together as my stomach bottoms out.

Please don't see me. Please, please, please.

"Esme!" Olly calls in the distance.

"Where are you?" Jake shouts.

Their voices echo through the forest.

My heart leaps. They're not too far away.

The figure—I'm fairly certain it's Lillian, even though I can't make out her face—turns in the direction of their voices.

"Call out, Esme!" Andy orders.

I can't!

I don't know how far away they are. I can't hear their footsteps and their voices aren't close yet. Lillian is maybe twenty feet away. I can't move an inch in case I make a noise.

Lillian looks around, the hood still obscuring her face. She doesn't appear to have a weapon, but there is no way I'm taking that chance. Just like there is no way I'm making a run for it. Stupid people run through a forest when their assailant is just feet away. Then they fall and we all know how that ends.

I don't need to outrun her, I need to outsmart her. And I will do that by pretending I'm not here.

"Esme?" Olly shouts again.

My eyes widen. His voice is much fainter than before.

No, this way! Come back. I wince, willing myself to breathe quietly. *Please come back.*

Lillian moves very slowly in my direction.

Ice-cold fear slithers down my spine.

I steady myself against the tree.

Branches and sticks snap beneath Lillian's feet.

We must be in the publicly owned section of the forest. The

camp's section is kept somewhat maintained. Now I'm out of bounds, away from any kind of safety.

I press my side against the tree and place one foot a step to the left. Lillian is going to pass me, and I have to make sure she doesn't see me.

It's too dark to make out her face. She's tall and slim. I can still only just make her out. She's like an evil paranormal presence in a horror flick. If she began to float and disappeared in a puff of black smoke it wouldn't surprise me. In fact, I would love that.

I want her gone.

Her footsteps are light, but I feel each one vibrate through me.

Crunch. Crunch. Crunch.

I curl smaller inside myself and say another silent prayer.

My grandparents would love to know that I'm praying.

Will I get a chance to tell them?

Flattening myself against the tree, I wait.

Please leave.

Her footsteps slowly get fainter and fainter.

I let out a quiet breath and swipe a single tear from my cheek.

Crouching in the mist, I count in my head.

She must be gone now.

I'm alone again.

My heart thumps.

It's scarier to be alone than it should be. I'd rather be on my own than have Lillian near.

How did she get away just now?

When I reach one hundred, I rise to my feet. The lingering

orbs are gone. I can see normally now, despite the fact that it's dark.

I look around and decide to walk forward. I'm sure that's the way back to camp.

You can do this, Esme. Keep moving.

I clench my hands and run to the beat of my thudding pulse.

28

My feet hurt from running on uneven ground. Sharp pains shoot along my shins. I round a thick bush and whimper, but I can't stop. If I stop now Lillian might catch me.

I run as if she's barely a foot behind me, as if she can reach an arm out and touch me.

Oh God.

"Olly!" I shout, spotting him up ahead.

He spins around and his eyes widen. A fraction of a second later, he's sprinting toward me.

"Esme!"

I'm vaguely aware of the others calling my name and saying how relieved they are, but all I can focus on is Olly.

His arms shoot out to catch me as I run straight into him. My legs give out and he's all that's stopping me from hitting the ground. I lean into him, feeling his warmth seep into my clammy skin. I sob, the relief of being safe drenching me.

The static from Andy's radio crackles as he makes a call to Cora to tell her we're almost back.

"What happened? Are you okay?" Olly asks.

You can't be a big baby now after insisting on coming.

I stand. "I don't know. One minute you guys were there, and the next I—I couldn't find you."

Should I tell them what happened?

No. No, I can't.

"We're so sorry, Esme, we thought you were with us," Andy says, stopping beside me.

I wipe my hands on my shorts and take a ragged breath. "It wasn't anyone's fault, and I'm fine."

"You sure about that?" Jake asks.

"Yeah."

"Did you see anything?"

My body turns cold. "Just a whole lot of trees after the lights."

And the dark figure of Lillian.

"Us too." Andy takes a big breath. "Looks like this person isn't done with their pranks, though."

I nod. "What do we do now?"

"We remain vigilant, stick together and make sure the children are safe," he says.

If I can't get my heart rate under control, I won't be doing anything at all.

"I agree," I whisper. But do I?

Jake scowls. "We ride this out, let this freak have his fun and keep the campers safe. The day they leave, we find out who's taking pictures and leaving notes."

Andy says, "That's settled, then. Let's get back to camp and have a hot drink and let everyone know there's nothing out here."

I look behind me. Somewhere in the distance, Lillian is probably livid because I made it back to the others. She was right near me. I shudder at the thought of her being so close. What would she have done if she'd found me?

I keep a small smile on my face and walk beside Olly, his hand in mine, trying not to crush his bones as I hold on.

"That was eventful," Jake says, his voice brimming with sarcasm.

I wish my evening had been as uneventful as his.

God, I wish I could speak with Kayla right now. She's the only person I can talk to about what just happened. Only I can't really, can I? I was supposed to talk to Lillian and clear this up. I was going to tell her how sorry we were that she got hurt and ask her to forgive us. But when it came down to it, when I was separated from the others, I was scared and hid rather than confronting her. I. Was. Scared.

There, I've admitted it to myself. Esme is a big chicken.

I pretended to be tough and unafraid, but I'm a phony.

Kayla can't find out what happened. She was counting on me to make this stop. I don't know how much more she can take if she knows that Lillian stalked me through the forest like she was stalking her prey.

No, this I have to keep to myself.

We walk into the clearing and the first thing I see is the

bright-white reflection of the moon on the lake. Small ripples in the water make it look jagged, like it could cut into you.

The second thing I see is the remaining group of counselors running toward the staff cabin.

"Shit!" Andy mutters.

What's going on?

We sprint around the lake.

"What is it?" Andy calls when we get close enough that he won't wake the campers up.

"The radio!" Cora says from the porch. "Someone just came on the radio telling us to get in the staff cabin or they'd start a fire. We heard rustling in the forest."

My eyes widen.

How did Lillian get back here so fast?

"What? Okay, I'm calling the police," Andy says.

His response is met with a wild and collective no.

"Get inside," Cora says. "I'll tell you everything."

We stampede into the multiuse cabin.

"What happened while we were away?" Andy demands, pulling the door shut. "We can't all be inside here. No one is watching the campers' cabins!"

Cora shakes her head. "It's not *them* this person wants. They're safer if we're not with them."

"What's going on, Cora?" I ask. "Where are Kayla and Rebekah?"

"They were very anxious out here, so I told them to go in and get some rest a while ago."

Bed? Kayla went to *bed*?

"About ten minutes ago, the first message came through the radio. This voice, it sounded like someone using one of those voice-altering things. They said if we contact anyone, wake the campers or alert the cops or anyone else, we're dead. *Dead.* We didn't know what to do, so we tried to look around, to see who was out there."

"How did this happen?" Andy asks.

"They must have our frequency."

"Why didn't you call me?" he demands.

"I knew you would be back." Cora drops her eyes as she speaks. I don't think she was certain that we would be back.

"When did this person threaten fire?"

Lillian, I correct him in my head.

"Before you came back, literally seconds before. He said, 'Everyone into the cabin or I'll send the food hall up in flames and call the parents.' Half went in the campers' cabins and the rest went in the multiuse to see if we could spot anyone lurking."

"Parents?" Andy's eyes bulge.

"This person has the parents' contact details?" I ask.

Cora shrugs. "I don't want to find out."

"It has to be a former employee," Andy says. "I just can't figure out why he would go to these lengths."

"Do we believe he would actually set the food hall on fire?" Jake asks.

Cora raises her eyebrows. "We *have* to."

"Whoever this is, they want us to be alone," Mary says from the back. "They want us trapped here, slowly going insane from paranoia, constantly worrying what we're going to have to do next."

"Wait, if they want that, then surely they won't set a fire?" Tia says.

"She's right," I say. "How would he do that and get away with it? There would be smoke, and the flames would be seen from town; the fire department would come. It would all be over for him. That one is for sure an empty threat."

Andy is a bobblehead as he agrees with me. "I think you're right. But we shouldn't ignore it. Four years—*four years*—I've been here, and it's always been a safe place. I can't believe this is happening."

"For what it's worth," Jake says, "I don't think this creep is going to hurt anyone. This bullshit is all about fear and every time we have conversations like this and run off into the woods, we're feeding his sick little fantasy. I'll have no problem kicking his ass."

"That may be true," Andy says. "Still, I don't think it would be right to ignore this."

"We can't ignore it," Marcus replies. "He's everywhere."

Lorenzo shakes his head. "Enough of this for tonight. Let's not give him any more attention."

Mary folds her arms and glares at Lorenzo. Catalina puts an arm around her shoulders. "Come on, he's right," she says to Mary. "We should get some sleep. Let's make it look like we're doing what he wants and keeping quiet."

"We *are* doing that," Olly says.

We have no choice.

29

I dig my fists into my stinging eyes and rub.

Man, seven- to ten-year-olds have a crapload of energy.

I'm drained. The incident with Lillian in the woods has me on edge. I woke about every hour, panicked that she was searching for me again. Everyone looks on edge.

But the kids are as excited and loud and bouncy as ever. I feel like I'm hungover, although the only thing I've had to drink since I arrived is water and coffee.

I don't know how the campers haven't realized that every one of our smiles is forced. I'm positive I look like I'm grimacing.

I care about them all, but I'm finding it really hard to bounce off the walls over a new fastest win of tennis.

Lillian is out there, somewhere close I'm sure, watching the morning after her night of insanity.

She's loving it, I'm sure. I bet she's drinking in every second that we look around for her.

It could come back to bite me and Kayla in the ass eventually, if Lillian decides that she wants to make herself known. Which, let's face it, she will. I just hope the others aren't around to hear it when she confronts us.

We're standing by the tennis court in the shade of the trees. Kayla's arms are wrapped around herself like she has to physically hold all of our secrets in.

"How are you doing?" I ask, still looking at the girls and smiling. My jaw aches. I don't know how models do it.

"All right," she mutters. She was awake in bed when I got back, chewing her nails to the quick. Mine are about the same.

"You can tell me the truth, Kayla."

"Can I?"

I fight the urge to push her. "Really, dude? We've known each other since we were obsessed with *High School Musical.* Hell, we have a blood oath!"

"Oh, now it's a blood oath."

Before we decided to become CITs, we hadn't talked about the accident for years. I hate that we spent so long ignoring what we'd done. I *hate* that we ran.

Dipping my head, I wince against the sting of regret.

"Kayla," I prompt.

"What do you want me to say, Esme?" She looks across the court as her girls cheer for another point and purses her lips. "I'm scared. We both know Lillian is going to do something bad. We burned her!" Her voice is low, a whisper, but I feel it in my bones.

"We don't *know* that." I don't say it with much conviction. I'm shocked to hear those words come out of Kayla's mouth. She's always been a total pro at denial.

"Yes we do! If we hadn't been out there that night, then none of this would be happening now. She wants revenge. I still don't think we're to blame, but *we* didn't get hurt."

"We never meant for anything bad to happen."

"Esme, can we not talk about this anymore, please? I'm totally over it."

We never talk about what we did anymore and it's slowly driving me crazy. You're supposed to talk, everyone says so.

Kayla storms off, leaving me with a burn in my chest that makes me resent my best friend just a little. I need her support right now.

I've spent so much time and effort making sure things aren't too much for her. I never get that in return.

Fine. Whatever.

After games outside, we go in for dinner and then to the beach for a campfire.

We finish up the day with s'mores. It's a pretty standard end; there haven't been many evenings that don't include marshmallows.

"Esme," Mary says behind her massive bangs, "can you pop into my cabin and see if Phoebe is there? She went to get her hoodie and hasn't come back out and I need to help Ava."

"Sure," I reply.

Kayla walks past me to join our girls by the campfire. They're mostly split up tonight, though, mixed heavily with the boys.

Jogging up the cabin steps, I twist the doorknob and let myself in. "Phoebe?"

My eyes bulge. Through a crack in the door to Tia and

Rebekah's tiny room, I catch a glimpse of Rebekah pulling her T-shirt down over her head. Her side and most of her stomach is burned.

"Esme?"

My pulse skitters as Phoebe walks up to me. She smiles.

I jump away from Rebekah and Tia's room. "Are you okay?" I ask her.

"I was getting a sweater."

Burns!

"You ready to join us?" I ask.

Rebekah has burns!

She nods. "Yeah."

What does this mean? I dash out of the cabin with Phoebe right behind me. I don't think that Rebekah saw me. She didn't turn around.

I walk with Phoebe until she sits down with her group. As soon as the other girls embrace her, I dart around the campfire and scan the crowd for Kayla. We need to have a conversation right this second. Whether she wants to or not.

"Kayla, can we walk?" I say when I find her.

Olly and Jake, who are sitting next to her, look up too.

Her shoulders slump like I'm the last person she wants to see. I'll try not to take that personally. "Er, sure, Esme. . . ."

She stands up and puts on a fake toothy smile that almost makes me roll my eyes. Doing the bitchy smile to me, really? Is she doing the popular thing now?

I grin back and grab Kayla's arm. "This will only take a minute."

The guys watch us suspiciously. Come on, we could be talking about anything. I'll tell the boys it's something menstruation related, that'll shut it down real fast.

Someone who knows the routine of camp and has access to cabins is doing this. . . .

"Jesus, Esme, what's going on?" Kayla asks, stumbling behind me as I tug her by the hand. She pulls out of my grip and glares.

"I know who Lillian is," I say.

"You what?"

"Rebekah."

30

"It's *Rebekah*!" I say her name again because Kayla is looking at me the way you look at people arguing in Walmart.

She blinks and shakes her head. "What are you talking about?"

"It's *her*! Lillian. Rebekah *is* Lillian. They're the same damn person. Catch up!"

Throwing her head back, Kayla laughs. "Oh, come on, Esme. Rebekah was with us when we were chased through the woods."

This is it, time's up. I can't keep hiding things. "But she wasn't there when I was stalked in the forest last night."

"*What?*" Kayla steps closer, tilting her head.

"When I got separated from the others, someone was stalking me. I saw her. Well, it was dark and misty, but I saw someone dressed in black. Tall and slim. She was so close."

"Esme, Rebekah was with us last night." Kayla says it like I'm slow.

"No, she went to bed early, remember? And she has *burns on her side and stomach. . . .*"

"Lots of people have burns. How do you explain the night of the photos? Rebekah was there that night."

"Right." I hold one finger up, cracking it. "There's two of them; that's how they're able to do so much. She—Lillian—would need help. There is no way she could do this alone. I don't know if Rebekah is Lillian or one of her cronies. Yet."

Kayla frowns, her once sparkly blue eyes now full of doubt. But I see it in there too, a little flicker. She's starting to believe me. Kayla is considering the possibility that we've been living with one of our stalkers for weeks.

"What did you see *exactly*?" she asks.

I don't like her emphasis on *exactly,* and her tone is the one she uses when she thinks someone is an idiot.

"Mary asked me to go to her cabin and check on Phoebe. Rebekah and Tia's door was open a little and I saw Rebekah putting on a T-shirt. There's a burn all down her side and her stomach. Like all down it, not just, 'Oh no, I spilled coffee on myself.' It was *bad*."

Kayla blows out a breath, her eyes darting to Rebekah's cabin. "Does she look like Lillian?"

I shrug when she looks back at me. "Maybe. Her hair is darker, but so is mine now. . . ."

"What color eyes did Lillian have?"

"I . . . Light-colored, maybe? Blue or green. It was dark that night."

I remember the orange reflection in her eyes from the flames and the look of terror in them.

"That's not good enough," Kayla says. "You have to be *sure* about it! We can't just accuse her of something like this. I mean, how many burn victims do you think there are? How could Rebekah do all this stalking anyway? The girl is petrified of confrontation."

"Yeah, well, even introverts can be crazy . . . and what better way for an introvert to attack than to watch from afar and send creepy anonymous messages. Besides, she's not working alone!"

Kayla shakes her head. "She would need pretty regular contact with whoever her partner is. I don't think I've seen her use her cell once."

"You and I used to text each other through entire classes and the teachers never knew a thing."

"This is—"

"Yeah, yeah, yeah, get past that. We need to figure out a way to prove that Rebekah is Lillian before anything else happens. From this minute on, we don't give her a second to breathe. We stay with her and watch her."

"Esme, if what you're saying is true, we need evidence."

"I totally agree. That's why I'm going to steal her phone."

"What? You can't. The burns might be a complete coincidence."

"And all the weird 'what's your biggest secret' crap that she was going on about when we first arrived? What was that about? She was trying to see if we'd lie."

"Which we did," Kayla replies. "We've lied a lot."

"Sometimes the truth can do more damage."

"Even if the truth is about an *accident*?"

I blink hard to stop myself from rolling my eyes. "Kayla, the fire and Lillian getting hurt was an accident, sure. Keeping quiet about it for ten years *wasn't*."

"I don't need the abridged version, I was there," she snips.

"Whatever. I need you to distract Rebekah."

"I really don't think that's a good idea. Why can't we just ask her about the burns?"

"How likely do you think she is to say, 'Yes, Esme, I am the one creeping off into the woods.' Come on," I say, throwing my hands up. "Rebekah isn't going to admit anything. We have to find out. Keep her busy."

I start to turn away, but Kayla grabs my wrist.

"Wait. How?"

"I don't know! Ask her to talk, tell her you're homesick. She likes to share feelings . . . even if they're made up."

"All right. Be careful."

I'll be the one in the cabin; she's the one who's going to be with Rebekah. It's not me who needs to be careful.

We part ways: she heads to the dock where Rebekah is dangling her feet into the lake, and I go inside Rebekah's cabin.

The campers are in the multiuse cabin having a dodgeball tournament.

A dodgeball game doesn't require every counselor and CIT, so we've split up. Half of us are supervising the campers and the rest are taking a break. That's code for watching the forest. Kayla and I have been tagged in for first watch.

Andy is flitting between checking the campers and making sure there's no further danger. He's clutching his phone and the damn clipboard like he has a clue how to handle this situation.

He hasn't mentioned the cops again, so I guess he's not telling them anything else besides what he's already told them about the guy on camp property. Which is hardly likely to be up there on the cops' list of urgent incidents.

"Esme," Andy says, walking toward me as he makes another round, "where are you going?"

"Oh, Andy," I say, pressing one hand to my throat and acting startled. "You scared me."

He didn't. After two weeks at camp, I no longer jump when he pops up like a ghost.

Think! Why are you going into a cabin that isn't yours?

"I'm sorry for frightening you," he says.

"That's okay, I was just going to go check inside, you know?" I scratch my jaw. "That makes me paranoid, I get that, but we have kids here."

"I think it's prudent to exercise caution, well done. I can take on cabin checks."

Seriously?

I run my hand through my hair. "Even the girls' cabins? The girls might be more comfortable if it was a female going into their room."

His pale eyes widen a fraction. I guess the thought of someone witnessing him looking through the girls' cabin does not appeal to him.

"Ah, right. I didn't think about that. Very well, I'll take the boys' cabins. Let me know if anything is amiss."

I smile. "Will do."

That was too easy.

Andy walks off, heading toward the boys' cabins.

After taking one quick glance over my shoulder and seeing that Rebekah is occupied, I open her cabin door and slip inside. I've been in Rebekah and Tia's room once, shortly after we arrived.

I press my lips together hard against the rolling in my stomach. Some people love snooping, but I hate it. It feels so wrong, and I always worry that I'll find something nasty.

If I find something in here that I don't want to see, how will I look Rebekah in the eye again?

I'd rather find evidence that she's the creep in the woods. At least then this would be over.

I walk through the main room and go into Rebekah and Tia's bedroom.

Their beds are made and there is nothing on the floor. Kayla and I are messy. I think I have at least three T-shirts on the chair.

Rebekah's is the bottom bunk; I remember her mentioning Tia was above her.

I pick up her cream-colored pillow and stuff my hand inside the case. If I were hiding things, they would be in here or under the mattress. Not original, I've made my peace with that, but our options here are limited. The floorboards are fixed tight, probably thanks to Andy.

The pillowcase is empty, aside from the pillow, so I drop it back on the bed and move on. I grip the thin mattress and tilt it, leaning it against the wall.

Wooden slats are all that's beneath.

Okay, Rebekah, where are your skeletons?

I drop the mattress and remake the bed. She has two drawers, but she shares the small dresser with Tia, so it's unlikely she would keep anything in it.

Or it's the perfect cover. Isn't there something about hiding in plain sight?

What would she hide in there, though?

A voodoo doll of me and Kayla would be a dead giveaway.

I open the first drawer. There's a photo of Rebekah with who must be her mom and dad. It's framed in pink glass, so I don't know why she wouldn't display it.

Why hide your parents?

I put the photo back down and root through the rest of her stuff. Deodorant, headbands, toiletries, a charger—Kayla and I keep ours in the wall socket—a notebook, wire-bound with doodles on the front.

Her diary?

I open the notebook, ignoring the pang of guilt in my gut. The first page has her name drawn graffiti-style.

I turn to the second page. There's a doodle of herself, I assume, and another little girl. Rebekah's good at drawing, her sketches are so lifelike, every pencil stroke is precise. I wish I could draw like her.

Turning the page again, I almost drop the book. Fire. She has drawn *fire.* No forest, no campers running away, just fire. Jagged flames take up the whole page. I run my finger over the raised, angry ink.

This is something.

Why would she have drawn this?

I know she's been burned. I have zero idea of burn victim statistics, but I'm willing to put everything I own on it being higher than one. Rebekah was burned; Lillian was burned. That doesn't make them the same person. But it does mean they have something in common.

I think about the flames that night—how vicious they were. If Lillian was burned—and I am pretty sure at this point that she was—and Rebekah is Lillian, wouldn't her burns be worse?

My stomach clenches as the memory flashes through my head over and over, like a horror flick on repeat.

As I start to turn the page, the cabin door creaks. Someone has opened it.

My heart leaps. I drop the notebook back into the drawer and push it shut.

"Rebekah?" Kayla calls from outside.

No!

Rebekah cannot find me in here.

I have no reason to be in here.

Rebekah calls back to Kayla from the doorway of the cabin.

Kayla replies with a question about going for a walk. I don't hear Rebekah's reply because the sound of her opening the door has my pulse racing.

I look around. The window in the bedroom is big enough for me to climb out of—it's a fire escape route—but it's too far away for me to make it there in time, and I certainly wouldn't be able to do it quietly anyway.

Her footsteps thud closer.

I freeze.

31

I'm about to be busted.

I scramble, shoving her sketchbook away.

Hide!

Dropping to my stomach, I wriggle sideways under the bunk bed.

Kayla says something, but her hurried voice sounds quiet from where I am. She's trying to stall Rebekah. I press my lips together as the door to the bedroom opens.

Rebekah steps over the threshold. Her gray and pink tennis shoes tread lightly, but they make a ridiculously loud noise in my ears.

What the hell do I say if she finds me under her bed?

Her feet pass me, and I bite my bottom lip.

What is she doing? *Please leave.*

Where the hell is Kayla?

Rebekah sits on the bottom bunk and the mattress depresses, almost touching my head.

I lie flat, with my head turned sideways.

Why didn't Kayla keep her outside? They had looked deep in conversation when I snuck into the cabin.

Does Rebekah suspect us?

No. If she did, she would be looking for me.

I can hear her fingers tapping something. Her phone?

She's hiding something.

"Hi, Mom."

She's calling home.

Listening to Rebekah talk to her mom feels like a step too far.

"Yeah, I'm okay," she says, though her voice is low and she sounds anything but okay. "Honestly, I am. Things are just kind of full-on, that's all. . . . No, I don't want to come home. . . . Some great friends, yeah . . ."

Will she say something about me and Kayla? If she is Lillian, will she say something that gives her away?

"How's Dad? . . . Good. Yeah, I'm using the cream. I never forget."

Cream for her burns? Does she use it daily?

I close my eyes. We did that to her.

Well, *if* she's Lillian.

"I'm remembering to take my meds, yeah. . . . Yes, Mom," she says in exasperation.

Rebekah hasn't mentioned anything about medication, but then, no one has. It's not something she needs to share. Still, I am curious.

Could it be a condition related to the accident?

"I have to go—we're about to head into the conference room. Okay, speak soon. . . . Love y'all too."

Conference room?

I hear her tap the screen and then she stands up. I can't see her, but I think she puts the phone in her pocket, because I don't hear her put it down.

I watch her tennis shoes walk past me and leave the room. The door bangs shut.

I wait until I hear the cabin door close before I slide from under the bed and stand.

In hindsight, I should have brought my phone with me. That way, I could text Kayla and ask if the coast is clear.

"Esme?"

I startle and grip the doorframe, my fingers digging into the wood.

Kayla opens the door and walks into the room.

"What are you doing?" I hiss.

"Don't worry. The others are walking around the lake."

"Why did you let Rebekah come in? I had to hide under the bed!"

Her eyes widen. "Let her? *Let?*"

"All right, all right, you didn't *let* her. What happened?"

"We were talking, and I mentioned that I miss my parents, like you said to, and then she suddenly got up. She told me she was late calling her mom. I tried to stop her, but she was adamant that she needed to speak to her mom that second."

I nod. "Let's get out of here."

"You *are* going to tell me what happened, right?"

"Yes."

We leave the cabin and I close the door, glancing around. Rebekah and Tia are with Jake, Olly, and the others, walking clockwise around the lake.

Kayla and I head in the opposite direction.

"Well?" Kayla asks.

"She sat on the bed. I was under it and she almost hit my head. Then she called her mom. I found out she uses a cream for her burns."

"Breaking news," Kayla mutters sarcastically.

"Did you expect a full confession? She assured her mom she's still using the cream and taking her medication."

"What medication?"

"She didn't say the name. Her mom would already know what it is."

Kayla sighs. "All right."

"Then she told her mom she had to go because she was needed in the conference room. That's weird, right?"

"Maybe she meant the staff cabin and just misspoke."

I shake my head. "I don't know, there are so many theories in my mind. Anyway, she keeps her phone on her, even though the rest of us leave ours in our room, and she's drawing pictures of herself and a little girl . . . and one of a fire."

"A fire?" Kayla rasps.

"Yep. I couldn't tell if it was in the forest, though, so I can't be sure she's Lillian."

"Who was in the drawing of the fire?"

"Rebekah and a girl around ten years old."

"Was Rebekah ten in the drawing too? Did she look like Lillian?"

"No, Rebekah was the age she is now." Maybe she's not Lillian but her helper?

"Maybe she knows Lillian? Maybe they're sisters?"

I shrug. "I have no damn clue. She said she only has an older brother, but she could be lying. Maybe she has a sister and that's Lillian. But what are the odds of sisters being burned in different accidents? Probably not that high."

"This is so messed up, Esme," Kayla says as we walk in the stifling heat.

"We just need to figure out Rebekah's deal."

"How do we do that?"

"Don't know." Why am I always the one who has to come up with the plans?

"Awesome."

"But now we know she keeps her phone on her. Constant contact. But with who?"

Kayla scrunches her nose. "Esme, what if we're wrong about her and she's just regular Rebekah with a burn?"

"Then we'll find no evidence and we'll say a very silent sorry to her."

I don't say it, but I *know* there is something wrong here.

We reach the halfway point around the lake; the others are heading toward us. The trees smell like freedom, and for once, the hot air doesn't prickle my skin. It's not as hot today, even though the sun is shining away.

Rebekah smiles freely, walking arm in arm with Tia.

"She looks very pleased with herself," Kayla says.

"Nothing like threatening your newest friends to relieve pent-up stress," I mutter.

"It sounds like you're already sure it's her."

"I'm not *sure* of anything, Kayla, and I hate that."

"Not having a party over here either."

I plaster a smile on my face as we reach the others. Since the note incident, Olly and I haven't spoken much. Things were looking good at first; he's sweet and supercute. Now . . . I'm unsure whether he wants to spend time with me or to run away. Maybe he's just spooked too.

"Hey, Esme," Rebekah says. Her smile is normal, but I look deeper. Is it genuine or does she know that I was just hiding under her bed?

"Hey," I reply. "Seen anything weird?"

"Not a thing."

"You want to walk back the other way together, Esme?" Olly asks.

Well, that sounds like he wants to spend time with me.

"Yeah," I reply. "Let's do it."

Kayla chuckles under her breath as she walks off with the others.

I wrap my arms around my stomach as we walk.

"You freaking out?" Olly asks.

Only a lot.

"There's a weird vibe here, you know?" I say. "All the campers are carrying on like normal, getting excited for *everything*, and we're pretending this is the best place on earth. It's a lot. I'm not sure if we can keep it up for weeks, let alone days."

"We might not need to. The cops might find out who it is," Olly says.

"They have one report of a trespasser who they think was an ex-counselor. Once they clear the two names Andy gave them, they'll write it off as someone getting lost on the trail. How much manpower do you think they're going to put into this?"

"I'll give you that. Are you saying we're out here alone?"

Sweat breaks out on my forehead. "Sorry to be the bearer of bad news."

"This feels so wrong, not going to the cops with all the information."

"Have you changed your mind?" I ask.

Olly shakes his head, taking a step closer to me as we walk. "No, I just don't think this is a good option either. You still think staying quiet is the best thing to do?"

"Yes," I reply.

I have to protect the secret I've been carrying around for ten years.

"We need a real break," he says. "Do you think anyone would be up for taking the trail into town?"

Laughter bursts from my diaphragm. "Is that a trick question?"

"You're not up for it, then?"

"After last time? And with someone in the woods?"

Why would he even suggest that?

"Well, I figure it's the best time to go. No one would think we'd be that dumb."

Because we're not going to be that dumb!

"Olly, really?" Why is he even going there?

Chuckling, he shakes his head. "Not one of my better ideas, I get it. Can we forget I said it?"

Not really.

"Totally, it's forgotten."

He really wants us to go back into the forest? That would be crazy.

"What's your favorite book?" he asks.

"What?"

"I realized we haven't had much time to talk about random normal stuff."

"*The Great Gatsby;* born June fifth, Gemini; tacos," I say, and his smile widens. "I don't know if I believe in God, but I do hope there's something after. Light blue; I hate sliders because they look like toddler shoes; Britney is still relevant; and Harry Styles should be my husband."

Laughing out loud, he replies, "All right."

"You go."

"*It;* May seventh; I have no idea about my star sign; with you on tacos; my family is religious but I'm unsure; dark green; sliders are the devil; Britney was hot; don't want to marry Styles."

I laugh, linking my arm through his. It feels like a bold move. Up until now, it's been him who initiates any physical contact.

"Where do you want to live after college?" I ask.

"Anywhere but here. If you could go on vacation anywhere in the world, where would it be?"

"I've always wanted to go to Iceland. . . ." I trail off before I can tell him it's because of the northern lights.

My stomach twists. Wait . . .

Anywhere but *here*?

32

Anywhere but *here*. That's what he said. His *exact* words.

Olly told me he lives in Missouri. Why would he say that if he lives in Texas?

Olly hasn't noticed the slipup. Maybe he just said it because we're here now and he wouldn't want to *live* in this heat?

"Iceland because of the northern lights?" He takes a guess at why I want to go.

"Yes," I reply. *Does he live around here?*

Why the hell would he lie about where he lives? He has a slight Southern accent but not what you would expect from someone from Texas.

Heat creeps up my neck.

What is going on?

Olly could be the one doing all of this. Maybe *he* is the accomplice.

I bite my lip as my mind storms with stupid theories.

Rein it in, Esme.

My paranoia is so strong that I'm suspecting everyone for little to no reason. Accents! That's what I'm basing my suspicions on.

I slip my arm out of his and shudder. "Jake just jumped in the lake."

"He's always in the water."

Olly was with us the night of the photos, though, and the time I saw Lillian in the woods. How could he and Rebekah be working together?

Unless only one of them is in on it and the other is innocent.

I need to find out where Olly is from.

And what handy ID lists your home address and state?

I have to sneak into Olly's room and find his driver's license.

But am I really ready to go there? I've already been through Rebekah's things. When I came back to Camp Pine Lake, I'd hoped to find a better version of myself.

"So you've only known everyone since we got here?" I ask. "You and Jake seem tight."

Olly side-eyes me, and I don't know whether I've said too much.

"I didn't know anyone before the beginning of summer. Jake and I are similar. I knew we'd be cool when he told me that Xbox has nothing on PS."

Of course.

"You're a gamer?"

"Yeah, but not massively. My brother is eleven and would play all day and night if our parents allowed it."

"What's his name?"

He replies a heartbeat later. "Daniel. Danny."

"Just you and Danny?"

"Yeah. Just me and him."

His posture is relaxed, voice light.

He doesn't have a tell. Why doesn't he squint, croak or look to the left—aren't people supposed to avoid eye contact when they lie?

Only that's not foolproof. My dad says since everyone knows that now, they make sure they don't do it.

I wish I'd been more interested in Dad's work. If he were here, he'd know in a millisecond if Olly was telling the truth.

"Who do you think is doing this?" I ask.

"I don't know, but I think we're on the right track, that it's someone who worked here. How else could they get into the locked cabins and know our routines, right?"

Or they might work here now and be feeding their partner in crime information.

Olly or Rebekah?

Or both.

Or neither.

Not him.

I blink hard. This is going well.

At this point I wouldn't be surprised if my brain imploded. Just a big *boom* and that's the end of Esme.

"What's your most-watched show?" Olly asks.

"*Friends.* Hands down. My mom watched it when she was

younger and starts from the beginning at least once a year. She got me into it."

He chuckles. "Here I was thinking you'd say *Riverdale*."

"Probably a close second. What's yours?"

"The Walking Dead."

"I think I stopped around season three thousand."

Laughing, he tilts his head back. "It's not that bad."

"I know, but you kill Glenn, you're dead to me."

"Never get attached to a character in *The Walking Dead* or *Game of Thrones,* Esme."

"Tyrion lived. I'm fine with *Thrones.* You know you can tour the city where King's Landing was filmed?"

"Croatia, right? We should go."

"Bit presumptuous to think I'll want to vacation with you, isn't it?"

He laughs again. "Who wouldn't want a trip to Croatia?"

I'm not going anywhere with Olly until I know he's not torturing me.

"Do you think Rebekah is okay?" I ask.

"No idea. Why?"

"I don't know, she seems weird," I say, and watch his reaction.

He shrugs one shoulder casually. "She's scared. No offense to her, but she seems like the type of person who freaks at everything."

"Don't you think there's a very good reason for us to be scared?"

If he isn't scared, why not?

"I do. Why do *you* think something is wrong with her?"

"I don't know. She seems . . . distant. I guess I don't know how she handles stressful situations. I forget we've only known each other a matter of weeks."

"Camps have that effect on you."

Is he speaking from experience as a camper or as a CIT? He couldn't have been here before, though. Andy, Cora and Mary are the returnees.

There is no way Olly could have been here before now; he's the same age as me. Unless he's lying and has a fake ID that says he's a year younger.

No, not Olly.

We reach the others. I have to get Kayla to sneak into the guys' cabin.

"Esme, want to go watch something? I brought my iPad and we have a couple hours until we have to be in the food hall for dinner," Olly says.

Result. I can be in his room without sneaking in.

Ignoring Kayla, Rebekah and Tia, who are waggling their eyebrows, I reply, "Sounds good. If we start a new series, we both have to swear not to watch an episode alone. *No* skipping ahead."

He holds his hands up. "I swear."

I nod. Today I snoop through his things. Tomorrow I go back to Rebekah's room and find her phone.

I follow Olly into his cabin. It smells like feet covered up with pine air freshener. The bedding is pale blue; the girls' is cream.

He stands outside the door to his room and lets me enter first.

I clench my fists as my palms sweat. Nothing is going to happen in here, so I don't know why my nerves are racing.

What if Lillian is someone he cares about and this thing between us is him trying to get me to trust him? He could shut that bedroom door and strangle me. Okay, obviously not. I need to start getting some decent sleep at night.

That does seem a little excessive over some burns. I really don't think Lillian died, and although my mistake was a big one, I was scared, and just a kid.

I want to believe that no one would kill over that.

Olly might be innocent.

"Okay, pull up Netflix," he says. "Mine is the bottom bunk. Jake shotgunned the top."

I turn to him and grin. "I did too."

He chuckles. "I believe it."

I grab the iPad sitting on his bed and open Netflix. "What do you want to watch?" I ask. "Ooh, what about *The Circle*?"

He shrugs. "Sure. Whatever."

"You have no opinion on this?"

"It doesn't matter what we watch, Esme."

I'd swoon if I weren't worried that he's been leaving creepy notes and chasing me through the woods.

But Olly couldn't have been the chaser either time. He was with me. There can't be three people involved, surely? Or more?

I shake my head and swallow bile at the thought of a whole group. I press Play, trying to ignore where my mind is taking me. The suspicious side of me really sucks right now. It's like it overrides logic and all I'm left with is a big pool of suspects who don't quite fit into the mold.

Olly sits beside me. We lean against the wall and I rest the iPad on my legs.

"Wait," I say, pressing Pause. "Do you think you could grab us some water before we start? I dehydrate in seconds here."

I don't think I've heard Olly mention the heat once.

Could my newest Netflix buddy be used to this climate?

He smirks. "Fine, but no snooping through my stuff. A guy's underwear drawer is private."

Damn it.

"I wasn't going to. . . ."

"I'm kidding, Esme!"

My throat goes dry.

His eyes linger for a second too long on mine, then he gets up.

33

Olly specifically told me not to snoop when he left.

Am I listening?

Nope.

The second I see him pass the window and head toward the food hall, I drop the iPad and slide off the bed. Olly isn't a mattress or pillowcase kind of guy, so I go straight for the dresser drawers.

Biting my lip, I pull open the third drawer down. The top two are likely to be Jake's since he took the top bunk.

Or that's what Kayla and I have done anyway. Rebekah and Tia too.

The wood makes a scraping sound as I gently tug the drawer toward me. Wincing, I slow down. Why is it so loud? But I'm alone; no one will hear it. I dig one hand in and root around.

I'm a terrible person!

An iPad case, pack of gum, penknife, deodorant.

Come on, Olly, you must have something personal.

I root deeper and come in contact with a small leather square.

Bingo.

The black wallet is worn and curled at the edges like he's had it a long time.

Okay, his license must be in here.

And that's the exact moment the door creaks.

Olly's rough voice asks, "What are you doing?"

I drop the wallet and close my eyes.

Shit.

Face up to it.

Standing, I turn to him. "O-Olly," I say, my heart in my throat. "I was just . . ."

"Snooping," he says. "Why?"

He leans against the doorframe, his expression blank. I don't think he's mad.

"I like you." I sigh.

Not at all a lie. I do like him, and I want my doubts to just be in my head.

"I'm sorry, okay? I saw an opportunity to see your stuff. That was crappy of me. I don't know why I did it."

He steps into the room, his eyes sharp. "I don't have anything to hide. No secret girlfriend's pic in there."

"That's not why I was looking." My cheeks flame. "Wouldn't you be curious if we were in my room?"

"Is this what girls do to guys they like?"

"It's what *everyone* does. When you like someone, you want to know everything. Sometimes you can tell more about a person by what they own than what they say." I'm lying. I don't enjoy snooping at all.

"I'll tell you anything you want to know, Esme. You don't need to sneak around."

I try to ignore the cold, sinking feeling in my stomach.

Well done, you've screwed this one up royally.

He takes another step and reaches out. I watch his hand curl around my wrist and unfold my arms.

"I just want to know you. The last guy I liked . . . it didn't end well."

"I'm not him."

"No, you're not. Can I have a do-over?"

He lets go of my wrist and pulls the drawer open all the way. "Go for it. Tell me what you learn."

"I don't want to," I tell him, and I mean it.

"Sure you do. I have nothing to hide. Snoop all you want. I'll even leave the room if you'd rather do it alone."

"No." I shake my head. "I'm sorry. I don't want to be that girl. I trust you."

I'm an idiot for thinking he's involved because of a slip of the tongue. He's been open with me and he's not even angry at me for going through his stuff. He wouldn't tell me to look if he had something to hide.

"Were you looking for something in particular?" he asks.

When is the ground going to swallow me? "No. You must think I'm crazy."

And I might be, you know. Since all of this started, the threats and stalking, I haven't felt very sane. I'm paranoid and jumping from one dumb theory to the next. It doesn't take much to make me suspicious, despite there being a serious lack of evidence with Rebekah and Olly.

"I don't think you're crazy. A little sneaky maybe," he says.

"I didn't mean to be."

That sounds so lame. I didn't mean to be sneaky? I freaking planned it!

"Ask me anything," he says. "Whatever you want to know."

"What song can you listen to over and over?"

His lips curl with a smile. "'Bohemian Rhapsody.' It's timeless and brilliant."

I touch my heart. "Hail Freddie. What's your sick food?"

"My what?"

"The only thing you can stomach when you're ill."

"Oh. Dry toast, I guess."

"Mine is plain pasta. What's your favorite thing about your hometown?"

"That it's called Springfield. I like *The Simpsons*."

There's a Springfield in Missouri. I know because my dad likes *The Simpsons*, too.

I nod. "My hometown has this little bistro called Dante's, and they serve the best Philly cheesesteaks in the world."

"How many calories are in those things?"

"About a whole week's allowance, but it's so worth it. Do you count calories?"

"Not religiously. Our old coach was big on living a healthy lifestyle. He liked to win."

"Football, right?" I ask.

"I was the running back."

"Did you want to be quarterback?"

"Never appealed. Besides, I was the fastest on the field. I could get that ball far."

"Do you love it?"

"I do. Football is big at home."

"Maybe I'll watch you in the Super Bowl one day."

"I'm not sure I'm *that* good."

"I wish I was sporty. I used to run track for school, but now I just do it for fun."

"I thought you had runner's legs." His eyes dip to my legs, then snap back up.

Smiling, I look away.

I don't mention him checking me out as I pass him. "If you could have dinner with any actor, who would it be?"

"The questions keep coming, huh?" Olly teases. "Dead or alive?"

I shrug. "Either?"

"Robin Williams. He was brilliant."

"Who is the person you can be one hundred percent yourself around? No hiding, no judgments? Mine is my nana."

"My dad. We're alike," Olly replies.

"What was your favorite thing to do when you were younger?"

"Six Flags Fiesta. Yours?' "

"The zoo with my nana. We went a lot, even sponsored some of the animals. Do you think we're in danger here?"

His attention drifts to his iPad. "I don't know."

I think we are, but I don't say anything to him because he's already clicking on Netflix.

So instead of pushing it, I watch *The Circle* with Olly until we have to go back to the food hall.

And I try to forget that I ever suspected him.

34

A slow two days later, I'm chewing my lip to the point of pain. No need for red lipstick when blood will do the trick.

The campers are asleep, and the day was pretty standard. Nothing out of the ordinary, unless you count one of the boys getting a Cheerio stuck up his nose.

Nothing out of the ordinary. That's what's making me sweat now. I'd prefer things to just happen. The wait for Lillian's next move makes my stomach churn constantly.

Kayla, Rebekah, Tia, Olly and Jake are sitting on the dock, dangling their feet into the water.

I'm supposed to join them.

Instead I'm sitting on the porch of the food hall, just out of sight of my friends.

"Esme?" Mary says as she walks past.

"Hi." I sit straighter.

She tilts her head. "Are you all right?"

"Fine. Just having a drink," I say, holding my mug of hot chocolate up.

She nods.

I'm sure she's about to leave—she should be in her bedroom with Catalina—but she sits next to me instead. "I thought you would be with your friends?"

Okay, she's staying?

"Yeah, I'll join them in a minute."

"You haven't had a falling-out, have you? Totally normal if you have, it happens from time to time when we're all in such close quarters."

"Nothing like that. I just needed a minute."

She huffs like an exasperated teacher. "Anything the matter?"

I shake my head, my long hair blowing around my face in the breeze.

"I know we haven't spent a lot of time together, Esme, but you can talk to any counselor here. Confidentially, if that's what you want."

Why does she assume I need a confidential chat? Because I'm sitting alone?

"I appreciate that."

Mary's big dark eyes watch me and wait, like she's thinking I'm about to spill my life story. I look away when her gaze starts to feel like it's boring into me.

Finally, she smiles. "Okay. I can tell something is wrong. Will you speak to someone if you need to?"

I don't want her to start telling the other counselors that I'm not okay.

"We haven't heard anything from this person in a couple of days," I say. "In theory that's a good sign. But it doesn't feel good, you know?"

"We were told to keep quiet and then nothing else would happen," Mary says.

"No, he said that if we don't alert the cops or anyone else, then the campers would be fine. What's the point of making us keep quiet and doing *nothing*? What does he get out of that? It doesn't make sense."

Not knowing what Lillian has planned is driving me *insane.* She could tell everyone what Kayla and I did at any moment. Would Andy kick us out? Right now, our friends think we're good people.

I drop my head. Am I not a good person?

Can one stupid decision really define you? Kayla and I never intended any harm.

Mary purses her lips, clearly turning my words over in her mind. I can see her making sense of them. "I don't think you're wrong, but none of this makes sense. Unless this person has a personal grudge against someone here, why would they continue to harass us?"

"You think they're just messing around?"

"No, I definitely think someone is out there and they want us to be scared. I'm unsure if I believe they want to hurt us."

I want to believe that Lillian just wants to scare us.

"Are you still Team Cops?"

Her lips slide into a smile. "Yes, I'm still Team Cops."

"They're not always that helpful. Sometimes the law doesn't allow them to be."

"Oh, I know. I had a friend once, this girl whose ex wouldn't leave her alone. There was nothing the cops could legally do unless he threatened her, or worse."

"What happened?"

"The ex strangled her to death, exactly one month *after* the restraining order expired."

I swallow. "Oh."

"It's not a nice story."

"So you're saying that the cops can't do anything unless this freak hurts one of us?"

It all sounds rather contradictory. If Mary knows that nothing can be done, why does she want to go to the police?

"There has been a direct threat, and children are here. I think more can be done in this case," she says.

"Even though we don't have a clue who it is? Or how many of them they might be?" I ask.

"How many?" With a shudder, she adds, "There's a chilling thought."

"I think it's more than one. Do you?"

"I doubt anyone could do this alone."

Good, she's got there, too.

"Do you think two people could do all of this?"

Her lips part in a small gasp. "I can just about deal with two, not a whole group."

Lillian lived around here. Who's to say she hasn't brought her friends in for a little revenge?

"You think they'll show themselves?" I ask.

"You said yourself that it doesn't make sense to threaten us, then walk away."

"Perhaps," I say, frowning. "You mentioned them having an issue with one of us. How would they know we'd be here?"

"It's likely teens from town getting their sick kicks from scaring us, Esme. But I don't think it's smart to ignore the possibility that one of us in particular is being targeted."

I need to change the subject.

"It's so pretty here," I say.

"Do you want to come back next summer?" Mary asks.

Absolutely not.

"I think so. How long have you been coming here?"

"Three years." She laughs. "I think Andy was born here."

"Yeah, he loves it."

"He's good at his job. There's a lot more to it than just making sure the campers have fun and learn new skills. He's managing staff too . . . and *this* situation. The past few days, he's looked tired."

"No one is getting much sleep. Besides the campers, that is."

"Ugh, my cabin is terrible for whispering until eleven at night."

"Mine too, but they usually quiet down before ten. I think all the physical activity wears them out."

"Whatever happens, we have to keep them safe," Mary says, wrapping her arms around herself.

"Of course."

The campers, the *kids,* are awesome. Some are cocky and full of attitude, but under the pretense, they're children. I won't let Lillian harm a single one of them.

I'd gladly expose my own secret before that happened.

And that could well be what she wants. The whole point of this is to make Kayla and me so paranoid we reach a breaking point, to watch us suffer before she forces us to speak up.

We can't even leave now.

We're completely at her mercy.

35

Mary walks along the beach. I watch her make eye contact with Catalina as she comes out of the cabin. Without a word, Catalina follows her. They said everything with a glance like some freaky Powerpuff juju.

They go into the multiuse cabin and close the door.

Okay.

"Esme!" Rebekah shouts, waving from the dock.

I plaster on a smile like the one Kayla used at school when talking to the popular kids. She was very good at their game. Sometimes a little too good.

Kayla stands and walks to meet me. "What were you doing?"

"Just talking to Mary."

"What about?"

"Three guesses, Kayla!"

"You look obsessed and soon people are going to be asking why."

"Don't worry about me, I have it under control."

"Do you?" she asks, her eyebrows lifting.

"I'm fine, Kayla."

"Maybe you should have an early night."

"Excuse me?"

"It's not good for you to be out here. You look pale and you're biting your nails again."

I hide my hands behind my back. "I told you I'm okay."

"And I'm telling you that you're not. I'm your best friend, Esme, and I can see what's going on. You're losing it." She steps even closer even though we're far enough from everyone else that they can't hear us.

I take a step back.

"People are going to get suspicious," she says. "You're constantly getting in the middle of every creepy situation and it's all you talk about to anyone."

"It's not *all* I talk about."

"It might as well be. Rebekah asked if you're okay. She said she's worried that you're not coping."

I bet she did.

"When did Rebekah say this?"

"Just now, while you were sulking over there."

My eyes slide over Kayla's shoulder. Rebekah and Olly are sitting together chatting. He throws a stick into the lake.

"Esme, I'll tell them you got too much sun and need to rest."

Kayla's hands are on her hips when I look back at her.

Am I unwelcome now? She's not really leaving me much choice. Not that I want to hang out with them right now. Not when Rebekah is analyzing me.

"Fine," I say through my teeth. "I'll go."

She sighs. "Don't be like that. I'm protecting us both."

"Night, Kayla," I say, and turn away from her.

No one calls my name as I head for my cabin.

≈

Dinner has been served after a day of baking, den building, dodgeball and tennis. The campers chat happily as they feast on Mexican food.

Taco Tuesday is the best day in camp.

But not for me.

Olly is finishing his fourth taco. The cooks here have to respect his and Jake's appetites.

Everyone's spirits are raised ever so slightly when we have a good meal. I pretend like mine are, too. This evening's conversation is about what we would do in the event of a zombie apocalypse. Half my table would go to the city and the other half would set up camp in a remote forest.

I'm Team Forest. Fewer humans to turn zombie and eat me. But I definitely wouldn't camp. I'd strap myself high up in a tree to sleep, like Katniss in *The Hunger Games.*

After dinner and music around the campfire, the kids go to bed.

It's my night off tonight, but Kayla and I have been asked to help tidy the outside area before we turn in. Cora is inside with the girls until we switch. I don't want to be outside; I'd rather be tucked up in bed.

It's not particularly messy out here, but I think Andy wants the creeper to see numbers. The more adults that Lillian and her cronies see, the less likely she is to follow through on any threats.

That's what I think, anyway.

I pick up a couple of tennis balls that have been hit over the fence.

As I turn to take them to the multiuse cabin, I see Olly walking toward me.

"Hey, Esme, you need a hand?" he asks.

I smile as he approaches. If I didn't need my friends right now, I would be pissed at them for how they treated me last night. "Yeah, can you grab those rackets, please?"

He picks them up and we walk back to the cabin.

"You shouldn't be out that far alone, especially not at night," he says.

"It's not too dark yet and I didn't go into the woods. There might be some balls in there, but hell no am I checking tonight."

"I'll take a look in the morning," he says.

We pass Mary, Catalina and a few others in canoes, letting off some steam.

They look so carefree.

I wonder what message that's sending to Lillian? We're still having fun. You don't scare us. Do your worst.

But how bad is her worst?

Olly holds the cabin door for me and I flick the light on. "Thanks."

He's acting normal. I'm not sure if they really were talking about me last night or if Kayla was just trying to make me feel bad.

We take the rackets and balls into the storage closet. It's full of sports equipment and smells like rubber and sweat. I turn to leave, but Olly steps in front of the door, blocking my exit.

"What are you doing?" I ask, my smile dropping.

"I've wanted to do something for a while."

Strangle me?

My eyes widen as he steps closer.

I brace myself for a fight.

Why aren't you running?

He looms over me. My mouth goes dry.

He *is* the one in on it with Lillian.

Fab time to find out that when it comes to fight or flight, I'm not a flight.

I've always had a lot of respect for the fighters. Turns out we're just stupid.

My heart races, and I clench my hands into fists.

I've taken self-defense classes, and I'm going to kick his ass.

His hands never reach my neck, though. They slide around my back.

What is happening?

It takes me a second later to really get it—I *am* that stupid—Olly doesn't want to hurt me. His lips touch mine.

Oh.

Code red! Code red! You're fraternizing with the enemy!

I relax into the kiss a second later and feel his smile against my mouth. He tastes like Dr Pepper and smells like a campfire.

Olly pulls back for a second. "I didn't expect complete shock, Esme. I thought I made it kinda obvious that I like you."

Do not tell him the shock is because he isn't choking the life out of you.

"I'm sorry," I say, shaking my head to try to get a little clarity.

"I'll stop if you want me to?" He looks at me, his eyes soft.

I don't swoon easily, but I am right now.

"You may continue."

He laughs and brings his lips down on mine again.

I step closer, closing any distance between us. I snuggle into him as he kisses us both breathless.

"We should get back," he says, minutes, hours later, I don't know.

He's taken my mind off last night and that's all that matters right now.

"Right. We have a job to do here and all that."

His mouth curls. "We should go and do that."

Neither of us moves. "Olly," I say. "I need to tell you something."

"Go on."

"The other day when we were talking about where we'd like to live after college . . ."

If we're going to start something, and it feels like we are, I want to be as honest as I can.

"Yeah?" he prompts.

"Well, you said you want to live anywhere but here, and for a second I thought you meant you lived here. In Texas. In this town."

"I'm not sure I'm following."

"We said that the person who could be watching . . . um . . ."

Lowering his arms, he breaks all contact and steps back.

"Me?" He turns and runs his hands through his hair. "Wow. You thought *I* was messing with camp?"

"No. Well, I'm sorry, but just think about how it sounded."

"I don't care how it sounded! Why didn't you just ask? I would have told you I just don't want to end up in a dead-end town like this. Jesus, Esme."

"I'm sorry."

Disappointment fills his eyes. "You actually thought I could threaten you all? That I would put *children* in danger?"

"No!" I say, but it doesn't mean anything because that is *totally* what I thought.

We haven't known each other long, but I really don't think Olly would be part of something as terrifying as this. Lillian wants to turn us against each other.

And I did exactly that.

"Please, can we just talk about this?" I plead. "I've been paranoid and scared. I like you and it was dumb. Like really dumb, but I haven't exactly been thinking straight."

He takes a step toward the door.

"Olly, don't leave, please?"

"I wouldn't hurt *anyone.*"

"I believe you."

He clicks his tongue against his teeth. "The first girl I've liked since my ex thinks I'm a deranged stalker."

I dip my head, wincing. I've made a huge mess of this.

"Olly," I whisper.

"Why didn't you just ask?" He sounds defeated, like this is all over and he's telling me it's my fault. I could have avoided this by talking to him. He huffs, his eyes flashing to mine. "That's why you were going through my stuff."

Crap.

"I was looking for your driver's license," I say. "I wanted so badly to prove my dumb theory wrong. The last couple of weeks with you have been awesome, and I was terrified that you might be the one doing this and that you hated me."

He tilts his head. "Why would that make me hate *you*?"

Oh God.

"No, I mean all of us. Whoever is out there clearly doesn't have warm and fuzzy feelings for any of us."

His sneakers thud on the floor as he walks closer to me.

"Why are you lying to me?" he growls.

I gulp. "I'm not lying."

"Then tell me what you meant by that. Why would this person hate you?"

I press my lips together.

"You acted weird when we were in the forest," he presses. "Sometimes you're off in your own world, and I can see the panic you're holding in. Last night you bailed on us and today you've been jumpy as hell."

"You're wrong," I tell him. But my words hold no weight because my voice cracks and betrays me.

"I'm not wrong. What's going on? You know more than you're telling me. Is someone threatening *you*?"

"Olly, no."

He shakes his head. "We're not leaving this damn closet until you tell me the truth."

I squeeze my eyes shut. I can't tell. I've never told anyone, ever.

"I can't," I whisper.

I keep my eyes closed, but I feel him getting closer. His breath cascades over my head and then I'm in his strong, warm arms.

"You're scaring me," he says into my hair. "If someone is harassing you, I can help. I won't let anyone hurt you, Esme. I promise."

After a mere two weeks, if something happened to me, he would get over it fast. We're not even together. I barely know the guy.

"Hey," Olly presses. "Please tell me."

His body is rigid.

I sink into him and feel my tears seeping into his T-shirt.

"You'll hate me," I mutter against his collarbone.

"Tell me." He pulls back. "It's bad?"

I nod. "I didn't mean it, though."

"What didn't you mean?"

"I lied about when I was last here as a camper," I whisper. "It was the year of the fire . . . and I was there that night."

36

The weight of the secret is heavy, but rather than feeling lighter now that I've told Olly, I want to crawl under a rock.

Realization hits and his jaw drops. "*You* were responsible for the fire?"

"It wasn't entirely my fault. I mean, it was, but it was an accident."

"What happened?"

"I—I was eight. The older kids had been sneaking out and bragging about it. I thought it would be cool if I did the same. It was so stupid."

Olly takes my hands in his and a glimmer of hope settles in my chest. Maybe he won't hate me. "What happened?" he asks.

"They used to sneak out the back window in the cabins and go down that trail. I didn't know it led into town back then. I went one night, past the camp's border and onto public land. I was a little scared but kept thinking about how the older kids would react the next day when I told them."

Meeting Olly's eyes, I wince. "I came to the clearing where people camp and no one was there. I lit a fire and it got out of hand."

Tell him what you and Kayla did to Lillian, you chicken!

"Whoa," he breathes. "Okay. Well, that was bad, but it was an accident."

"I never meant for it to happen. I added too many sticks to the fire. It collapsed as the sticks under the new ones gave way and the whole thing toppled sideways and hit that small group of trees." I gulp. "It was almost like adding gasoline, the trees caught fire that fast. It had barely rained all summer."

Olly squeezes my hands, telling me it's okay.

Nothing about that night was okay, though. He doesn't understand that because I can't find the words or the strength to tell him the rest.

We're new friends. What if he doesn't keep my secret?

"I hated myself for a long time after that," I say.

"What did you do once the fire spread?" he asks.

"I ran. Like a little coward, I ran back to camp and slipped through the window. By the time I heard sirens, I was back in bed. The whole forest didn't catch fire purely because of the number of rocks around the trees and the lack of debris. Any longer, though, and one of the trees could have fallen over and reached the others."

"Who called nine-one-one?"

"I don't know. There was a lot of smoke, so it could have been anyone. I heard a rumor that it was some people outside a bar who noticed the fire."

"You never told anyone?"

"No, never. In the morning there were a couple of cops at camp. I thought they'd come for me, but it turned out they were just asking the counselors if they'd noticed anything. Over breakfast we were all told there had been a fire off-site."

"And you decided not to tell."

Olly isn't asking me a question.

"I was so scared of what would happen. It was an accident, so there was no point in getting myself into trouble, getting kicked out of camp *and* giving the camp a bad name. How would it look when the counselors didn't know the campers were sneaking out at night?"

He frowns. "Do you think they're doing that now?"

"There never used to be locks on the windows. Now the only window you can get out of in their room is a fire escape with an alarm on it."

"Jesus," Olly mutters, dropping my hands.

"I regret it. Every day I've regretted what I did that night. I wish I could go back and stop it from happening. I was *so* stupid."

"You were eight."

"I still knew right from wrong."

"Damn, Esme." He rubs his jaw. "All this time . . ."

"I think whoever is doing this might know it was me that night," I whisper.

Olly's eyes snap to me and widen like an inflating balloon. "Why would you think that?"

"'The lake never forgets'? What other crap has happened

here besides the forest almost being burned to the ground?" *And someone getting hurt.*

"Probably lots of things."

I arch an eyebrow. "Such as?"

"I don't know, but I doubt you're the only one who has ever gotten themselves into trouble here." Olly blows out a long breath, as if there's something else he wants to say but won't.

I tilt my head, my eyes piercing into his as if I'll actually be able to read his mind. He looks away.

When he remains silent, I sigh. "Maybe we should go to bed."

"Are you for real? You think I'm hiding something again. You search my room because you think I'm a stalker, then you off-load your secret onto me, and still you think I'm hiding something."

"I can see that you are!"

"How?"

"Because you can barely look me in the eye!"

"I don't know what you're talking about."

I reach for him, but he backs up, shaking his head. "Please tell me if there's something, Olly," I say. "All of this is driving me insane and if we know for sure, once and for all, what this craziness is about, then we might be able to stop it."

"Esme . . ."

"Please?"

"There's nothing to tell," he says, scowling.

My jaw drops as he turns and walks out of the cupboard. He shuts the door a little harder than necessary.

And I know one thing for sure. Olly's keeping secrets too.

37

What is he hiding? Olly is lying to me, and I'm still half-lying to him.

When confessing my horrible secret, I left out the most important part of that night, and right now, I'm glad I did. Why would I tell him every gory detail when he's not telling me *anything*?

I open the cupboard door, flick off the light, and make my way outside.

Everyone is still in the same place as before. Olly is nowhere to be seen, so he must already be in his cabin.

I don't know what's happening with us now. I went in wary of him, then we were kissing, now he's mad at me. There's less back-and-forth in a game of Ping-Pong.

"Esme, you okay?" Kayla says as I walk into our little room, ready for bed.

The girls are still whispering to each other. Lights-out isn't for another thirty minutes.

"Ugh, not really." I drop onto Kayla's bed and put my head in my hands.

"What's going on?"

Tilting my head to the side, I peek up at her through my fingers. "I told Olly."

Her light blue eyes bulge. "You did *what*?"

I drop my hands. "Not about Lillian and I didn't mention you. I told him that I was in the forest and accidentally set it on fire."

"What the hell! Why?"

"I don't know. He could see that something was up, and he'd just kissed me."

"Wait, what? He kissed you? How was it?"

Really? I shake my head and ignore the question. "Anyway, he was understanding about the fire. He knew it wasn't intentional."

"Then what? You *definitely* didn't mention Lillian? We were supposed to take that to our grave."

"I'm sorry. It all got a bit much. I swear I only told him that I did it, no mention of you."

"Why do you look so down if Olly doesn't blame you for the fire *and* he kissed you?"

"Um . . . so I told him the truth about why I was snooping in his room, that I was suspicious. That annoyed him, but he got over it. After the kiss, when I dropped the bomb and said maybe what's happening now is due to that, he said something odd."

"Well?"

"He said that I'm probably not the only one to get into trouble at camp."

Sitting taller, Kayla tilts her head closer to me. "Like something else has gone down?"

"Thank you! That's exactly what I thought, too, but he got all shady and left in a huff, slamming the door."

"He's overreacting, right? That means the dude's hiding something."

"Do you think he was a camper here?"

"We'd remember those eyes."

"Yeah, I would, but maybe he was here after we were?"

"Isn't that a little too much of a coincidence? Bad stuff happened to three campers who all find themselves shiny-new CITs at the same time in the same place?"

"I guess."

"Ugh, I hate that I'm being sucked back into this . . . but what's the theory here, Esme? Olly's involved like Lillian, or he's like us?"

I'm not going to apologize for "sucking her back into this." She never should have left.

"I have no clue." I throw my hands up. "It's *so* frustrating because I know he's keeping a secret even after I told him mine. It wasn't easy to spill. Now he has a confession . . . maybe. Does it even matter?"

Kayla seems to consider this. "You have to talk to him. We need to know what he's hiding."

"How, though?"

"I vote for the direct route. Rip the Band-Aid off, Esme. Walk up to him and demand answers."

"Thank you," I say sarcastically. "That was superhelpful."

"Well, I don't think he's going to have it all written down for you to snoop again and steal!"

"That reminds me, I should try to get another look at Rebekah's diary."

"I love that almost getting caught isn't a deterrent for you."

"Getting caught just makes me sneakier. Besides, next time you're going to do a better job of keeping her busy."

"What do you want me to do, lie on the ground and hold her ankles?"

"No, start crying and she'll comfort you."

Kayla opens, then closes her mouth. Then she says, "That's actually a good idea."

"I know!"

I strip my clothes off and get into my pajamas.

"Fine, I'll do that," she says. "What do you want to do first tomorrow, interrogate Olly or ransack Rebekah's room?"

She makes us sound so delightful. At least she's with me again. I'm not sure how long it will last, though. She'll probably spook again with Lillian's next move.

"I'll start with Olly," I reply. "There's a hike tomorrow afternoon, and I'm going to have a very bad headache."

"I don't know if I should be proud of you or fear you."

I smile. "Think you can talk to Jake and find out if Olly has mentioned anything to him?"

"Sure."

"Just don't be obvious about it. Oh, and if you tell Jake about the fire, that's okay."

"Do you think Olly will tell him?"

"I hope not."

"I hope Jake doesn't know anything," Kayla says, sighing dreamily.

"That's going well, then?"

Her expression turns mushy. "I picked a good one that day. He's sweet and also has that alpha male thing working for him."

"Because he wants to go into the forest and pummel the person doing this?"

"He wants to protect us."

"Stop swooning long enough to keep a straight head, yeah?"

"What does that mean?" Kayla demands.

"Olly's not being honest about a lot. I think he might know Jake better than he says he does. They're very . . . in tune. They're a little too close for having only met a couple of weeks ago, don't you think?"

"Jake wouldn't lie."

"You've known him for, like, three minutes, Kayla."

"He *wouldn't* lie."

"You can't be certain of that."

"You need to stop pissing off all your friends, Esme."

Oh, come on!

Is she really arguing with me over a boy she barely knows? This is the last thing we need with all that's going on.

"Not trying to. I want to get to the bottom of this, same as you do," I tell her.

"Then can we agree to not accuse my boyfriend of being a liar?"

Boyfriend? Since when? Something tells me not to focus on that part or she might get cranky with me again.

"Yep," I say, smiling with gritted teeth. "We can agree to that."

I climb up onto my bed and scoot under the blanket.

"So, our suspect list is currently sitting at two? Rebekah and Olly?" Kayla asks.

"Yes," I reply, silently adding a third as I curl up.

Jake.

38

I jump awake, clutching the thin blanket to my chest.

What was that?

There was a crash. I'm sure I wasn't dreaming.

I throw the blanket off and climb down the ladder. Kayla is still asleep—she wouldn't wake if there were an atomic bomb. Surely I can't be the only one who heard the crash.

The girls are also asleep. But the noise was too real to just be my imagination.

Frowning, I pad toward the cabin door and slide the dead bolt open. The metal scrapes and I clench my teeth. *Shh.*

When I get the lock off, I pull the door open.

Be brave.

Stepping onto the porch, I glance around. It's early; the sun is still a while off from rising.

I look to my left. Olly is outside his cabin. Are we the only light sleepers?

"You heard that too?" he asks.

"Yeah, it woke me up. What was it?"

"I don't know. I think it came from your direction."

I glance the other way. Nothing looks off.

"Do you think something fell?" I ask.

Olly walks toward me. "Maybe. The thud sounded like something against wood, right?"

"Look," I say, as my eyes land on the food hall. Its door is wide open. "The door wasn't open when we went to bed."

Olly's eyes narrow. "Great."

What has Lillian done this time?

Olly stops when he reaches the steps of my cabin. "Okay. You wait here, and I'll go check it out."

"Wait, what?" I jog down the steps and grab his wrist. "You can't go in there alone. We don't know what's happening!"

"Esme, you can't go in there at all. Just wait until I've seen if it's safe."

My back stiffens. "Yes, I can go in there."

"I love that you have this super-chick thing going on and you don't need saving, but right now can you *please* stay here?"

I cross my arms. He's right about one thing. I don't need saving.

I watch him walk toward the food hall. Then I follow because there's no way I'm going to stay put. This is my mess.

Creeping closer, I try to look around the door as Olly opens it.

He looks over his shoulder and lifts his eyebrows like he knew I wouldn't do as I was told. "I mean it, Esme, wait until I've gone in."

"What if that's what they want to happen, huh?" I whisper, wrapping my arms around my stomach as I look back toward the lake.

"Don't be an ass," he hisses.

A smile touches my lips as I follow closely behind him.

Groaning my name this time, like he's beyond frustrated, he tilts his head back. "Can you not just do as you're told?"

"No. It's a curse."

He turns around and I follow close behind him.

Lifting his hand, he flicks on the light and we both gasp.

39

Is that what I think it is?

I blink hard, but when I open my eyes the image is the same.

This is very, very real.

The carcass of a deer lies in the middle of the floor between two tables. Blood pools in a circle around it like a grim rug.

I grab Olly's hand as my pulse thumps in my ears.

"What the hell is that?" he says.

I stare unblinking until my eyes sting. "It's a deer."

Doing a double take, he stares at me like I'm insane. "I know it's a deer, but *why* is it in the middle of the cabin, dead?"

Because Lillian is sick.

I should've known she would do something like this. The night of the fire, she terrified me and Kayla by showing us a poor animal that she'd killed and mutilated. It was the reason Kayla lashed out at her in the first place.

I should call an Uber right now.

"We eat in here. *Children* eat in here," I mutter. "I can't believe anyone would do this."

Olly covers his mouth. "I think I'm going to hurl."

Okay, get it together. You're not supposed to know who is behind this.

"L-let's look around. There might be a note like the one we got on the door."

He exhales. "Our resident psycho is getting bolder."

I walk around the tables, making sure to put as much distance between me and freaking Bambi as possible.

The deer isn't huge, but it's probably heavy. It's also covered in blood, so getting it here couldn't have been easy. It had to be a two-person job, surely.

"Esme, here," Olly says.

I turn to see him pick up a piece of paper from a table. He scrunches his nose. "Damn, that's gross. It's written in *blood*."

"What does it say?" I ask, jogging over.

"It says, 'Someone here wants to talk.'" He looks up. "Who wants to talk?"

Someone. "Maybe it's about Mary? She's been very vocal about going to the cops."

"She's been vocal when we're around the campfire. How close is this person?" Olly asks, holding the note up.

I wave my hand at the dead deer. "Pretty damn close, Olly!"

In my room too.

"We need to get Andy," he says.

"I—I'll go."

Olly looks down at the deer with wide eyes.

Whatever his secret is, I don't think he was involved in putting the deer in the food hall.

I turn on my heel and race outside, down the steps and to the staff cabin, where Andy is sleeping peacefully. I almost feel bad for waking him up with this news.

Almost. I need someone else to deal with this, because I'll clean up the blood, but I'm *not* touching that deer.

I rap lightly on his bedroom window.

A minute later, the curtain is pulled to the side. Andy's eyes land on me, and he startles.

"Esme?" he says, opening the window and rubbing his pale forehead. "What are you doing?"

"I need you to come to the food hall," I say breathlessly.

His face falls. Shutting the window, he drops the curtain and I hear him bumping about, getting his clothes and shoes on.

I walk around to the front of the cabin and wait.

"What happened?" he asks, dashing through the door and down the steps.

"A deer," I say. "Dead."

"A dead deer?"

"Dead. Murdered. I don't know. It's *in* the food hall!"

"In it?"

"Yes, come on."

He runs past me and I follow, sprinting up the food hall steps.

I hear Andy say Olly's name and then he cusses the air blue.

"How did you find this?" he asks, sinking to his knees near the animal.

The blood is close to him. I squirm. *Move back a little.*

Olly crouches down. "I heard a crash. It sounded like chairs falling over or being thrown. Esme heard it too. The door was open, so we came in here and found this."

"Whoever it was, they couldn't have gotten far," I say, pressing one hand against my rolling stomach.

They both turn to me.

"God," Andy breathes. "All right. I'm going to get my phone and take some pictures, then we're going to clean this up. No panicking, we're not giving this person what they want."

"Okay." Nothing is okay, and that sounds like an awful plan, but I don't have a better one.

"You two stay here," Andy tells us.

I walk around the deer when Andy leaves, and Olly rises to his feet.

"Are you all right?" he asks.

"Are *we* all right?" I counter.

He was mad at me five hours ago.

Olly grabs my hand and pulls me in for a hug. I sink against him and my muscles relax. "We're cool, Esme. Does the deer mean anything?"

"What?" I mutter against his shoulder.

"You think the person doing all this knows about the fire? Is a deer relevant to anything that happened that night?"

Wow. What a question to ask. He's perceptive.

"What is it, Esme?"

"There was a dead deer near the fire site. But it wasn't significant."

Another lie.

The deer *was* significant.

My head spins. Of course it was significant. I should have known back then how troubled Lillian was. I was scared of her then. I'm petrified of her now.

"What do you think it means?" Olly presses.

I shrug. "I don't know!"

It's a warning just like that night: Fear me.

"Everything okay?" Andy asks, walking back into the cabin.

Olly looks up and rubs my back. "She's just a little freaked."

"It'll be fine, Esme. This person is just trying to scare us."

I turn around and Olly drops one of his arms from around me. "It's working," I say. "I'm scared for the campers. What if they'd found this?"

Andy shakes his head. "They're *never* in here first. Whoever did this knew that it would be staff who found it. This was all for us."

That makes sense. We always set up before the campers come in to eat. Lillian's knowledge of the camp is too great for her to not have been here. Or not to have an accomplice who's here.

There was no one else with Lillian that night in the woods. If Lillian isn't Rebekah, she must have told her everything.

I take a breath.

Andy shakes a blanket out. "Are you ready to get this deer into the woods, Olly?"

Wrinkling his nose, he replies, "Sure."

That is such a crap job. "How far will you take it?"

"Not too far. There's an area between two trails that's filled with bush. It'll be hidden in there."

"Great. I'll go and get buckets and cleaning supplies," I say. "The quicker we clean the blood up, the less likely it'll be to stain."

There are a lot of stains on the floor anyway. Hopefully the blood will blend in with them.

Or I could bleach the bloodstain and it would be lighter. That's preferable to a faded patch of blood.

I'm almost to the kitchen when I hear the front door creak open.

40

I spin around. Andy and Olly are already facing the door.

Oh crap, she's out there!

"Was that someone?" I ask.

Olly takes off running.

"Olly, no!"

Andy catches me as I make a run for it too.

"Stop, stop, stop. Esme, you can't go out there," he says, wrapping both arms around me.

I wriggle in his firm hold. He does not look this strong. "Let go! Olly could get hurt!"

This is all my fault. It should be me chasing her.

"Stay here. I'll go." Andy twists us around and pushes me deeper into the room. "I'll go, Esme."

Pressing one hand to my chest, I pant and my eyes sting with the threat of tears.

Do not cry.

Andy dashes from the cabin.

Walking backward, I let my legs hit a bench and then I sit.

I take a long breath and release it slowly as my head swims. This is all getting to be too much.

If Olly gets hurt because I wouldn't let go of my secret, I'll never forgive myself. Kayla and I need to have a chat, because we can't keep this up. We can't let someone else get hurt because of what we did.

I watch the door, willing Olly and Andy to come back. Maybe I should follow them? My getting lost in the woods isn't going to help anything, though. I've done that already.

What if Lillian's leading them away so she can get to me?

Calm down. Breathe.

With my heart racing a million miles an hour, I get up and walk into the kitchen. The cupboard with cleaning supplies is padlocked for safety. I twist the numbers to 9-4-5 and the lock springs open.

I grab two buckets, new sponges, rubber gloves and strong chemical cleaners. I've noticed the products used on the tables are *much* more eco-friendly. They won't cut it for this job, though.

I fill one of the buckets with hot soapy water and chuck the sponges into the empty one. Then I carry them both into the room, ready to clean when Olly and Andy get back.

I can't believe I'm having to do this.

Now there is nothing I can do until they return.

Unless . . .

No, there is no way I can roll that deer onto the blanket and wrap it up myself.

No. Way.

My eyes slide to the deer. It stinks like death, all musty and gross.

I can't sit and do nothing. I think about the last time I was this close to a dead deer and steel myself.

Taking shallow breaths, I pull on the black latex gloves, pick up the blanket and press my lips together. I wish I didn't need to breathe during this. The closer I step, the stronger the smell.

Laying the blanket out, I shake my head.

What the hell am I doing?

I walk around to the deer and reach down. My hands circle a front and a back leg.

The stench hits the back of my throat, and I swallow a gag.

Why would Lillian do this?

Leaning back, I pull the deer and it rolls effortlessly onto its other side.

Stepping to the side, I turn my head away and try to breathe some fresh air.

"Right, I need to wrap you now," I mutter, walking around to the deer's back. I can't get too close—I don't want to step in the pool of blood. But I manage to lean over and grip the edge of the blanket and then tug it up.

Gritting my teeth, I lift with every ounce of strength I have and push. The deer rolls again, and I cover it with the blanket. Now it can't be seen.

"I'm sorry," I whisper as if it can hear.

I pull the bucket of water close and get on my knees. Gripping the big yellow sponge tight, I wipe the blood with it. The sponge glides gracefully, picking up a line of gloopy blood as it goes.

So, so nasty.

The water turns pink as I dip the sponge into the bucket and squeeze it out.

Oh God.

"Esme?"

I drop the sponge and stand up as Olly and Andy come back into the room.

"You're okay," I say.

She didn't get them.

"We couldn't find whoever it was. No one else is awake," Andy says.

"You wrapped it?" Olly asks, smiling with pride.

"Yes. It was awful. You might want to roll it a couple more times before you take it out."

Andy clears his throat. "Thank you, Esme. Good job." He turns to Olly, who nods at his unspoken question. Yes, he is ready for them to dump the deer in the woods. I want to ask them to bury it, but that seems ridiculous and time consuming.

I get back to the cleaning and sneak a glance at Olly as he and Andy make light work of rolling the deer further into the blanket.

By the time they have the thing all rolled up and ready to go, I've got most of the blood up.

"I'd like to come," I say, taking the gloves off and putting them in the other bucket full of blood-soaked sponges.

Olly looks up through dark lashes.

"I'll bleach the floor after," I say.

"Of course, Esme," Andy says. "We'll all help with the floor once we get this little girl to the woods."

My heart pinches. I wish he wouldn't refer to the deer as "little girl." It's sad enough that Lillian did this to her. We don't need to make her sound like a pet.

Andy and Olly lift the deer and walk slowly outside.

I follow close behind. It's so dark out; the only light is the reflection of the moon on the lake. I squint to see. As it creeps closer to five a.m., we'll have some light.

Andy and Olly walk down the steps and we go around the food hall and into the forest.

"How far are we going?" I whisper, treading carefully.

"Only a couple of minutes," Andy replies, his voice strained due to the deer's weight.

We dodge smaller trees and bushes as we walk through the forest rather than on a trail.

"All right, about here, between those heavy bushes," Andy tells Olly.

They lay the deer down and gently pull the blanket, rolling her onto the ground. Andy gathers the blanket in a ball and sighs. "How has it come to this?"

I dip my head, guilt stabbing me in the chest, feeling Olly's intense gaze on me. Does he want me to fess up right now? Spill everything about that night to Andy? He must suspect there's more to it.

"Let's get back," Olly says. "We can discuss who, what and why later."

He says it to both of us, but I know it's for me.

We head back to camp in the dark. I breathe easier the more distance we put between us and the deer.

"Are you two okay?" Andy asks. "You should never have had to do that."

I nod and Olly tells him he's fine.

"If you need to talk, my door is always open. As CITs none of what happened tonight is your responsibility. I appreciate you helping me take care of it."

"No problem," I tell him.

"I don't really feel like a CIT anymore," Olly says.

"Yeah, me neither."

"I've got to say, you don't seem like it either. There has been so much more you've had to deal with than any other CIT any other year. All of you have taken on every challenge with grace and maturity. You're a credit to this camp," Andy says.

I'm a curse to this camp.

Olly and I glance at each other, then I look away. We're both thinking the same thing. It's my fault this is happening in the first place.

We get back to the food hall and put on rubber gloves. We need this place clean and sterile so that everyone can eat in here in four hours and thirty minutes.

I get onto my knees with tears in my eyes, while Olly gets a new bucket of water and Andy chucks the blanket in the trash. There's still a wet sponge on the floor near the trash bucket. I pick it up and freeze.

Written in blood are the initials LC.

41

Lillian snuck in here to write this when we left. If I hadn't gone with Andy and Olly . . .

Don't think about that.

"Esme?" Olly says, his tone asking what's wrong with me. He kneels down. "Oh my God. This wasn't here before, was it?"

"No. I *definitely* would have noticed."

"Andy, do you know anyone with the initials LC?" Olly asks as Andy walks toward us, snapping on a pair of rubber gloves.

"I'm not sure, why?"

"Look." Olly points to the letters on the floor.

"My goodness." Andy shudders. "Well, this could at least help narrow the search further. I'll have a look through the staff files and see who fits."

"Can I clean it up now?" I ask.

"Just let me get a picture." Andy takes his phone out and as soon as I hear a click, I dunk the sponge in water and scrub it over her initials.

"Didn't you want to bleach?" Olly asks.

"After this is clean," I reply, gritting my teeth.

Just. Go.

Whose blood did she write it with? I cleaned the deer's up. All that's left is a stain. Her blood? Am I washing away forensic evidence?

I use both hands and scrub as hard as I can. Andy and Olly help. Only one of them is aware that I'm unraveling.

If Lillian never worked here, Andy won't find her in the files. She'll want to remain hidden. I don't think she has been to the camp other than to snoop. I think that her accomplice is the one who worked here. Maybe *still* works here.

"All right," Andy says as we finish cleaning up and then wash our hands. "We should all get back to bed."

You would never know anything happened here. The floor is lighter and patchy where the blood was, but unless you were looking for it, you probably wouldn't notice. And if anyone does notice, we'll say food was spilled. The campers sure can make a mess.

Andy clears his throat. "I'll take the trash out. You two get some rest. Thank you for everything you've done tonight. It won't be forgotten."

That's what I'm afraid of.

Olly and I leave first. We walk in silence out of the food hall and down the steps.

I swallow a sob. *Don't break down!* "That was intense."

"Who is LC?"

"Olly, please," I whisper.

"Not happening." Grabbing my hand, he pulls me in the opposite direction to my cabin.

"What are you doing?" I tug my arm, but he doesn't loosen his grip, just keeps dragging me along with him. "Olly, let me go!"

"*Shh.* In here."

The multiuse cabin. We were in here last night.

"This is becoming our thing," I grumble as Olly shuts the door behind us and finally releases me.

He flicks on just the far lights, the ones that won't be visible from outside. The thick blinds are down too.

I fold my arms and glare at him. "What do you want?"

"The truth."

That's rich.

"Ditto!"

His eyes darken. He's mad . . . again. Well, so am I! "Esme, who is LC?"

I remain silent. Olly stalks closer. I narrow my eyes and hold my ground.

Stopping right before the toes of his shoes touch mine, he says, "LC just left a dead deer for us."

"I remember!"

Sighing sharply, he looks up at the ceiling.

"I didn't sneak out with anyone called LC," I tell him. "Now it really is your turn."

"Then who is it?"

"Olly! Where are you from?"

"Missouri."

Not buying it.

He said he wants to be away from "here" and he's super evasive. He probably chose Springfield because it's the same name of the town in *The Simpsons,* his favorite show.

He must be from Texas.

Oh God. That's it! How did I not connect the dots earlier?

"You said your favorite thing to do as a kid was visit Six Flags Fiesta. *Fiesta.* That one is in Texas," I say.

He winces, grinding his teeth.

"Tell me the truth. *Now.*"

"Esme, you're—"

"No! I don't want any dumb excuse or bullshit story. Tell me the truth, Olly."

"All right! Fine." He takes a long breath. "I moved from Texas to Missouri when I was fifteen."

I take a step back. I knew it. "Why would you lie about that?"

"I haven't been back here in a long time."

"Three years isn't a long time, Olly."

"It feels like it."

"You lived here? In this town?"

"No, the next one over. The towns share this forest. I wanted to come here without baggage."

Oh God.

"You said you didn't know your way around town."

"That wasn't a lie. I've only been there a few times in passing."

"Where is Jake from?"

"Texas."

Of course he is. Both of them are popular and athletic, and they're too close to be two-week-old friends.

"Right. So you *did* know each other before coming here."

"I've known him since we were about five. We kept in touch after I moved."

Great, twelve *years*, not two weeks.

"This makes no sense. Why would you lie about either of those things?"

"I used to go into the woods with my friends and older brother at night," Olly says. "Since I was about eight, we'd sneak off and hike or make a campfire. There was a large group of us."

My stomach clenches.

Where is he going with this?

"Olly . . . were you there that night?"

I turn around, unable to look at him. Shame washes over me, and I feel sick.

His footsteps creak on the wooden floor as he gets closer.

"Yes," he whispers, his breath blowing across the back of my neck.

I close my eyes.

"What did you see?"

"I got lost in the woods that night for the first time ever. We were walking, and I heard something. The others told me I was crazy and kept going, but I ditched them and came back. I saw the most beautiful girl—she looked like an angel—about my age, hanging out with her friend. You were both wearing pajamas, so I figured you had to be campers."

I look over my shoulder and he wraps his arms around me, hugging my back to his chest.

"It's okay, Esme."

"You saw the fire?"

"Yes. I saw you stack too much wood on the fire. I saw that girl come and talk to you and Kayla. I saw the fire get out of hand, and . . . I saw the fight."

I lick my lips, my heart thudding against his arm. "What else?"

"The branches fell, and the fire took the trees." He lowers his head, resting his forehead on my shoulder. "I watched you go to help the girl, but Kayla pulled you back and you both ran. Did you know that you are the only one who looked back? Kayla didn't."

Tears prickle behind my eyelids.

"What happened to the girl?"

"She was burned, but she eventually got up. But that's when I heard Jake shout my name and I left. I wish I had gone over to her. I'll always regret not helping her. What?" Olly asks as my body turns to stone.

"Lillian *was* hurt."

I have the same regret as Olly. The guilt of not helping her is something I live with every day.

"Lillian? LC? What was her surname?"

"Campbell. I tried to look her up on social media, but she's not there. Why didn't you tell me this when I confessed about the fire?"

"That was only yesterday, Esme, and we got into an argument. Remember, you thought I was the one messing with the camp." I start to pull away, but he stops me. "No, we're not fighting again," he says.

"I'm tired," I tell him. Suddenly I feel like I could curl up on the floor and sleep for a month. My head is going to explode.

"Me too, but we still have a lot to discuss. Lillian. That's who you think did this?"

"You knew this *whole* time."

"Yes. I was waiting for you to tell me the *whole* truth."

"I was waiting for you to tell me *any* truth."

Olly lowers his head closer to mine. "Lillian was burned. That's motive enough."

"I hate this."

His expression softens. "I know you do. What happened was an accident. You're not a bad person. In fact, you're one of the best."

"What do we do now, Olly?"

"I'm going to kiss you and then we're going to figure this thing out together."

I can't think of a better plan right now.

He closes the small distance between us and I sink into him.

Suddenly the light turns off with a snap, like the power has been cut.

I gasp, and Olly stands taller.

Lillian is still here.

42

"I swear if you suggest we go outside, I will throw you in the lake," I whisper while my heart tries to break out of my rib cage.

I can't see well in the dark, but Olly's arms are still very secure around me.

"I wasn't going to suggest *we* go out there."

"No way."

"She's just a girl, Esme."

I elbow him hard in the chest and he hisses through his teeth. "See, women can hurt too," I say.

"Unnecessary," he growls. "We can't stay in here, but who knows what she's got planned out there?"

"She's dangerous; we both know that. Let's call Andy for help," I say, checking my watch. We don't have long before sunrise.

"There are four cabins full of sleeping children between this cabin and Andy's."

He unwraps his arms from around me and I faintly make out him rubbing his chest. That will teach him for insinuating that women are weak.

I don't want to praise Lillian and Rebekah for what they've done here, but all hail girl power. I wish they would just use it for something good.

Rebekah might not be involved! I remind myself.

"What if we go out there and she has a gun?" I ask.

"How would that be revenge?"

"Isn't that, like, the *definition* of revenge?"

"No, and you don't believe it is either. You're letting fear talk now. She doesn't want to kill anyone; she wants to screw us up and turn us against each other. We're already divided: half want to go to the cops and the other half are scared to."

But Lillian must have an end game. In four weeks, we leave.

"What are we supposed to do with that, Olly? We need to do *something*. She could be out there now sacrificing more animals or writing threats all over the cabins!"

"I'm going outside."

"Bad. Idea."

He takes my hand. "Come on, let's look through the window and see if we can spot her."

The cabin is drenched in darkness. I can barely see an inch in front of me.

Olly and I shuffle forward. I reach my free hand out to feel. When it touches the wall, we move sideways. The window is only just visible, a thin strip of dull light around the dark fabric blind.

I hook the blind with one finger, wincing as I shift it out of the way. Olly's temple touches mine as we lean closer and look out.

My heart seizes and I jump back, letting the blind fall shut as a scream rips from my throat.

Olly makes a sharp *bah* sound and grabs hold of me, pulling me closer.

Lillian and whoever her accomplice is are outside, dressed head to toe in black, hoods up, facing us.

"Oh my God, they're out there!" I mutter.

"Okay. It's okay. Hey, look at me, Esme."

I can just about make out his face and meet his eyes.

"Don't panic."

"They're out there and they know we're in here! I *am* panicking! What are they doing? Waiting for us? To do what?"

I don't ever want to see Lillian again.

"Hey, shh. Nothing bad is going to happen to us. They're two girls our age. It's going to be fine."

"Y-you think we should go out there and talk to them."

"Yes."

Taking a breath, I place my clammy palms on his chest and focus on not freaking collapsing.

"All right," I say, and then regret it instantly. "Finding out what she wants is the only way to stop this."

"We go out together, but stay behind me. Please."

Holding my hand, he leads me to the door.

My pulse skitters as he pulls the door open.

Should we grab a weapon? There are plenty of bats in here. Though I'm hoping there won't be any need for that.

We step out onto the porch.

"They're gone," I breathe, doing a three-sixty to try to see *where* they went.

Olly creeps forward on the porch to peer around the side of the cabin. I do the same on the other end.

My footsteps are too loud, though I'm practically on my tiptoes and walking like a sneaky cartoon character. I place one hand on the corner of the cabin, my fingers digging into the rough wood. I peer around the corner and see nothing but darkness.

I turn to Olly.

Only, he's not there.

"Olly!" I whisper. Where the hell did he go?

I pad lightly along the porch, my side practically scraping along the cabin wall. "Olly?"

What is going on?

I strain my ears, trying to hear his footsteps, but I can only hear my ragged breathing. No matter how much I try to control it, I can't.

My stomach clenches.

I'm leaving tomorrow.

"Olly, where are you?" I whisper.

Please say she hasn't hurt him.

It's still dark out. I don't even know where the circuit box is to turn the electricity back on. That's what they've done, tripped the circuit . . . I think. It must be in the staff cabin. If I can find it, I can turn on the outside lights and find Olly.

"Esme?"

I startle, my body almost leaving the damn porch floor.

Pressing one hand over my pounding heart, I snap, "Jesus, Olly!"

"Sorry, I didn't mean to scare you."

"Where did you go?"

"Around the back of the cabin. They disappeared so quickly, I thought they went that way instead of around the lake. I couldn't see anyone, though."

I shudder. "It's so creepy knowing they're out here."

Not that I'll be doing much sleeping from this point on.

"The cabins are locked," Olly says.

"They have a key," I remind him.

"Which they wouldn't use with the campers inside. They seem to have a conscience when it comes to that, at least."

"What do we do now?"

"Andy."

We traipse back to the staff cabin again. I don't know what time it is, but I don't think we'll be seeing the sun anytime soon. It's not quite light enough.

Something catches my eye as we walk past the lake. "Olly, there's something in the lake."

I can just make out lumps of . . . something floating in the moon's reflection.

"Andy will have a flashlight," Olly says. "Stay where I can see you."

I wait while Olly runs to get Andy. When I say *wait,* I mean that my legs won't move anyway. My eyes strain as I try to see what's floating out there. It looks like a few small objects.

Andy comes rushing up with Olly a heartbeat later.

They take the steps quickly. Andy trains his flashlight on the lake.

"They were outside?" he asks.

A shiver rips through my body. "Yes."

"What were you doing in the multiuse cabin?"

"I needed to talk to Esme," Olly replied.

"I was freaking out a little," I add to give our story more weight.

The flashlight catches something that makes me lose my footing. "What the hell is that?"

Andy gasps.

"Oh my God, it's a doll," Olly says.

A *doll.*

No. It's not just one doll. There are five.

"Why?" Andy whispers.

"This is hideous." Five naked plastic dolls float on the lake. "There's something on two of them. Can you see?" I ask.

"Yeah," Andy replies. "I can't make out what."

"We need to go and get them," Olly says.

I knew that was coming. Of course we need them to be gone by the time the campers wake up. Can't say I'm particularly looking forward to fishing these out of the water.

"Esme, you hold the flashlight," Andy says. "Olly and I will retrieve them."

They wade into the lake and I shine the flashlight on the five dolls.

As I raise the light, it bounces off them and I can see clearly what's on the ones that are marked. Eight big black crosses over their eyes.

43

Creepy. Disturbing. Sick.

Five naked baby dolls, four with their eyes crossed out.

Who do they represent?

Me? Kayla?

Lillian?

Jake and Olly too?

Lillian was the one who was harmed that night.

"Are they American Girl dolls?" I ask.

Olly and Andy look up at me with identical frowns. Yeah, they wouldn't know.

"It's a brand. I had a couple of them when I was little. There are much cheaper dolls they could have used. Either they belonged to one of them or they spent a fortune to chuck these in the lake."

"What are we going to do with them?" Olly asks.

Andy huffs. "I'll bag them up and put them in my office. Once summer is over, we can go to the cops."

"Shh," I scold. "If they're watching, and I have a feeling they are, they'll hear you. No cops, remember?"

"God," Andy breathes. "This is out of hand."

"The next time we see them, we go for it," Olly says.

"Go for what?"

"Grab them, tie them up, hold them somewhere."

That sounds fun.

Olly's eyes meet mine. "We can take them."

"I think a woman is doing this. Or at least one of them is," Andy says.

Wow, he is several chapters behind.

"Why do you think that?" I ask, playing along with his great discovery.

"The dolls. Would a man think to use dolls?"

I shrug. "Maybe. Dolls aren't just for girls."

"Perhaps not. But it's most likely a female."

"Yes," I say. He's *not* wrong.

"Let's get the dolls inside." Andy looks Olly and me over and seems to make a decision. "You are both going to help me go through the staff files. We're looking for someone with the initials LC. Even better if we find a woman with those initials."

"Are CITs allowed to look at staff files?" Olly asks.

I want to punch him in the throat. I'm sure we're about to break all sorts of confidentiality laws, but *who cares*?

"Not technically, but I need help here," Andy says. "The faster we find out who LC is, the better."

"Can we please get some coffee before we start?" I ask as we walk to the staff cabin, each of us holding plastic dolls.

Andy nods. "That might be a good idea. It *is* five-thirty in the morning."

Fab, I've had about an hour of sleep. Will this night never end? Lillian's ramping up, her taunts coming thick and fast now.

Grumpy Esme will be coming out to play tomorrow. Or rather later today. Not that I'm planning on staying at camp.

We drop the dolls in the staff cabin.

"Would you two go make the coffee? I'll get the files out and we can get started," Andy says.

The last time Olly and I were alone in a cabin . . .

Olly senses my unease. "I'll go. It's probably best if Esme stays with you."

Andy's eyes drift to me and then Olly. "I agree. Take this radio and let us know if you have any trouble."

I have *no* objections. I don't want to go back out there. I want to sit in here, snoop through staff files and wait for my coffee. Maybe we won't find an LC in these files, but I might get some information on who Lillian's accomplice is. I'm pretty sure it's Rebekah, but I need evidence.

Olly takes the radio and clips it to his jeans. "I'll be right back."

"The files are in here," Andy says, leading me into his office. "Let's take them into the staff room and put them on the table. We'll need the space."

"Do I have a file?"

He smiles and unlocks the metal cabinet. "Yes. It's not very thick."

"Is that good?"

"This is your first year with us and you haven't done anything wrong, so I'd say yes, it's good."

"Does anyone have a thick file?"

Smirking, Andy says, "Take these to the staff room."

He stacks a bunch of files into my waiting hands and I carry them to the table. In the staff room there are two comfortable couches, a vending machine, a battered foosball table and a CD player. Yep, CDs. I don't think I've ever owned one. This room is stuck in the nineties.

"Do you think Olly is okay?" I ask.

"He would radio if he wasn't."

Olly has only been gone a couple of minutes. The coffee probably hasn't finished brewing yet.

I flip the first file open and stifle a yawn.

Misty Allen.

She's too old.

"Not this one," I say, putting the file on the floor. That can be the No pile.

"Nor this one. I remember her, lovely girl," Andy says.

I look at Andy over the top of the next file. "Please tell me you're not basing this on who you remember liking?"

"Her name is Sandie. No LC."

"Okay."

Andy leaps up to unlock the door as Olly returns. It's locked again straightaway. Olly comes into the room holding three cups of coffee. They're stacked on top of each other and his chin is resting on the top one.

Andy jumps up and helps him.

The second I thank Olly, I take a sip. Wonderful caffeine-laced liquid burns my tongue. Fatigue has begun to set in, and I need a pick-me-up badly.

Olly sits next to me.

"You okay?" I ask.

"Tired but ready to find our hugely unwelcome friends."

Me too. "I suggest we look for someone who's been here in the last few years," I say. "Things change at camp, and this person knows our current routine. And remember, this LC isn't alone, so we can't limit our search to just those initials."

"Why do you think only those initials were left?" Andy asks.

Olly clears his throat. "Maybe they didn't have time to write the other ones? I don't know. We shouldn't rule anything out, though, right?"

"Agreed."

I put my coffee down and open the next file.

Rebekah's file.

My face falls.

I pull the folder closer to my chest and scan it. I quickly find what I'm looking for—her home address. It isn't in Kansas. It's in Texas. *In this town.*

I close the file with a racing heart and put it in the No pile, but not before I memorize her address.

"Not this one," I say out loud.

Slowly, we make our way through the files. Even though I've found what I was looking for, I continue, which is tedious, but I need to keep up the pretense. I don't want Andy to know yet.

I'll tell Olly when I get him alone.

I roll my neck and yawn.

"It's six," Andy says. "We should try to get an hour of sleep."

"I *really* like the sound of that," I reply, covering my yawn with the back of my hand.

Olly stands and stretches. "All right, let's put these away first." He looks at me out of the corner of his eye. I pick up my stack of files and stand. Does he know that I'm hiding something? Hopefully he will understand that it's because of Andy.

By now he must know I'll tell him. I hope.

Andy locks the cabinet and we part ways. He goes into his room; Olly and I head out.

We walk to my cabin and I stop on the porch. "Go to yours and we'll head inside at the same time."

His lips quirk, amused. "You worried about me?"

"Yes. I'm worried about all of us."

I have so much to tell him, but right now all I can think about is sleep. Olly seems to sense this.

His fingertips trace my jaw. "Get some rest, Esme."

"I'll try."

I'm sure he's going to kiss me, but he doesn't. Instead he bites his lip, drops his hand and turns. I watch him walk along the trodden path to his cabin. He looks over his shoulder when he opens the door.

I do the same and we both slip inside.

44

An hour later, I wake with a foggy head but a clearer mind.

I found out that Rebekah is from this town. That at least gives me somewhere to start. This is something. I finally don't feel so far behind Lillian. We're closing in.

"Morning," Kayla says cheerfully.

I roll over and see her head peeking over the top of my bunk.

Whatever. It's been morning for what feels like five days already. I think I managed to get about forty-five-minutes' sleep. It's almost seven.

Groaning, I rub my tired eyes. "Morning. I need coffee."

She laughs. "Let's go get some then. Whoa, babe, you look awful."

"I didn't sleep well."

"No shit. Your eye bags are suitcases and you're washed out."

"Thank you."

I sit up and slide my legs over the ladder. Twisting, I climb down and stretch my arms over my head.

Do I tell her?

She'll find out. I don't think Andy and Olly will keep last night's insanity a secret.

We both get dressed and then head to the food hall for breakfast. Some of the girls are dawdling, getting ready slowly and messing around with their hair. That's pointless, we're swimming today.

In the lake of dolls.

Which I'm glad to see is American Girl–free.

The lake looks peaceful, as if it's frozen in time.

"Let's eat lunch outside today," I tell Kayla.

"Huh? It's hotter than lava."

"Trust me, Kayla."

She does a double take. "Why are you so tired? Oh my God, is it Olly-related?"

"*Nothing* like that."

"Then, what?"

"Not here. Too many people around."

Her eyebrows knit together.

"I'll fill you in on everything then, I promise."

"Okay," she says slowly. "Let's get you fed."

Olly is sitting at our usual table with a big plate of bacon and eggs. He's gulping down a mug of coffee like it's air.

I load up a plate with croissants and fruit. Then I get my beloved coffee and take a seat. Kayla has opted for a big cup of tea.

She didn't spend most of the night running around dodging Lillian's every move.

"Morning," I say to Olly.

He looks sideways with guilty eyes. "How are you doing?"

"I'm exhausted. You?"

"Same."

I sip my coffee.

"We need to talk today," he says, keeping his voice low so that the others won't hear. They're engrossed in their own theories about the person in the woods anyway.

"I agree." I turn to him. "Kayla too . . . and Jake?"

Olly subtly shakes his head. Does Jake not know about this? He was there the night of the fire, but Olly said Jake didn't see anything, that he called Olly from somewhere deeper in the woods. Maybe Olly never told him. But then why did Jake agree to lie about how long he's known Olly?

"All right," I whisper, nipping off a chunk of croissant.

"Morning, campers," Andy says as he enters the food hall with way too much energy for someone rolling on one hour's sleep.

I'm a zombie.

Olly and I exchange a tired glance.

"Who's ready for music and swimming?"

Not me.

The campers cheer, and I wince.

No one is particularly hyped about walking the trails anymore, so we've been keeping close to camp. This week, we're supposed to camp out in shelters we make ourselves. No freaking way.

It's on Andy's color-coordinated schedule that he printed for counselors and CITs. I want to scribble crosses all over it like the creepy dolls' eyes.

I don't know if he's thrown the dolls away yet or if he plans to store them. I couldn't care less about that, what I want to know is why Lillian put them in the lake. What kind of mind thinks that up? It's sick.

I pick at my food.

"You tired, Esme?" Rebekah asks.

Are you?

Tia must sleep like the dead if she's not waking up every time Rebekah sneaks out of their room and back in.

I have the upper hand here. Rebekah doesn't know that I've found out she's Lillian's accomplice.

"I'm fine," I reply with a smile. I probably look like I've been drugged.

She knows I'm not fine because she knows that I was outside removing the dolls from the lake. But neither of us can admit it.

We have to keep on playing the game.

"I'm going to go find the particular guitar that Ellen likes." Rebekah rolls her eyes. "She doesn't do well if she doesn't get that one."

"I'll come with," Tia says. "I need the bathroom before the campers make my ears bleed."

My eyes slide to Jake. He's still lying too.

Why, though? I guess he doesn't know that Olly told me the truth.

But why would he need to lie about where he's from in the first place?

It doesn't make sense.

There is something I'm missing, or rather something Olly hasn't revealed yet.

I watch Rebekah and Tia leave, and then I turn to Olly. It's on the tip of my tongue. I'd love to grill them both on why they lied.

"Let's go, man," Jake says to Olly. "I need to piss."

Lovely.

Olly doesn't look at me when he leaves with Jake, but he does chuck a "see you later" over his shoulder.

Is he mad at me again?

We were fine when we left for bed . . . I think. It was early and I was tired. Am I forgetting another argument we had?

"Something wrong?" Kayla asks.

"I don't know."

She glares. "Yes you do. Fill me in."

"I'm not sure that now is a good time. We're in a room full of people."

"No one else is at our table and no one is paying us any attention."

"I bet the diva inside of you is so mad about that fact."

Narrowing her eyes, Kayla replies, "Shut it."

Shuffling closer, I lower my voice. "Okay, so last night was . . . eventful. I woke up in the early morning because of a loud noise. Olly did too. We found a dead deer in the food hall."

"What? In *here*?"

"Yep."

"Like, it had died in here?"

"No, like Lillian had killed it and dumped it here. We're sitting quite close to where it was, actually."

Her pink-painted lips part.

"It was bleeding. Olly, Andy and I cleaned it up and put the deer in some bushes in the forest. When we came back, there were initials written in blood on the floor. You can probably guess which ones."

"LC," Kayla breathes. "Oh my God! Well, she *does* have a thing about deer."

I shudder, not wanting to think about that. "When we were all going back to bed, we saw five dolls floating in the lake."

Her eyes widen, but I don't slow down, because I'm on a roll.

"We got them out, and four had crosses drawn over their eyes, Andy hid them, and we went through the staff files. Kayla, I found out that Rebekah lives in town. Which means she lied about where she's from. She's definitely helping Lillian.

"Oh, and Olly admitted that he and Jake are from one town over. They were in the woods the night of the fire and Olly saw everything, including Lillian get burned by the fire."

"What?" Kayla hisses. "Are you . . . What? Last night? This all happened *last night*?"

"I finally got to bed at, like, six in the morning and had just under an hour of broken sleep. Tonight you and I have to sneak out and go into town."

"What? *No way.*"

"Yes way, and we have to do it without anyone else. Just me and you."

She pales. "In the forest at night?"

"You up for it?"

"Not a chance, Esme," she replies, her voice thick with fear.

I raise my eyebrows. "We *have* to, Kayla. We need to end this."

We have to find Rebekah's house. I have the feeling that if we do, we're going to find Lillian.

45

Kayla is so not down with the idea of us sneaking through the woods alone at night while two people try to ruin our lives.

Can't think why.

I'm not entirely sure why I want to go. All I can think is that I'm so exhausted, I'm delirious. That's the only excuse for what I'm about to do.

I'm not ready to face the very real possibility that I'll be doing this alone tonight. I could take Olly. He would come, I know that for sure, but there is something about his secret childhood home that bothers me. And the fact that he and Jake are still pretending they don't know each other is shady and crazy suspicious.

I paddle in the edge of the cool lake, trying to keep myself awake by picturing all the ways Lillian could screw with me in the forest tonight. The sun shines brightly over camp as if it has no clue of the darkness lurking here.

Kayla is near but she hasn't said much to me since I told her I want us to go into town.

Nothing like fear to keep you alert.

My group is in the water and being taught by the swim instructors.

If they find a sunken doll, I'm going to throw up.

"How are you?" Andy asks, stopping dead in front of me. One more step and he'd be in the water. He's possibly paler than me this morning. But I think I win with the dark circles under my eyes.

I saw him walking around the lake with his clipboard earlier. He looked like he was checking things off, making sure equipment was safe and everything was in order. But I think he was actually looking for Lillian.

She won't be here now. Not after last night. She knows we're even more on edge, that we'll be watching like hawks.

"Exhausted but okay. You?"

He nods. "About the same. Who does something like this to a camp of kids?"

"There are a lot of crazy people out there, Andy."

"Yeah, no kidding. I just want to go to the police, but I'm too scared that this LC will realize what we're doing and react." He sighs and moves on, stopping by the kayaks and pretending to check them over.

Kayla grabs my hand. "Okay, my head is going to explode, and I'm still worried that you want to go back into town. Jake is being his usual sweet self to me, and I don't know how to be around him now that I know he's lying."

"Slow down, you really *are* going to explode."

"I can't believe he and Olly were there that night."

I nod. "Me neither. You know, there is one thing that is still bothering me."

"One thing?"

Rolling my eyes, I clarify, "Okay, one *new* thing."

"What's that?"

"Why are we all here? Lillian didn't just luck out that the three of us who were there that night are here now. I think she set this up."

Kayla frowns. "You're *beyond* obsessed with this, Esme."

Oh, I'm so far past obsessed it's not even funny. "How are you not? She's been stalking us and threatening the whole camp. Now we have an address. We know who her BFF is."

"We *think* we know."

I raise one eyebrow. "I have Rebekah's address! She's *from town.*"

Kayla's doing that thing again where she tries to deny the truth, and it's infuriating.

My chest burns. "Rebekah is the definition of BS. Look it up. Are you coming with me tonight or not?"

Kayla twirls her long ponytail around one finger. "Well, I can't let you go alone, can I?"

"You could. Maybe that would be better, actually. Yeah, I could swipe two radios from Andy's office, and you could keep watch. It's a bad idea for both of us to go."

"You're not going alone."

"I need you here. If Lillian thinks we're here she won't go looking for me. It's our night to be outside, unless Andy orders another freaking lockdown."

She opens her mouth to challenge me.

"Kayla, you know I'm right."

"Will you at least take Olly?"

"Hell no."

"It's him or me."

I roll my eyes. "We'll discuss this later, but I don't think Jake and Olly need to know any more than they do already."

"So it's all on me and you."

Now we're a team, huh?

"That's the way it's been from the start, Kayla. This is our responsibility."

"It was an *accident*."

"That doesn't mean we're not to blame. We didn't help Lillian."

"Because she was crazy and we were *scared*."

That's not a very good excuse.

We'll end up going around in circles if we keep talking. "Whatever. You should get back to the beach, your group is playing."

With a huff, she wanders off, whipping her hair the way mean girls in movies do. She's really playing the part now that she's dating the quarterback.

I've annoyed her. She wants a say in what happens next, but she doesn't want to step up and try to figure this out.

If she's not with me, then she can't make any demands. I'm

going into town tonight and she can stay here. And I'm not going to think about it so that I can't talk myself out of it. All I know is that I can't keep doing this.

"Esme, can I have a word?" Olly asks.

Cora looks up from where she's standing waist-deep near the girls. "Take ten, Esme, I've got this."

Well, I can't say no now.

I give her a tight smile. "Thanks."

Slipping my flip-flops on as I step out of the lake, I ask, "You want to walk?"

"Let's go to the food hall instead. I told Andy I would get the snacks ready for after the activity."

"Okay."

We walk up the steps and into the kitchen.

"What are we having?"

"Orange wedges, watermelon, crackers and yogurt are on Andy's list." Olly holds up a piece of paper with today's snack highlighted in case Olly didn't see the date beside it.

I bet Andy's never been late or unorganized in his life. Lillian is really messing with his order.

"I'll grab the fruit. Can you get the rest?" I ask.

"Uh-huh."

We work in silence at first. Olly glances at me occasionally as I slice oranges into wedges.

"What did you find?" he asks.

"Sorry?"

"Last night, in the files. What did you find?"

I put the knife down. "What do you mean? We didn't find anything."

His eyes narrow. *"Esme."*

"Can we please not have the same argument over and over? I didn't find anything. But while we're talking, do you want to go into more detail about why you and Jake lied about knowing each other? It can't just be because you were there the night of the fire. Why have you never said anything about knowing me? Didn't you think it was weird that we all just happened to be back at camp at the same time?"

He chucks the box of crackers down on the countertop and turns away from me.

"You'll think whatever the hell you want anyway, so forget it, Esme."

I watch with my mouth catching flies as he shoves the door open and storms out of the kitchen.

46

I used to love the mystery of night.

Things can exist in the dark that can't in the light. Elves and unicorns could be running around for all we know.

No, I haven't lost it. I know logically that's not true, but if you can't see something, then how can you be *sure* it doesn't exist?

Five-year-old me loved the thought of her toys coming alive at night and mythical creatures flying around outside.

It's not such a fun thought anymore. Not since I know what is lurking in the dark.

I'm currently sitting around a campfire listening to a conversation about football. I like football as much as the next non-obsessive American, but I don't want to spend hours talking about it.

I tap my fingers against my soda can and wish everyone else would get up and do something else. When we break off and go our own ways, I can get away. The radio is in my pocket already and Kayla has one too.

While Andy was briefing everyone, I swiped two radios from the staff cabin. It was embarrassingly easy to do. I can see how Lillian managed to get keys.

Olly watches me from the other side of the fire.

I don't know what he's thinking, but we're still in a fight. Usually, he would be sitting next to me. Tonight, however, he sat as far away from me as he could.

His little tantrum over my simple question hasn't been forgotten. I still have a lot of questions and he clearly doesn't want to answer any of them. There has to be a reason for that.

"Why is he staring?" Kayla asks, looking anywhere but at the boys across from us.

I shrug, not really in the mood to talk to her about it. "I don't know, but it's starting to freak me out. He's going to have to find something else to look at if I want to get away."

"You remember at school when you needed to call your cousin about Bieber concert tickets, so I told the teacher you were about to hurl? She let you go to the bathroom."

"Please don't tell everyone I'm about to hurl."

She laughs. "I just mean I've got your back." She takes a breath. "You have to be careful out there, Esme."

Kayla will always be my best friend, and I love her, but she is blowing so hot and cold at the moment. I don't know how much I can rely on her.

"I'll be careful. This could all be over tonight."

Sighing, she looks up at the sky. "I hope so. I hate being scared."

"We're going to be fine."

"I can't die," she whispers, curling her hands into fists.

"You're not going to die." I can practically see her heart rate spike. "Kayla, it's going to be all right, I promise."

She purses her lips, and I know she's thinking of her grandma. It was awful. Kayla watched her nana die in that car and thought she was next.

Taking a deep breath, she gets up and plasters on a big smile. "Okay, let's end this tonight."

We both raise our hands in a little wave at the same time.

A wave of nausea almost makes me double over.

"We're going to bed, guys," I say, rising to my feet.

Olly looks up at me with a slight frown, but he says, "Night," with everyone else.

Kayla and I tiptoe through the main room where the girls are sleeping and into our room.

I pull the door closed and turn to her. "Right, I'll go out of the window. They won't see me from this side of the cabin."

Kayla's eyes dart from the door to the window. "Please, please, please be careful."

"I'll be fine. Rebekah is out there with the rest of them."

"You still think she's involved?"

"Hopefully we'll know soon."

"Should I go back out and make sure she doesn't leave?"

"Nah, I don't think she's going anywhere tonight. She's been yawning for the last hour." I'm still tired from the never-ending deer-and-doll night too.

Let's not think about that.

"I'll keep watch out the window and see if she sneaks off," Kayla says.

If Rebekah does sneak off, Kayla will see her from our bedroom.

"Radio me if she does. Like the *very second,* but use a code word in case any of the girls from the main room hear."

"What code word?"

"Er . . . clover."

Kayla scrunches up her face. "That lucky weed?"

"I need all the luck I can get."

"Okay. I'll say 'clover' if I see Rebekah heading your way."

I open the window, haul myself up and swing my legs out. "I'll be as quick as I can."

"*Careful,* Esme."

"That's my middle name."

"Your middle name is Mallory and it means 'unfortunate one'!"

It's a family middle name. We haven't *all* been unfortunate. Just me, actually.

I wave my hand, dismissing her. "See you soon."

Dropping to the ground, I watch Kayla close the window, and then I creep through bushes to meet the little trail into town.

I walk into the night, the trees my only company. The air is warm and silent. I take light steps and look up when I hear a hoot. Damn owl nearly gave me a heart attack. It takes flight and swoops through the trees.

I've been in the woods for about thirty seconds and I already regret my life choices.

It's dark as hell, the air is cooler than usual, and I'm alone.

The dark and I don't feel like friends anymore.

I put one foot in front of the other, following the trodden man-made path toward town. I dressed in dark colors and left my flashlight on my bed, so I'm walking slowly.

The less noise I make, the less likely Lillian is to find me. I think she and Rebekah have been coming from the other side of the lake, where the fire was.

This was by far my dumbest idea since I was fourteen and thought a perm would look great. The curls were so tight, I looked like a poodle.

The forest feels alive tonight. When I'm too far to hear any sounds from camp, I hear the soft breeze dancing between the trees. Small animals scurry away from me before I see them.

When I reach the end of the forest, I roll my shoulders. I made it. I look around and cross the deserted road.

The trees finally give way to houses—big stone houses with large, manicured lawns—and my shoulders lose tension.

Rebekah's house is right on the edge of town.

I make a right and stop. My eyes flit to my phone screen, where the map is showing a dot for Rebekah's house and another one for me.

Besides a few people out walking, I don't see anyone. No one gives me a second glance, probably because I'm not in camp clothing. I blend in. I'm even pretending that the heat isn't making me want to run for the nearest AC.

It takes me two minutes to walk around the block and come face to face with Rebekah's house.

Rebekah is wealthy.

I walk up the drive, clutching my phone. Wiggling my fingers, I take a breath and press the doorbell.

If Lillian answers now, I'm probably going to pass out.

The lock on the door clicks and my muscles tense.

A little old lady with rollers in her hair and wearing a fluffy pink robe answers the door. Definitely not Lillian.

Rebekah's nana?

"Yes?"

"Hi, um, my name is Chloe." My little Pomeranian's name. "My car broke down a block away. I've called Triple A and they'll be here soon, but"—I hide my face with my hands—"ugh, this is so embarrassing, but I'm kind of desperate for the bathroom."

I drop my hands and smile.

"Oh, sugar," she drawls.

"Would it be at all possible to use yours? Please?"

"Of course. Come on in and I'll show you where it is."

"Thank you."

She points to a dark wood door on the right. "Just there."

"I really appreciate this," I tell her, and disappear into the bathroom.

I lock the door, close my eyes and lean against the wall. Clawing at my suddenly itchy skin, I look around. I don't want to be in this house for a second longer than necessary.

Okay, you can do this. I need to find out as much as I can about Rebekah without making her nana suspicious.

After a minute, I flush the toilet and wash my hands.

When I come out of the bathroom, Rebekah's nana pops around the corner. "Over here."

Okay, she's inviting me deeper into the house.

I walk into her little country kitchen.

"Your house is lovely," I tell her. Old people love it when you compliment their home. My nan goes full-on bashful.

"Thank you, darlin'," she replies. "Can I get you an iced tea?"

"Oh, that would be awesome, if you don't mind?"

She waves her hand. "Of course not. Take a seat over there."

I do as I'm told and sit at the round table in the corner. From here I can see the living room. There are little pink flowers all over the sofas.

On the wall behind me is a massive collage. There must be about fifty photos.

"This all your family?" I ask.

She looks over from the fridge. "Oh yes. I have five children and thirteen grandchildren. My first great-grandchild is due in the fall."

"You all look so happy," I tell her, scouring the collage for pictures of Rebekah.

And, *bingo,* there she is. Smiling in a picture with people I assume are her cousins. Her face steals my breath.

"Do they all live close by?"

"Oh, we're scattered, I'm afraid. Every one of my children chose different colleges across the country. The grandchildren have done the same, but they all come back to visit."

"That's good you get to see them."

She nods. "My granddaughter Rebekah spent some time here

over a few summers, but she's older now, so she's got better things to do."

So that's how Rebekah and Lillian know each other. They must have met when Rebekah came to stay with her grandma. They spent summers together plotting.

"Are your grandkids coming this summer?"

"Some of them might. Rebekah has an internship. Some accounting firm. She's always been good with numbers."

Internship? That's why she told her mom she was needed in the conference room.

Wow, Rebekah's nana doesn't know she's just ten minutes down the road. No wonder Rebekah was acting so shifty at the arcade and hiding in corners. She was afraid she'd be seen by locals.

There are so many more questions I want to ask, but I'm very aware that it's going to seem weird if I keep going. I don't want her to call Rebekah and talk about the stranger whose car broke down and who asked lots of questions about her.

I have what I need for now.

I smile at Rebekah's grandmother. "Thank you so much for letting me into your home. I should get going now. Triple A will be here soon."

"All right. You be careful out there at night, Chloe."

The night isn't my problem. Your granddaughter is.

47

Sneaking out was fine. Well, fine-ish. Except I gave absolutely no thought to the fact that I have to get back.

I've been gone for about an hour. Kayla is on the lookout, and I haven't had any message or a call to say that she's seen something. Our bedroom has a great view of the path toward town. She was in the best place to see Rebekah and Lillian.

You are fine.

It's dark. I'm at the edge of the forest, staring at the trail as if it's going to bite me.

I've always loved adventure. On every vacation with my parents I'm the one who wants to explore the area and go on day trips.

I can now confirm that adventure is highly overrated.

Give me my sofa, snacks and Netflix any day.

Is the forest thicker than it was an hour ago? The damn thing is alive and growing. Maybe the forest doesn't forget either.

One foot. *Just move one foot.*

You can't stand here all night!

I step into the mist.

I want to move that foot backward and head to the bus station. I could be at the airport in a little over an hour. Of course, with no ID, I can't actually get on a plane.

Whatever my next move is, I have to go back to camp and get my stuff. And I can't leave Kayla on her own. I have to stay with her. Bestie solidarity and all that. I can't leave Olly and Jake either. We're all here for a reason.

The hairs on the back of my neck stand as I realize something: why Lillian is doing this now. In one of my first conversations with Olly, he mentioned that he also got a CIT pamphlet. He probably got the same one I did, with the creepy threat on the back. Lillian must have sent one to all of us. Jake had to have seen what happened that night for Lillian to send him a pamphlet.

Which means Lillian knows that Olly and Jake were there the night of the accident.

I have to get back to camp to warn them.

Tapping my fingers against my legs, I take a deep breath, inhaling a lungful of courage and dewy air.

I step forward slowly and take one last look over my shoulder before I walk into the woods.

The air is heavy. I feel like I could choke on it.

I squint to see more clearly as I follow the little trail and try to keep my eyes everywhere. Literally. I swivel my head from left to right constantly, looking for Rebekah or Lillian through a thin screen of mist.

I want to curl up and make myself as small as I can, but I don't want to look like I'm scared. If Lillian is out there, at least she can't hear or feel the thumping of my heart.

Ahead of me, something rustles.

I dash to a tree and plant myself against it. Jagged bark digs into my back. I cower as my heart pulses. It could easily be an animal. It's probably an animal.

Stepping around the tree, I make my way to the next one, almost tripping over my feet.

No falling!

The noise is gone. I'm sure it was a deer. The poor thing is probably in danger too.

Crunch.

I whip my head around. That was behind me.

Gasping, I turn and bolt toward camp.

I dodge trees, steeling myself for the flash of a camera . . . or worse. Nothing comes. I sprint, my sides burning with the exertion.

I break through the trees and sob. I'm back. I'm safe.

Stumbling, I slow and creep toward the cabin, I wipe my tears and keep to the wall, bracing myself against it. When I reach the window, something sitting on the windowsill catches my eye.

A little roll of white paper. I gulp and curl my hand around it and stuff it into my pocket.

Kayla unlocks and opens the window when she spots me. I haul myself up and Kayla grabs my arms to help me in.

"You okay?"

I nod. "Fine. Nothing happened. Rebekah's nana was lovely but said nothing we didn't already know. Rebekah knows the area and must have met Lillian here."

"Sorry you had to do that."

"It's fine. I'm going to get some sleep."

I get ready for bed clumsily but in record time and climb the bunk ladder with the rolled-up paper still in my palm.

With a yawn, I get under the blanket and lie down.

The thick paper is soft between my fingertips as I peel it open.

Squinting, I read the red ink on the paper.

Nothing you do goes unnoticed—LC

The writing is neat and tall, with slashes that spike at the end of each letter. I press my lips together as fear runs ice-cold through my veins.

Not only did she know that I'd snuck out and leave a note on the windowsill, but she probably followed me too.

Lillian or Rebekah must have crawled on the ground close to the wall so Kayla wouldn't see them plant the note.

Did Lillian follow me to Rebekah's nana's house? I was careful to check my surroundings. I didn't get that twitchy feeling like someone was watching me.

I gulp.

She's everywhere.

Maybe she realized I was gone when it was too late for her to follow me, and now she's trying to freak me out. She knew I was up to something. The fact that she hasn't burned the camp to the ground proves that she knows I haven't gone to the cops. I would expect more of a retaliation if she thought I'd spent the evening at the police station.

"Did you see anyone while I was out there?" I whisper in the darkness.

"No one at all," Kayla replies, handing me a bottle of water. She takes a sip from hers. "What was Rebekah's nana like? How did you get in?"

I take a long swig of water. "I pretended that my car broke down and I needed to use her bathroom. Thank the Lord for Southern hospitality. She invited me in and made me iced tea."

"What did you find out?"

"Rebekah stayed with her nana for a few summers."

"So that's how Lillian met Rebekah."

"Yep." I cover my yawn with the back of my hand. "Man, I'm so tired."

"Wait, you can't go to sleep yet. What else did you find out?"

"Not a lot. I wanted to bring up Rebekah's burns, but I didn't know how to without it sounding weird. Her nana thinks that Rebekah is interning at some accounting firm."

"She really doesn't know she's here?"

"Not a clue. I doubt anyone does."

Kayla laughs humorlessly. "God."

I down the last of the water. "I'm really mad. Lillian should just talk to us if she's pissed."

And, of course, we should have said something ten years ago. That doesn't justify what they're doing now, though. They're not just messing with me and Kayla anymore, they're messing with all of us.

"I was thinking . . . I think we should try to leave a note for her." Kayla says.

"That's risky. We can't have any evidence of us contacting her."

"We don't have to write 'Love, Esme and Kayla' at the end."

I scratch an itch on the back of my head. "Right, but wouldn't it be obvious?"

"We can't keep quiet and take all of this for another four weeks, Esme."

God, that's a long time when you're being terrorized.

"I'm with you there. When we talk to her it has to be face to face."

"When? Everyone is so on edge. We play games and roast marshmallows, but we're also constantly looking into the forest."

"I don't know *when*."

Kayla's looking at me for all of the answers when I don't have a single one. How should I know how to handle this situation? This is the first time I've been threatened.

We do need to start beating Lillian at her own game, though. We have to get ahead of her and turn this around.

There's no reason why we can't play too.

What we did is going to come out eventually. Going along with her crazy is only prolonging the inevitable.

Making that leap is scary. I like the people I'm here with, and I'm scared of how they're going to see me and Kayla when they find out the truth.

Lillian left her creepy little note for me. Maybe Kayla and I can get a camera and set it up to catch her? I need to know when she's in our room and what she does here.

I blink heavily, my eyes begging me to close them. My head is swimming. Rubbing my forehead, I groan. I'm getting a headache or I'm getting sick.

Being ill right now is the last thing I need. I have to be on my A game. No, E game, because Esme is going to take Lillian down.

I frown as my muscles turn so heavy, I can barely lift a finger.

My eyes close and I'm gone.

48

Groaning, I rub my foggy head and roll over.

The mattress is cold and damp.

What . . . ?

My eyes flick open and for a second, I see a blur of brown and green and white.

When my vision sharpens, the first thing I see clearly is moss.

Gasping, I jolt and scramble to my feet.

I'm in the forest.

I stumble to a tree, frowning as my brain tries to catch up.

Kayla and I were talking and then we went to sleep. What happened?

My back hits a tree and I glance around. The forest is silent, eerily silent.

I shake my foggy head as my heart races.

Lillian. The crazy bitch *drugged* me.

How? It couldn't have happened at Rebekah's nana's house.

It's been too long. I think. I don't really know how long it takes to drug a person.

My pulse whooshes loudly in my ears.

Stay calm. Stay. Calm.

I have to get back.

Lillian will be watching.

Taking long breaths in and out, I try to ground myself as my stomach flips.

Don't give in.

She's here. How else would I have ended up out here?

All I have to do is show her that I'm not afraid. That I'm not interested in her game and I'm not feeding into whatever sick fantasy she's trying to play out here.

I retch silently.

I want to run and scream and leave.

What do I fear most, Lillian or letting Lillian win? Letting her win. Though the other is a very close second.

Lillian is a hunter, and I'm her prey.

I curl my hands into fists and feel something like dried paint on them.

My body tenses.

No, please *no.*

Slowly, I raise my trembling hands in front of me. They're red. I look down and see dark splatters on my white pajama top.

Blood.

Oh God. Whose blood is it?

I frantically swipe my hands down my top, but it does little to get the dried blood off.

I look up, my head swiveling in every direction.

Where is she?

Clamping my teeth together, I take long breaths so I don't hyperventilate.

Stay calm. Breathe. Think.

Somehow, I need to get back. Lillian put me here, so there must be evidence of the path she used.

You can do this. Focus, Esme.

I crouch down and trace my footprints back to the imprint my body left in the moss. I run my hand over the dip where my head was. This is where she left me.

I look around. Which direction did they carry or drag me from?

There. Two sets of footprints pressed into the mud and moss. They're not deep, so I must have been out here a while. It's still dark; I can only just see in front of me.

You. Can. Do. This.

I have to get back to camp before sunrise.

Crawling on my hands and knees, I find the next set of footprints and the next.

Please let this take me back to camp and not to wherever Lillian is hiding.

I place one palm down and then the other and shuffle forward.

My breath swirls in front of me.

The ground is cool and damp, and my knees are probably covered in mud by now. I sink softly into the ground every time I move. I wish I would sink completely.

A rustling in a tree above me makes me freeze. Shit. My stomach rolls.

Long pine tree branches reach out, some touching the branches of other trees like the whole forest is connected.

It was just a bird.

Move.

I crawl again, following the indentations in the moss.

A cackling that sounds like it's coming from every direction rings through the woods, bouncing off the trees.

I sit up and look around, but I can barely see anything through the mist.

Nope. Screw crawling, I need to go *now.*

Forcing myself to my feet, I take off. My head is clearer, and I don't feel dizzy anymore. I have a better chance of finding camp now. I can do this.

Lillian can go to hell.

I fly between trees, following the footprints.

The cackling sings out again. I whimper, pushing myself even faster.

She's *not* going to get me.

Rounding a tree, I stop dead in my tracks and I dry heave.

I clench my fists. Lillian has killed another deer. I blink hard, hoping the image will disappear. It doesn't. She tied the deer to a tree upside down.

Gagging, I press one wrist to my mouth. The deer has been cut open. A large gash stretches the length of its body and everything that should be inside is outside. The gory red mess of organs lies on the ground beneath it.

Lillian is a psychopath.

And I *have* to get out of here.

I pant, sprinting through the forest as if I know where I'm going. Mist parts as I run through it. My arms swing with every step, sending me flying a little faster. My gym teacher swore by pumping your arms to increase your speed, and I'll try anything.

Images of the deer and the blood on my hands flash through my mind, spurring me on. I might be scared to the core, but I won't give in to her.

Whatever she throws at me, I will fight.

Yes!

I whimper as I come to the edge of the forest. I've made it.

"Esme." Lillian laughs from behind me.

Go.

I race along the lake, never slowing.

Kayla and I need to do something drastic and soon because Lillian is getting *way* worse.

I sob as I run up the stairs to my cabin, and then stop. I just want to get to my friend.

Placing my hand on the doorknob, I take a breath and quietly open the door. I lock the damn thing behind me and tiptoe into my room.

She could have killed me tonight.

Jesus. Lillian *kidnapped* me.

We were wrong. She *does* want to hurt us.

49

In my room, I lean against the door and then sink to the floor. My breath comes out heavy and desperate. She had me and she could have easily killed me.

She's in control and there is nothing we can do.

That *can't* be true.

"Kayla," I rasp as quietly as I can manage, clawing the floor.

I need help.

I blink and burning tears streak down my face. "Kayla, *please*."

She jumps awake, flicks on the lamp and props herself up on her elbows. "What? *Esme?*"

The room floods with light and I slump against the door.

I'm back and safe.

You are not safe here!

When Kayla's eyes land on me, her mouth pops open.

Slipping out of bed, she pads toward me.

"Oh my God, what happened to you?" she asks. "You're covered in dirt and . . . blood!"

"I woke up in the forest."

"You did *what*?"

I shake my head, trying to make sense of it. "I went to sleep here and woke up in the middle of the forest with blood on me."

"Jesus."

Kayla rushes to close the distance between us and wraps her arms around me.

I fall into her embrace. "I didn't know what was going on. I was so scared," I sob. My chest caves and I almost drop to the floor again.

"It's okay. It's okay," she hushes me, her hands shaking. "Come on."

She helps me walk to the bed and sits me on her bunk. I stare at the window, half expecting Lillian's face to be on the other side.

"How did you get there?"

"I—I don't know," I tell her. "I don't remember anything other than what I told you. I think Lillian drugged me. She must have!"

Kayla stands and grabs a bottle of water off the chair. She opens the lid and takes a towel from a pile in the closet.

I watch as she kneels in front of me and wets the towel.

"You're going to be okay, Esme."

Am I?

It doesn't feel like it. I'm cold and tired and I just want to go home.

What we did that night was bad, but we don't deserve this.

"She must have drugged you as well," I say.

Kayla nods. "Yes, I figured."

Her voice is small and squeaky.

She's scared.

She wipes my hands with the towel and smears some of the blood.

Clenching my teeth, I turn away.

"She did this to me," I say, my vision blurring with tears.

"And you survived." Kayla scrubs a little harder. "Whatever the little psycho is doing, we can beat her."

Can we? She drugged us and hauled me into the woods.

"Esme, where did the blood come from?"

The deer flashes in my mind.

"When I was running, I found it."

"Found what?"

"A deer, a small one. It was tied to a tree."

Kayla scrubs even harder, like she's trying to take off a layer of skin. "Tied?"

I close my eyes. "Upside down, cut all the way down the middle and—"

"Stop! Please don't finish telling me, Esme."

"I'm sorry." I snap my teeth together.

She doesn't want to hear it. I had to *see* it.

"There, all clean."

I look at my hands. "Thank you."

"Take your clothes off. I'll bag them. You can wash in here with the towel and water, and then we'll get you changed."

"Keep the clothes. In case."

"In case of what?"

"In case they're needed for evidence."

"We're not telling anyone what we did, Esme!"

"We might not have a choice. We'll hide them for now."

"Fine. You get yourself washed."

What I really want is a shower, but it's four in the morning.

I stand and strip off my clothes. Kayla stuffs them in a plastic bag, which she hides at the bottom of the cupboard.

She hands me the bottle of water and towel. I manage what's probably the least effective wash of my life, but it's the best I have right now.

"Here, put these on," she says softly, handing me fresh pajamas.

I curl my hands tightly around my heart pajamas and hold them to my chest. "Kayla, what are we going to do?"

We're too calm. I want to freak out properly.

Yeah, because that's going to get us far.

"We figure this out in the morning," she says.

"Are you suggesting we go back to sleep?" I look at the bottle in my hand and my face falls. "Where did you get this water?"

Kayla drops the plastic bag in the trash can. "From the kitchen."

I whip a pile of clothes off our chair. There are two more bottles of water beneath them.

"Oh shit," Kayla says, turning the open bottle around.

"Lillian drugged these and left them in our room."

"How did she know we'd drink them tonight?"

"Because it's summer in Texas . . . and because she's watching us."

"I can't deal with that." Kayla shakes her head and clutches her hair in her fist. "I hate her. We have to do something. We can't live like this, and we can't let her get away with what she's doing to us."

"Can we just get through the night and then we'll come up with a plan."

"When do we call it quits and dial nine-one-one?"

"I don't know," I reply.

"I'm scared of people finding out. Things are going great with Jake. I finally feel more myself after being in therapy for years."

"This won't change that, Kayla."

"It will. Of course it will change that. It changes everything."

"You care too much about what people think."

She snorts. "And you don't?"

"I did. But I'm caring less and less these days."

Kayla turns. "Sleep with me?"

"Oh, I was planning to."

I stuff the spiked bottles of water in the bag with my bloody clothes. Kayla gets into bed and scoots to the wall. I turn off the light and slide in beside her.

"She's worse than I could ever imagine," she whispers.

"I knew there was something wrong with her that night, but I never imagined she would be this sick."

"I need this to be over. I can't take it."

I nod. "Me too. She's crazy and dangerous and threatened the campers if we go to the cops. They're just kids. We need to do this ourselves."

"Do *what* ourselves? What does that mean?" Kayla asks, the fear in her voice ringing through the air.

"It means we take control."

"Like how? That doesn't sound like a very good idea. What do we do precisely?"

"We're going to *her*."

50

Kayla and I are about to do something mighty stupid.

We talked last night—or early this morning, rather—and we know that if we take Lillian on ourselves, she won't have any reason to harm the others.

It was a pretty crappy realization as we're both petrified.

We just barely made it through another day. I didn't get any time alone with Olly to warn him about Lillian, but it doesn't matter now. Kayla and I have a plan to end all of this tonight.

"Night," I say to Cora as we cross paths. She is heading toward the other counselors, who are sitting by the campfire, and I'm going into our cabin.

"Sleep well, Esme."

Not likely.

Kayla jumps as I walk into our room.

"Whoa."

Her eyes are round.

"This isn't a good idea," she says.

"You want this to be over too," I remind her. "We have to make contact. No one else can stop this."

"But now? Like, you want to go outside *now*?"

"All the girls are in bed, but I think I heard some whispering. We'll leave it a little while longer."

Kayla's fingertips dig into the wood. "Esme, we should wait. Come up with a real plan, one we've thought about for longer than three minutes, and then we'll go have a chat with Lillian."

"We'll talk ourselves out of it."

"Maybe we should."

I stare at her. "Really? You're the one who wanted to send her a note."

"A note. Not go out there and find her. I'm not sure if you've realized yet, but she's not exactly a reasonable person. Don't you think she'll have something planned for when we do come face to face?"

"Yeah," I say. "That's why we need to do it on our terms. We can't give her time to plan anymore. We'll be right there, and she'll be the audience in our show."

"You need to sleep, Esme, you're delirious."

I wish I could, but I'm too wired.

"Keep a lookout for the others. When they go to bed, we're out of here."

Kayla sighs, defeated.

Walking to our window, she peeks around the blind. "The

light is still on in the multiuse cabin. Everyone around the campfire has either gone to join them or gone to sleep."

"Ugh, they need to go to bed. Are you coming with me?"

Kayla looks over her shoulder. "Yes, you're not doing this alone."

I smile at her even though my stomach does a flip.

What if our going together isn't a good idea? Should we let Lillian have the two people she wants to hurt alone?

We could be feeding her sick fantasy.

We're definitely doing that.

≈

Two hours later, Kayla and I both watch from the main room windows as the rest of the counselors and CITs filter into their cabins to sleep.

"Go," I whisper as Cora comes toward ours.

We dash into our room and hide behind the door.

I listen, biting my lip as Cora tiptoes into her room and closes the door.

"Now?" Kayla whispers.

"A few more minutes. Wait until she's in bed."

Kayla leans back against the wall and looks up at the ceiling. In the silence, I hear her breathing grow faster.

"Okay, let's do this," I say when the rustling in Cora's room stops.

Kayla follows me as we tiptoe out of the cabin.

The room is louder tonight, a few of the girls snoring.

The very second we step onto the porch, my plan feels weak and really stupid. Really, *really* stupid.

I close the door behind us, wincing as it clicks shut.

Am I going to let that stop me? *Nope.*

"All right," I say, zipping up my hoodie. "Let's go do this thing."

"Wait," Kayla says, gripping my wrist. "What if she turns violent?"

"We are so past that. From what we've seen, Rebekah hasn't left her cabin, so Lillian is alone. Two against one. This time we know what we're walking into and we won't underestimate her."

"What if what she wants is to harm us?"

"How much worse can it get?"

I don't know if I'm getting a fresh dose of adrenaline or of stupidity, but I know we have to do this. Lillian is becoming bolder and it's only a matter of time before one of the campers sees something or gets caught in her crazy games.

This started with Kayla and me, and it has to end with us.

We step onto the grass and quickly duck around the back of the cabin.

"Where now?" Kayla whispers. "The forest is huge."

"We start looking at the site of the fire damage."

Kayla shivers despite it being hot out. "I hate it there."

"Not my favorite place either."

"Can we not go through the woods to get there? Let's walk around the lake."

I narrow my eyes. "That's a great idea, if we want to get busted. Andy probably looks out his window periodically."

We walk along the edge of the forest, just deep enough that we should be hard to spot, especially in the dark with black clothing on.

"I should have texted my parents," Kayla mutters.

Don't bite. Don't respond.

"Really?" I say three seconds later. "We're not going to die. You don't have to say goodbye to anyone."

"Y-you don't know that."

"And if you really thought we were going to *die* tonight you wouldn't have left the cabin."

"Can we not argue, Esme?" she snaps.

"Can you be a little less pessimistic, Kayla?"

"You're arguing with me."

Yep, and while we're arguing, you're not stressing out about Lillian.

I bet she's somewhere watching us. I want to look for her, but, one, I don't want to freak Kayla out, and, two, I think Lillian will want to see where we're going before she reacts.

The feeling of being safe at this particular moment clashes with everything I've felt over the past week.

"How do you think Rebekah has been able to keep up this lie the whole time?" Kayla asks.

I shrug, even though she can't see the movement. "Some people lie as naturally as they breathe. Rebekah thinks she's on some revenge mission with Lillian. They both hate us for what we did."

Kayla looks at me. "But this isn't really Rebekah's fight, right? How far would she go for someone else's revenge?"

"We'll be fine."

I don't want to answer her question, or I'll turn around and hide under my bed.

Kayla whips one arm out. "What was that?"

I look around and bite my lip. "What? I didn't hear anything. What did you hear?"

"Someone walking."

My pulse thuds. "Lillian. That's not surprising. Come on, we're almost there."

"You're not scared?" Kayla asks, her eyes wide.

"Did you really think she wouldn't show? She's probably been behind us the whole time."

Wrong thing to say, Esme.

Kayla gasps.

"Don't freak out yet," I tell her. "We're going to be fine. I promise."

She stumbles beside me. "You can't promise that. I don't want to die." Her voice trembles.

"You won't die."

I can't promise her anything, but I would do anything to protect her.

Kayla grabs my arm, her fingertips digging into my flesh.

We pass a wooden Private Property sign. We're at the camp's edge.

"I hate walking past these," Kayla says, running one hand over the sign.

Another three minutes and we're there. We walk into the circle.

"What now?" Kayla mutters, her eyes large and alert.

"Now we wait. She'll show."

To be honest, I'm sure she's already here, watching.

My stomach lurches.

Where was Olly watching from that night? What tree did he hide behind? Why didn't he help Lillian? She knew he wasn't with us and that he wasn't responsible.

Did Jake really see nothing?

"Olly had nothing to lose by helping Lillian that night," I say.

Kayla turns to me. "Huh?"

"He said Jake called him and he ran, but why? I don't understand why he wouldn't help."

"We didn't help either, Esme."

"We were responsible for the fire and needed to run. But if we stumbled across a fire and saw a person hurt, we would help."

That, at least, I can say with absolute certainty. We didn't know how bad she was hurt.

"Esme," a low musical voice sings.

I whip my head around to where I think it came from.

"What the hell?" Kayla mutters.

"Looks like Lillian is here."

"Rebekah too?" she asks, gasping.

"I don't think so," I whisper. "Remember, she didn't leave her cabin. At least not before us. Maybe she has the night off from villain duty."

"Esme."

Kayla squeezes my hand so hard my fingers grind together.

Okay. Be brave.

"Lillian, we're bored with this," I say.

"What are you doing?" Kayla's voice is low.

"No one is impressed with your stupid juvenile games," I continue. "You're stalking a camp for *children.* Grow up and show yourself so we can deal with this rationally."

Words are coming out of me as if I've summoned every ounce of courage I own.

I wish Kayla would slap her hand over my mouth.

But this has gone on long enough, and I'm so done. I can't spend another day half watching four girls and half watching the woods.

"You're going to get us killed!" Kayla snaps.

"No, I'm going to finish this."

"Perfect Kayla and Esme, loved by everyone at camp."

Kayla and I look up at the same time and see a girl, a couple years older than us, appear from the trees.

She's here.

She's angry.

And she's armed.

51

My dad owns a gun. I've fired guns at the shooting range. I've never been particularly scared of them before.

It's very different when you're staring down the barrel of one as your stalker points it at your face.

Kayla steps closer, her side plastered to mine.

I lift my chin to appear unafraid, but my skin is crawling.

Don't show fear.

"Hello, Lillian," I say.

She steps into view and tilts her head. She's wearing a black hoodie with her dark hair in a ponytail and hanging out from the hood. "I'm honored you remember me."

"It's hard to forget when your initials are carved into my bedroom wall."

Lillian glowers.

I'm being catty.

I'm pissed.

"There is a gun aimed at your head," she says.

"You've put children at risk."

"I would never hurt a child!"

"You've scared plenty of them."

"Collateral."

Nice.

"Why didn't you come talk to us?"

"Why didn't you stop and help me?"

My stomach drops. *Rein it in, Esme!*

I wince, my face heating with shame. "We are so sorry about that night, Lillian. It was . . . the worst night of our lives. I wish I could turn back time and do everything differently. It's a poor excuse, but we were young and petrified."

"It *is* a poor excuse. Half of my body is scarred for life. I spent a month in the hospital. My family ended up bankrupt and we lost our house because we didn't have enough money for medical care. I've been following you two on social media for two years. Your lives are perfect."

That's not true.

"Almost everything on social media is perfect," I say. "It's not reality. My life isn't perfect, and I'm far from it."

Lillian's lips curl viciously. "You definitely aren't perfect, Esme, but no one knows that because you never told anyone what happened."

"I'm sorry. We were *scared*."

"You ruined so many lives that night and you don't even care."

"We care. We—"

"Shut up!"

I jump back at the acid in her voice.

Her free hand meets the one around the handle of the gun, steadying her aim.

I raise my palms. "Okay, okay. Look, we can talk. Please believe me, Lillian, we never wanted you to get hurt that night."

"Did you see Jake and Olly that night?" Lillian asks.

"No," I tell her. So she did see Jake. What did he and Olly do that night?

And since when did Kayla lose the ability to speak?

"Have you been watching us at home?" I ask, afraid to hear the answer.

"Of course I have. Since Kayla's disastrous cheerleading tryout."

God. That was when we were sophomores. Lillian has spent days, months, *years* coming up with the perfect revenge. She found us in Pennsylvania.

"Your friend mute?"

Kayla pushes harder into me.

"Scared," I say. "You have a gun pointed at us. Why don't you lower it and we can talk? We'll answer any questions you have. I'll find a way to make you believe how sorry we are."

"Let's take a walk," Lillian says.

Kayla shakes her head.

Lillian's cold blue eyes turn black. "No? You're saying no to me?"

"Where do you want us to go?" I ask, to get her mind off Kayla's reluctance.

She wants us on her terms. We decided to confront her and

now she's trying to take back control. Surely the gun gives her enough of that?

"I have a place," Lillian says.

I grit my teeth. "Okay. Where is this place?"

"In the forest. An abandoned cabin that's mine now. You two should be used to cabins in the woods. Let's. Go." She inches her chin to the side.

I take Kayla's hand and pull her along. "No, Esme," she whispers, trying to tug me back toward camp.

"We have no choice. It'll be fine," I tell her.

"You don't know that!"

No, I don't.

"Hurry up, ladies! We haven't got all night."

Why haven't we got all night?

What exactly does Lillian plan to do before sunrise?

52

We slowly walk deeper into the forest with Lillian right behind us. I can't see the gun, but I feel its presence like a dark cloud following us, ready to shoot daggers of lightning.

Beside me, Kayla's body shakes violently, her breath coming in short pants. Her fear is feeding mine.

We can't give up.

I try to make eye contact with her so I can calm her down before she has a panic attack.

What do we do? We could fight Lillian now and speed this whole thing up. Maybe we'll get away. Or do we go along with her and hope a better opportunity to run comes up? Once we reach her destination, she will have full control. That's not a position I want to be in.

I should try to get the gun, to knock it away from her and grab it. We'd be in charge then.

Seems like a semi-decent plan. Unless she's further back than she sounds, and I can't reach the gun.

In that case, Kayla and I are both dead.

Squinting, I see the outline of something big and square in the distance. A building.

I swallow. "Are we going in there?" I ask.

"Keep walking," Lillian barks.

That's a yes.

"Esme," Kayla whispers, her voice trembling.

"It's okay."

The pine trees around us blow in the soft breeze, like they're alive and leading the way. The only audience to whatever Lillian has planned.

Whatever she thinks is going to go down, I have to keep a clear head and fight back. Kayla and I are not going to die tonight. If that's what she even wants. Lillian is understandably angry, but *murderous?*

There's a big leap between wanting to kill someone and actually doing it.

Hunting people isn't like hunting deer.

We approach the building. It's a cabin, about the size of the staff cabin at camp.

"What is this place?" I ask.

"An old ranger's cabin. They built another one closer to town along with the new camping site. No one comes here anymore."

No one comes here anymore.

I take a breath. We're all alone out here. But we're not alone, not really. Kayla and I have each other and we're strong.

"What are you going to do?" I ask.

"Get inside, Esme."

I can hardly refuse, can I? I turn to her and I'm met with the barrel of a gun. Swallowing my nerves, I look past it to meet her eyes. "Lillian, please. You can't take this back. Whatever you do, you'll have to live with it. That's not going to be easy, it eats away at you. Trust me."

"Trust you?" Her hollow eyes round. "After that night, you expect me to trust you?"

"No, I don't, but I'm telling the truth. Living with guilt is hell. I know it's what I deserve."

"You deserve much worse than to live with a little guilt. I have burns over forty percent of my torso. It was *agony*. I'm scarred for life. What do you think living with that is like?"

I want to curl up inside myself.

"Lillian, I'm so—"

"Don't say sorry! Do *not* say sorry. Just get inside!"

Kayla whimpers and grabs hold of my arm. "Esme, we can't."

Lillian tilts her head.

"It's okay, Kayla, follow me." I take her hand. She grips mine so hard it almost crumbles.

I turn back around, and Kayla and I walk side by side, both stiff with fear, toward the door.

Kayla reaches out. I watch her hand shake around the doorknob.

"Inside," Lillian barks.

I don't look at Kayla as we step inside the cabin because I don't want to see her fear. I told her that everything would be okay. I'm not sure it will be.

The room looks warm and inviting. There's a stone fireplace, and a lamp sitting on a table, glowing orange. There's a fluffy white rug on the floor and a small leather sofa with a red blanket draped over the back.

In one corner is a little kitchen with a kettle and a microwave. Two doors are at the back of the cabin. I assume one is a bathroom. The other I don't want to know. It was probably an office before, but who knows what Lillian is using it for.

The cabin looks quaint and comfortable. Not exactly what you'd expect for a villain's lair.

"Sit down," Lillian instructs, pointing with the gun toward the love seat. Kayla and I don't hesitate. We have to be careful.

There will be no silly and disorganized escape plan.

I sink into the soft, worn leather and look up at Lillian. She stands close to the fireplace and faces us. That's when I see what's on the wall behind her. A photo collage. Loads of photos of me and Kayla. Ones from when she was chasing us through the woods, ones of us at camp, and even ones of us sleeping.

I press my lips together so I won't react.

The fire is littered with ashes. She's been lighting it. It's too hot to need a fire, even at night. What has she been burning?

I'm certain I don't want to know.

"What are we doing here, Lillian?" I ask.

"We need to have a conversation."

"We could have had that anywhere. You know where we live. Why all this?"

Kayla nudges me as if she thinks I'm going too far. *Me.* Lillian has been messing with us for weeks. She slaughtered a deer, drugged us and left creepy notes and messages. She scared a camp full of kids and now she's freaking kidnapped us and *I'm* the one who has gone too far?

"Do you really not get it? You ruined my life!" Saliva sprays from her mouth as she bares her teeth at us.

I meet her eyes. "I get that, and I can tell you how sorry we are and how much we regret it, but it seems that's not good enough. You won't accept that we wish that night could have been different. Nothing we say or do will make this better, so why are we really here?"

Her head tilts again like she's unsure. But I know she has absolutely thought this through. She knows what she wants from us. She can exact her revenge, but that will never make things right. Is she just now accepting that?

"Look, whatever you do here tonight isn't going to make up for the fact that a terrible thing happened to you. Hurting us will make you feel better for about two minutes and then you're back where you started. It changes *nothing*."

She levels the gun at my forehead. "You don't know what you're talking about!"

"Yes, I do, and you know I'm right."

"Shut up, Esme!" Kayla hushes me.

What are we supposed to do if we can't talk to her? Lillian wants something from us; otherwise she would have just shot us in the forest.

"Kayla's very close to getting a bullet in her skull," Lillian says to me.

I feel Kayla shudder. She whimpers, then clamps her mouth shut.

"She's scared and confused," I say. "We don't know what you actually want. Do you just have questions?"

"Do I have questions?" Lillian's manic laughter cuts through my heart. "I have a lot of questions."

"We'll answer anything," I say softly. Maybe I can get her talking about that night and draw some emotion out of her other than rage.

"Why did you sneak out?" she asks.

"There was this group of older kids and they would sneak out. We weren't actually friends with them; they were too cool to be seen with us. But we thought if we snuck out too, they might like us. It was stupid, but we were kids."

Lillian scoffs.

"We're sorry that things got so out of hand . . . but you made mistakes that night too."

I'm dancing on the edge here. Calling her out isn't my finest idea, but Kayla and I aren't taking all the blame.

Lillian's eyes narrow. "You let me burn. You *ran*."

I close my eyes against the image of Kayla throwing Lillian backward. In that second, she was just reacting; we never intended for Lillian to get hurt, but she landed in the fire, knocking the wood onto the ground.

Lillian tilts her head. "Now I'm going to light a fire and do the same to you."

53

My eyes fly open.

"Burn us? No. No, no, no!" Kayla gasps for air.

I squeeze her hand. *Please calm down.*

"Or I could just shoot you."

My mind spins so fast I can barely catch my breath.

Five dolls. Four with their eyes crossed out. She wanted us dead this whole time.

Bile hits the back of my throat.

Lillian's eyes look straight through us. "You think I'm crazy, but you have no idea what that night was like for me. I can still feel the overwhelming pain and smell my burned flesh. I couldn't call for help. My dad is . . . not a nice man. I was scared what would happen."

"What did you do?"

"I couldn't call for help," she repeats. "Everyone would know that I had run away. You don't understand, I couldn't let that happen."

"What did you do?" I ask again.

"I dragged myself to the lake. I tried to soothe my burns in the water, but it only made things worse."

Kayla gasps.

"Someone else must have called the cops, because I eventually heard sirens. I ran with everything left in me. When I got home, I set fire to my bedroom and that's how my parents think I got burned. We all got out, but our house was ashes." She smirks. "My hair straighteners were blamed."

"Jesus."

I press one hand against my rolling stomach.

Lillian was ten. She did all of that before she hit puberty. The hunting, mutilating animals, and burning down her freaking house! She set fire to her home so she wouldn't get into trouble. And she thinks she's better than us?

"Why didn't you tell anyone? The fire in the woods wasn't your fault."

"That wouldn't have mattered to my dad."

"Okay," I say, trying to wrap my head around this. I need to talk to her as if this is all totally normal behavior. "He would have blamed you?"

"He's not a forgiving man. A lot of people respect and look up to him. They think he's an amazing husband and father. No one knows the truth. If he knew I'd snuck out of the house . . ." She shakes her head and I have to fill in the blanks.

Things would've been very bad for her.

"Are you sorry too, Kayla?" Lillian asks. "You pulled Esme away. I saw her turn back to help me."

"Kayla was scared," I say.

"I wasn't asking you!" Lillian snaps. "Kayla can speak for herself."

"Of . . . of course, I'm so sorry," Kayla says, her voice husky. She clears her throat. "W-we never meant for anyone to get hurt. We liked . . . we liked hanging out with you."

Kayla is making it sound like we were all friends that night. It's a good move.

We didn't like it, though. Lillian showed us the head of a deer that she had hunted and killed. It made me nauseous. I was instantly petrified of Lillian. Kayla completely freaked out when she saw the deer's head. She started screaming at Lillian that she was a freak.

Lillian lowers the gun to her side.

I press my arm into Kayla's, willing her to understand what I can't say. *Do not move yet.* That gun can be raised quicker than we can reach her. She's not close enough.

Kayla seems to get it or she's just thinking the same thing, because she sits perfectly still.

"Did you send that CIT pamphlet to everyone there that night?" I ask.

"Yes. I wanted you, Kayla, Jake and Olly here."

"Rebekah?"

"I met her a few years ago at a group for burn victims. She's too easy to manipulate. So desperate for a friend she would do anything."

"Why Jake and Olly?" Kayla asks.

"They watched and did *nothing.* Jake was the worst. I saw him later, when I was on my way home. He and Olly were wandering in the forest again. This time they looked right at me and saw the burns. Jake called me a psycho and pulled Olly away. They both ran. I knew then they were there the whole time. Jake's not sneering now."

Olly hadn't mentioned that.

I steal a glance at Kayla. Her eyes are wide.

"What did you do to Jake?"

Jake might have made mistakes, but he was just a scared kid. How could Lillian not see that?

Lillian's eyes sparkle as she looks at the doors in the back.

Oh God.

"He's in one of those rooms," I whisper.

Slowly, she nods. "He's very quiet."

"What did you do?"

"Go and see, Esme."

My heart stalls.

"What?"

"I'll wait here with Kayla. If you even think about escaping, I'll put a bullet through her head."

I lick my lips. "Lillian, please."

"Get up, Esme!"

With my heart in my throat, I stand up and turn toward the doors. "Which one?"

"Bathroom. Door on the left."

What could she be doing with him in the bathroom?

I wrap my trembling fingers around the doorknob and turn it slowly.

"Go on," Lillian says.

The door creaks as I nudge it open.

There is a bathtub.

Jake looks at me from the tub, eyes wide, pupils dilated.

54

I stumble back and grip the edge of the doorframe. Jake. She's killed him.

Dried blood trails from his mouth to his chin. It looks like it would flake away if you touched it. His face is pale, like a porcelain doll's.

"Find him?" Lillian asks.

My blood burns. I want to scream at the laughter in her voice.

Turning, I look at Kayla first. She shakes her head, her face crumpling.

Then I look at Lillian.

Lips pursed, dead eyes alight with satisfaction.

"Why?" I rasp.

"He doesn't care about anyone but himself. People like that make me sick. Star of the football team thinking he's better than everyone else, worth more."

"He was probably scared that night too."

Lillian scoffs. "Yes of course he was. Little Esme, always

looking for the good in people. Who are you kidding? You're not even good."

"I'm not the same person I was back then. It's been *ten years.* I've grown up, I'm stronger, and I would never make a mistake like that again. No one is the same as they were when they were eight!"

In the back of my head, I can't stop thinking, *She is a murderer.*

I was stupid to ever think we could talk this through. The revenge she wants isn't the kind that Kayla and I are supposed to survive.

Lillian thinks our deaths will make things right.

"You haven't changed that much," she says. "Neither of you told the camp that all of this involved you."

"We never thought you would do something like this," I say, nodding back toward Jake. "He's dead, Lillian. You *killed* him. How long ago?" It couldn't have been longer than a few hours. No one knew Jake was missing.

She waves her free hand. "About an hour before you came to me. He was an asshole."

"He didn't deserve to die. You could have dealt with this another way."

She rolls her eyes. "Don't advocate talking when you've spent ten years hiding your sins. It makes you a hypocrite."

"What does all of this make you?"

"*You* are the ones who hurt *me*! All I'm guilty of is speaking to you that night!"

"You terrified us with that deer's head. You ran at Kayla when she called you out on it. She only pushed you out of self-defense.

She never meant for you to fall into the fire. And now you've *killed* Jake!"

"I didn't have a choice, and he deserved everything he got. I wouldn't harm an innocent person. That's the difference between you and me."

I push away from the door. The smell from the bathroom is making my stomach churn.

"You were scared of your dad and we understand that. We were scared of our parents too. Can't you see, Lillian, we didn't feel like we had a choice either."

Her face freezes.

We all feared something that night.

I've made it sound like our parents were cruel as well. Maybe she'll relent if she thinks we shared a similar childhood.

"Shut up!" she screams. "Shut up, you bitch. You have *no* idea what you're talking about."

I raise my hands, palms facing her. "Okay, I'm sorry. I didn't understand."

Except that I do. I understand fully. Fear can be debilitating.

"Okay," Kayla says. "Here's what we're going to do. Jake was a bully to you, so you did what you had to."

Lillian looks surprised but nods. "He was evil."

"Yes," Kayla replies. "But thanks to you, he will never hurt anyone again. We need to get rid of his body, though. If the cops find him, he can be traced to you. Your DNA will be everywhere."

My jaw drops.

What is she saying?

Kayla shakes her head at me. "Esme, this is the only way. We have a responsibility to help Lillian cover this up after what we did to her. We'll scrub Jake clean and bury him deep in the woods. Then, we'll burn this cabin to the ground."

What the hell? She was madly in love with him five minutes ago.

Lillian watches Kayla as if she's some complicated puzzle.

It's not complicated. Kayla is in full survival mode and it's disturbing. I've never seen her like this.

"You're just adding another secret to the one we've been carrying! We can't do this. It's *Jake,* Kayla!" I say.

I ignore Lillian's smirk as she watches us disagree.

"What she had to do was our fault and this is what we deserve for not doing the right thing all those years ago." Kayla stands and Lillian makes no move to stop her. "Now, let's strip his clothes off and put them in the fire."

"Stop! Do you hear yourself?"

"What's the alternative, Esme?" Kayla snaps.

Lillian kills us. But how do we live with ourselves if we help hide her murder? How do we walk away from this? What is she going to do after we bury Jake? She's never going to let us walk away.

"There has to be some other way."

"You could die with him," Lillian says. "Kayla is the one willing to do what's necessary . . . but would she help me clean up and hide her bestie's body too?"

Kayla eyes widen. She looks at me, pleading.

"Kayla?" I whisper.

"Don't make me do that, Esme. We made a pact ten years ago to never talk about that night. We can do that again. We'll help Lillian, and we can go home knowing that this is all over."

My head swirls with conflict and confusion.

If we do this, would Lillian really let us walk away? We can't do that to Jake or to his family.

Maybe this was Lillian's plan all along. She could be setting us up for Jake's murder.

"Kayla, this might not be what you think," I say.

"What do you think it is, Esme?" Lillian asks.

Kayla's face is red, like she wants to throw something at me. We are not going along with this blindly.

"I don't know. What happens if we help you?"

Lillian's lips curl, but her smile isn't friendly. "You go home."

"What, and we never hear from you again? Or are you now thinking that with Kayla's offer comes an opportunity?"

Kayla looks at us both.

"I'm not stupid, and neither are you, Lillian. Eventually people will start asking questions, wondering who was terrorizing the camp, why an old cabin is on fire, and where Jake went. . . . The cops will come looking. They might link it to you; after all, your DNA is all over this place. But if we help, our DNA is on his body too."

With wide eyes, Kayla looks from Lillian to me.

She was never going to let us walk away. If we're convicted of a murder she committed . . .

"I tell you what," Lillian says to Kayla. "If we kill Esme too, we'll bury her and Jake, and no one will ever know. If you refuse, you both die here today. Two bodies, three bodies, I don't mind how many I get rid of."

My stomach turns. She can't be serious.

"No," I say.

Kayla is my best friend; she would never do that.

Tell her, Kayla!

Why isn't she telling Lillian to get lost?

"Kayla!" I snap.

Tears well in her eyes. "I'm sorry. I can't die. I can't."

Her words punch the air from my lungs.

"Kayla, you're my best friend," I whisper as fear grips my throat.

She wipes tears from her cheeks. "I'm sorry, Esme, but I choose me."

55

I know I should run. I should shove Kayla into Lillian and make a run for it.

Will my legs move? *No.*

"You can't, Kayla," I say.

Lillian's smile grows. She is loving this.

Fire burns in my veins.

Turning us against each other is a bonus for her.

Kayla wipes her tears again.

"Kayla!"

She doesn't look at me; instead she turns her head toward Lillian.

"How does that feel?" Lillian asks. "To have your best friend in the whole world turn against you so easily. There was barely any hesitation."

Kayla may be petrified of dying, but I *never* expected this.

"That's not my best friend talking," I say.

Kayla cowers.

She's consumed by fear. Lost.

I step closer to the sofa.

Lillian aims the gun steadily at my head but makes no move to pull the trigger. Instead she watches what I'm about to do with Kayla. . . .

Kayla doesn't meet my eyes, but she turns her head, showing me that she knows I'm there.

"Don't, Esme," she whispers. "I hate this."

Lillian is a few feet from Kayla, and the fireplace is a step or two behind her.

I shove Kayla with every ounce of strength I have. She flies backward with a scream and into Lillian.

Get out.

I take off without looking back. Something slams against the wall. The thud sounded like a head, but I can't be sure.

I yank the door open and sprint outside.

My legs burn as I try to get away as fast as possible.

Behind me, I hear Lillian shout.

Then I hear two sets of footsteps.

I look back, but the thick forest is dark. I can't see them, but I know they're coming. I take a path similar to the one I remember, but now I'm deeper in the woods.

I have not been out here nearly enough to know where I'm going without a map and compass.

I can figure this out. I can get away from Lillian—and *Kayla*—and get help.

Stay calm. Don't overthink.

Stepping around a tree, I run to the next one and plaster myself against it.

I take a breath and listen carefully, willing that sense to take over. Lillian has a gun and Kayla is broken beyond recognition.

She's scared right now. The thought of imminent death has made her lose herself. When she stops and thinks, even for a second, she will see what a monumental mistake she has made and beg for my forgiveness.

Above me, the sky rumbles. I raise my eyes and see a fork of lightning through the leaves.

A thunderstorm. That's going to make it harder to hear them, but it will also make it harder for them to hear me.

I peer around the trunk in the direction I need to go. No one is around; the forest is dead quiet.

They could be hiding and watching me. Lillian has been watching in the shadows for weeks. For *years.* Kayla doesn't know how to sneak around, though; she will be tripping and falling all over the place.

She's a liability to Lillian. What happens when Lillian realizes that?

I press my hand to my stomach and breathe through the wave of nausea. What if she kills Kayla?

The sky rumbles again, and the thunder is followed by a quick flash of lightning.

Forget Kayla.

I look around again. Nobody. Pushing off the tree, I sprint to the next one, planting my feet on the ground quickly and quietly like a deer escaping a predator. My heart thuds faster with every step.

I'm not supposed to be the prey out here.

The sky lights up again and thunder rolls.

I still don't know exactly where I am, but I think I'm close to camp.

Trees whiz past in a blur of brown and green.

I pant harder, trying to get enough oxygen.

You need to hurry up.

Lillian could be anywhere.

If I don't get out of here, I'm going to die.

Go, Esme! Now!

With my stomach tied in knots, I push myself to go even faster. My feet hit the ground harder and my pulse thuds so fast I can't hear anything else.

I dodge trees, bouncing off each leg to get around each obstacle as quickly as I can. The sky lights up. I push harder.

A slicing pain in my side makes me double over, but I don't stop. I can't stop.

Thunder cracks through the air.

Breaking through the trees, I fall to my knees. Camp.

I raise my head and gasp.

"What is going on?" I whisper, vision blurred.

With my last ounce of strength, I haul myself to my feet and grab a branch so I don't fall.

Four cop cars. Red and blue lights flash across the camp, bouncing off trees.

What happened here while we were in that little cabin with Lillian?

We were gone for only two hours.

Turning, I lose my footing and slam right into Rebekah.

56

I leap backward and she shows her palms. "I'm not goin' to hurt ya."

"You were working with Lillian!"

"Yes, but I never expected . . . *this.* She was so broken when I met her at a support group a few years ago. I thought she just wanted to frighten y'all, to make you think about what you did and to be sorry. She said she wanted you to be as scared as she was that night. I got that, so I agreed to come here as a CIT and help her."

I back up, my eyes scanning the forest. I haven't heard Lillian or Kayla for a while. That's both reassuring and unnerving.

"What changed your mind?"

Rebekah takes a breath. "When I went to the cabin to find her a little while ago, I saw . . ."

"Jake."

She nods, wide-eyed. "I knew she saw him that night too, but I never thought . . . This is crazy, Esme. We need to get away from her. Where's Kayla?"

I swallow the urge to throw up. "She's with Lillian."

Rebekah gasps, one hand flying to her heart. "She killed her, too?"

"No," I say. "Kayla's on her side. We were in the cabin and Lillian said either we both die or just me. Kayla chose herself."

Rebekah's jaw drops. "What? How could she?"

I don't know, but she did. Somehow I need to get Kayla back.

"What's happening here?" I ask, looking around.

"It's been evacuated. The cops got an anonymous call about an hour ago about someone stalking the camp. The cops took all the kids to the police station until their parents can pick them up. I came back to find you and Kayla. I'm sorry, Esme. I didn't know how out of hand this would get. Lillian never made it sound like she wanted to hurt anyone."

"She wanted revenge."

"I swear I didn't know that she was so dangerous."

"Is anyone still here?"

"Andy. He's talking with the cops."

"Who would call the cops? We all agreed we wouldn't. It doesn't make sense." I lean into the tree I'm holding and try to make the pieces fit together.

"I don't know, Esme, but we need to get away from the forest."

"Esme!"

Rebekah and I jolt at the same time and swing around.

"Olly." My jaw drops. I start to run to him but stop myself. "What really happened the night of the fire? Jake was with you the whole time?"

He looks over my shoulder. I do the same. No one is there.

"I left him out of the retelling, just like you left Kayla out. After the fire started, Jake and I didn't go back to my brother. We stayed and watched the whole thing. Lillian saw us. We ran and eventually bumped into her again a little while later. Jake told her off. I didn't want to admit that we were scared of a girl, but we so were. After that, Jake and I agreed to keep quiet," Olly says.

"You saw her after, when she was burned, and didn't help her or tell me!"

"You're lecturing me on morality?"

"Hey, y'all can't do this now!" Rebekah snaps. "Lillian could be here any freakin' second!"

A shrill siren cuts through the air as another cop car races along the road and into camp. We watch from across the lake as it screams to a halt.

"Let's go," I say, and start running for help.

At least that's what I want to do, but I'm stopped by the bang of a gun.

The hollow sound radiates through me.

I turn. Rebekah and Olly are looking at me with wide eyes.

Was it me? Did Lillian shoot me?

I don't feel pain.

Then I see it. A red circle spreading across Olly's shirt.

"No!" I scream as he falls to his knees.

Lillian walks into view with Kayla right behind her.

I drop to the ground in front of Olly and place my hands over the wound.

His blood is red-hot and seeps between my fingers. "You're going to be okay," I tell him.

His eyes travel behind me and he whispers, "Esme."

Turning slowly, I look over my shoulder. Lillian is close. Kayla cowers behind her, eyes trained on the ground.

"Now you can join your disgusting friend Jake," Lillian says to Olly.

"You're a psycho," he spits.

Her lip curls. "I'd finish the job for that, but you'll bleed out soon and I need the bullets."

"Lillian, what happened?" Rebekah asks.

"Oh my God, stop. Do you know how tragic you are? Quit the poor-me act, Rebekah, it's boring. Get on the ground beside them."

"Lillian, can we talk about—"

Bang.

I blink in horror as blood splatters from Rebekah's forehead and she falls heavily to the ground.

I whimper, pressing my lips together.

Rebekah's eyes lose focus and her jaw drops open.

"You have to get out of here, Esme," Olly croaks, wincing in pain.

How?

"I can't leave you. I can't move my hands. She's right, you'll bleed out."

"Don't worry about me. Try to get back."

I shake my head, my eyes welling with tears until Olly is a blur. "Please hold on."

"Esme," Lillian sings.

My body ripples in disgust at the excited tone in her voice.

"Hold your hand over the wound and press hard," I tell Olly.

Olly replaces my hands with his hand and winces.

I rise to my feet and face Lillian. "You're sick."

I'm done trying to play nicely with her.

Lillian smirks. "Do you think I care what you think of me?"

"You were burned, something terrible happened to you, but everything that's happened since then has been on you. No one else is at fault here but you. Stop pretending what you're doing is justified. It's not. You're a *murderer.*"

"Shut up!" she screams.

"Wait," Kayla says.

Lillian stills and glances to her side.

Kayla opens her mouth and her eyes widen when she realizes she has nothing to say.

"Go ahead, Kayla," Lillian instructs.

"Um . . . I was thinking . . ."

Lillian turns her head.

I take the chance. Screaming, I launch forward and knock into her.

Lillian falls back, shouting out.

I spot a rock. *Do it.*

Without hesitation, I pick the rock up and smash it against the side of her face.

"Run, Esme!" Olly shouts.

I leap to my feet and turn to him. "I'll help you up."

"She's not dead. Go and get help!" he shouts, still pressing his hand against his wound.

Olly . . .

"Go!" he rasps, spluttering. Dying.

I take off, my eyes stinging with tears. Maybe I should have killed her. But I don't want to have to live with that.

I sprint toward the lake, but a third gunshot brings me crashing down. I freeze.

Gasping, I see Kayla stagger toward me holding her side. I run to her.

"Kayla, no!"

Her legs give way as I reach her.

"Go, Esme," she croaks.

I fall to the ground and cradle her. "Oh my God, Kayla. I'm so sorry. I'm so, so sorry."

"No, I'm so sorry, Esme. I was scared and I didn't think."

"Why did she shoot you?"

"She told me to shoot you, and I refused. I was trying to run away with you."

"Kayla," I whisper as tears stream down my cheeks. "You're not going to die, you know that, right?"

"I—I feel cold," she murmurs. "It's okay, though, because I just realized I would do anything to protect you."

When it came down to it, she chose me.

Curling around her, I sob. "Please don't leave me."

Her breathing rattles and my eyes widen. "Kayla!"

Something lands beside me.

I look down. *What?*

Squinting, I reach down and pick up something black from the grass.

My breath is knocked from my lungs when I realize it's the gun.

Suddenly, I know who called the cops.

Kayla's body relaxes, her full weight laying in my arms, and she takes one final, ragged breath.

No. I sob, my heart splintering into pieces.

"Police! Freeze!"

My heart stills. I look up and see Lillian smiling from between the trees. She turns and silently disappears into the forest.

Then, with wide eyes, I turn to find five gun barrels pointing at me.

Kayla, Rebekah, Olly and Jake are dead, Lillian is gone . . . and I'm holding the gun.

ACKNOWLEDGMENTS

As always, I would first like to say thank you to my husband and sons. I love you guys.

Sam and Vic. What would I do without you and our "Ungodly Hour" morning sprints? Though recently we've been spending more time drinking coffee and sending each other GIFs than writing!

Kim, thank you for keeping me organized and taking care of my Facebook reader group. Tasha's Tribe is an awesome place for my readers because of you.

Ariella and Molly, thanks for being part of this journey with me. You are the best team.

Wendy, Alison, Colleen and Heather. Thank you for working with me on this book. You guys are my rock stars!

And to my readers, THANK YOU SO MUCH.

Published by Delacorte Press, an imprint
of Random House Children's Books, a division
of Penguin Random House LLC, New York.

1

I dig the tips of my yellow-painted fingernails into the firm leather seat as Dad drives us home on the verge of breaking the speed limit. He's anxious to get back, but I would rather he slowed down. My stomach dips, and I hold my breath, squeezing my eyes closed as he takes a sharp corner.

With my muscles locked into place, I raise my eyes to the rearview mirror. Thankfully, Dad's eyes are fixed on the road, but there's a tightness to them that's unsettling. He's a good driver, and I trust him with my life, but I'm not a fan of this speed.

The car, a black Mercedes, is immaculate and still smells brand-new a year on, so I'm surprised that he's driving so fast on dusty country roads.

Everything is going to be different now, and he seems to be in a hurry to start our new life.

It's not right. We need to slow down, savor the ease of what our lives used to be, because the new one waiting for us in just five minutes, I don't want. Things weren't perfect before, but I want my old life back.

The one where Mom was still alive.

It's spring, her favorite season. Flowers have begun to brighten our town, turning the landscape from a dull green to a rainbow of color. It's my favorite time of year, too, when the sun shows itself and the temperature warms enough so you don't need a coat.

I'm always happier in spring. But right now, it might as well be winter again. I don't feel my mood lifting, and I definitely don't care that I'm not wearing a stupid coat.

My twin sister, Iris, is in the front passenger seat. She's staring out the window, occasionally starting a short conversation. It's more than I've done. There's been nothing but silence from me. It's not because I don't care; it's because I don't know what to say. There are no words for what has happened.

Everything I think of seems dumb and insignificant. Nothing is big enough to fill the enormous void left by our mom.

The warm spring sun shines into the car, but it's not strong enough to hurt my eyes. I don't want to close them again anyway. Every time I do, I see her pale face. So pale she didn't look real. Her once rosy cheeks gone forever. It was like staring at a life-size porcelain doll.

I wish I hadn't gone to the funeral home to see her. My last image of her will be her lifeless body.

When I go back to school, I'll be fine. I'll swim and study until it doesn't hurt anymore.

Or I'll want that to work, but I know it's going to take more than a couple of distractions to make the pain disappear.

We turn down our road and my toes curl in my tennis shoes. I swallow a lump that leaves my throat bone-dry.

Dad slows, pulling into our drive and parking out front. Our house feels like it's in the middle of nowhere, but there are about ten houses nearby and it's a five-minute drive into town. I love the quiet and the peace of my hometown, but I feel like it's going to drive me crazy. Right now I need loud and fast-paced. I need distractions and lots of them.

Iris gets out of the car first, her butt-length, silky blond hair blowing in the warm breeze. She's home with me and Dad forever now.

Our mom died after falling off a bridge while out running two weeks ago. She was by a farm and the land was uneven and hilly. It had been raining and there was mud on the ground. The rail on the steep side of the short bridge was low, there more for guidance than safety, and she slipped off. The bridge wasn't very high, apparently, but she hit her head and died instantly. That's what the police told us.

Mom ran to keep fit and healthy so she could be around for me and Iris longer, but it ended up killing her.

Her death is still impossible to process. I haven't lived with my mom or Iris for six years, since she and Dad divorced, but her permanent absence weighs heavy in my stomach like lead.

When I was ten and our parents sat me and Iris down to explain they were separating, I had been relieved. It had been coming for a long time, and I was sick of hearing arguments while I pretended to sleep upstairs. The atmosphere was cold at best, our parents barely speaking but smiling as if I couldn't see through the crap mask.

Iris and I have never had a conversation about it, but the separation was a surprise to her. She shouted and then she cried while I sat still, silently planning how I would tell them I wanted to live with Dad. It wasn't an easy choice for anyone, but we had to make one. Dad and I had always been close; we share a lot in common, from movies and music to hobbies and food. He's the one to give us clear guidelines, without which I would crumble. Mom was laid back, sometimes too much, and I would never get anything done.

Besides, Mom always wanted to live in the city, and I never liked how densely it's populated.

Mom and Iris moved out; then they moved away to the city. I have spent school holidays flitting between houses, sometimes missing out on time with my twin thanks to conflicting schedules. She would be with Dad while I was with Mom.

None of our family members, friends, or even neighbors could understand it. You don't separate twins. I get it—we're supposed to be able to communicate without speaking and literally feel each other's pain. But Iris and I have never been like that. We're too different.

We're not close, so although she's my sister, it feels more like a distant cousin is moving in.

She still has her bedroom here, which she and Dad redecorated last year when she visited for the summer. But she's brought a *lot* of stuff with her from Mom's. The trunk is full of her things.

I watch her walk to the front door as Dad cuts the engine. She has a key to the house, of course, so she lets herself in.

Dad scratches the dark stubble on his chin. He usually shaves every morning. "Are you okay, Ivy? You've barely said a word the entire time we've been on the road."

"I'm fine," I reply, my voice low and gravelly.

Fine, the modern *I'm not okay* definition of the word, is what I mean here. Everything has changed in the blink of an eye. Two weeks is all it has taken to turn my world upside down. And what about Iris? She was closer to Mom than anyone. What right do I have to fall apart when she has lost even more than me?

"You can talk about it. Whenever you want."

"I know, Dad. Thanks."

His eyes slide to the house. "Let's go inside."

I take a long breath and stare at the front door.

I don't want to go inside. When I go back in there, our new normal starts. I'm not ready to let go of the old just yet. Until I walk through that door, my twin isn't living with us again because our mom has died.

That's all total rubbish, obviously. Not walking through that door changes nothing, but I can pretend. I need longer.

"Ivy?" Dad prompts, watching me in the mirror with caution in his blue eyes, almost afraid to ask me if everything is okay again in case I crumble.

"Can I go to Ty's first? I won't be long."

His brow creases. "We *just* got home. . . ."

"I'll be back soon. I need a little time. It will give you an opportunity to check in with Iris too. She's going to need you a lot, sometimes without me."

He opens his door. "One hour."

I get out, my heart lighter knowing I have an extra sixty minutes, which I can stretch to seventy before he'll call. "Thanks, Dad."

Shutting the car door, I look back at the house.

What?

The hairs on my arms rise. Iris is watching me from the second-floor window.

But she's not in her bedroom.

She's in mine.

2

Tyler lives down the road, so I get there in under a minute and knock on the door.

He opens up and his leaf-green eyes widen. "Ivy." Reaching out, he tugs me into the tightest hug. His arms wrap around my back, and I sink into him. "Hey," he whispers. "You okay?"

"Not really," I mutter against his Ramones T-shirt.

"Come on." His arms loosen but he doesn't let go completely, his fingers sliding between mine as he leads me inside. "When did you get home?"

"A couple of minutes ago. I haven't been in the house yet."

He eyes me curiously as we walk up to his bedroom, his head turning back every second step. Even though his parents are at work, he leaves the bedroom door open. Rule one. If we break it, we'll never be allowed to spend time together without a chaperone.

Neither of us will break it.

I let go of his hand and collapse onto his bed. His pillow is so soft, and it smells like him. It's comforting and everything I need right now.

The bed dips beside me as Ty sits down. Running his hand through his surfer style chestnut hair, he asks, "Do you want to talk?"

I press against the ache in my chest. "I don't know what to say."

"I'm not your dad or sister, Ivy. I'm not looking for comforting words. You don't need to pretend you're okay for me. Tell me how you feel."

I roll from my side to my back so I can see him. "I feel lost, and I feel stupid for being such a wreck."

"Babe, your mom died. Why do you feel stupid?"

Shrugging, I shake my head and swallow so I don't cry. "I don't know. I'm supposed to be more together. Don't I have a reputation for having a cold heart?"

"No, that means you don't cry when whatever boy band breaks up, not that you're made of stone and don't cry for your mom."

I love that he doesn't know the names of any relevant boy bands.

Iris has always been the emotional one. I'm the logical one. Unless something *really* affects my life, I'm not going to cry over it. What I rock at doing, though, is stressing and overthinking.

"Iris hasn't cried once that I know of," I tell him. "And all

I've done is cry. It's like we've reversed roles." Dad and I arrived at their house eleven days ago, the day Mom died. Iris was like a robot. She got up, showered, dressed, and ate. She tidied and watched TV. Iris continued her routine as usual, but it was all in silence as if Dad and I weren't there. She only started talking properly again this morning.

"Everyone handles grief differently."

I look up at his ceiling. Everyone deals with all sorts of things differently; I just didn't realize that Iris and I would walk through this totally out of character. We may look the same, besides her hair being about five inches longer, but we're nothing alike. Now we're swapping parts of our personality?

Sighing, I stare straight into his eyes and whisper, "I don't know how to help her. I barely know her anymore."

"You can't fix it. You only have to be there for her. There's nothing anyone can do to accelerate the grief process; you have to let it happen."

I don't like that at all. I like my control. If there's a problem, I find a solution. I don't handle it well when there's nothing I can do.

He chuckles. "You'll learn how to do that, I promise."

Sighing, I blink rapidly as tears sting the backs of my eyes. "My mom is gone."

"I know, and I'm so sorry."

Get it together.

"Mom asked me to visit for the weekend last month," I tell him.

"Ivy, don't do this."

"I told her I couldn't because I was spending the weekend at the pool to prepare for a swim meet I missed because she died."

"Ivy," he groans. "You had stuff to do, and it's not like that's never happened before."

I sigh into the sinking feeling in my gut. "Logically, I understand that."

"There's no way you could have known what would happen, babe."

I'm not all that good at forgiving myself. Everyone else, sure, but not myself.

Ty shakes his head. "You can't live up to the standards you hold yourself to. No one's perfect."

All right, I'll give him that. But I constantly strive for perfect. The perfect grades, fastest swimmer, solid circle of friends, real relationships. I'm setting myself up to fail, I get that, and I would stop if I could.

"It feels like Iris is only back to visit. We haven't lived together in *six years*."

His fingertips brush my blond hair. "You'll all adjust, I promise."

We will but we shouldn't have to. Mom was too young to die. Iris and I are too young to be without her. "I want things to go back to the way they were."

"You don't want Iris there?" he asks softly.

"No, that's not it. Of course I want her with us. I wish she didn't have to be, you know? So much has changed, and I'm not ready for any of it. Mom is supposed to be here. Who is going to take me prom dress shopping? She was going to scream when I graduate and totally embarrass me. Who will cry first when I try on wedding dresses or when I have a baby? There is so much that she's going to miss. I don't know how to do it all without her."

I have Dad, but all those things won't be the same without Mom.

"Ivy," he says, brushing his fingers across my face and down my cheek. "She will be there for all of that and more."

Yeah, only she won't. Not in the way I need.

"Iris was in my room," I say, changing the subject before I lose the control I've only just regained after yesterday.

"Okay . . ."

"She was watching me from my room when I left to come here."

"Did you tell her you were going out?"

"No."

"Maybe she was curious."

I bite my bottom lip. Maybe, but what was she doing in my room in the first place? Hers is right next to mine, so she could see me outside from her window too.

"Hmm," I reply, not entirely sure where I'm going with this. I've been in her room, so it's not a big deal. "Yeah, maybe. It just seems weird."

Ty lies down beside me. "It's not weird for her to want to be close to you. There's a lot of change for her, and she's the one who's had to move, leaving behind all of her friends."

I wince at his words. "Yeah, I know."

Iris has lost so much, and if being around me and my stuff helps her even a little bit, then it's fine with me. Oh God, and I'm here. She was in my room probably wanting to be close to me, and I left.

I left her!

My heart sinks to my stomach. “I should go.”

His hand freezes on my jaw. “Already?”

“I have an hour, but . . .” I’ve already been a terrible sister, no need to continue that.

He nods. “You need to be home with your dad and Iris.”

“Thanks for understanding, Ty.”

Well, this was brief, but worth it. We get off the bed and walk downstairs past the line of pictures showing Ty growing up. The last one is of us both, arms around each other smiling at the school Christmas dance.

Ty put things into perspective for me. I’ve been cooped up in a bubble of me, Dad, Iris, and Mom’s side of the family—I haven’t gotten enough distance to give myself any clarity.

I follow him out of the house, chewing my lip as I go. I’ve been so focused on me and how I feel that I haven’t really thought about Iris. Maybe we will grow closer, and that can be the one good thing to come out of this tragedy.

“Call me if you need anything,” he says, holding on to the edge of the front door.

I lean in and give him a quick kiss. “I will. Thanks.” Then I turn and run along the sidewalk all the way back to my house.

My feet hit the asphalt so hard it sends sparks of pain along my shins, but I don’t slow down. I pass our neighbors’ houses in a blur, their pruned hedges and rosebushes flashing by. Sucking in air that burns, I reach out and almost slam right into the front door. Bowing my head, I grip the door handle, my lungs screaming for the oxygen I've deprived them of during my sprint.

"Dad? Iris?" I call as I walk into the house.

"In the kitchen," Dad replies.

I swing left and find Dad sitting alone at the table.

"Where's Iris?" I ask, breathless.

"Upstairs. She didn't want to talk."

Oh. It was selfish of me to run off the second we pulled up. "I'm going to check on her."

Dad nods. "And I'll start dinner. What do you want?"

I shrug. This past eleven days have been nutrient free. We've grabbed whatever food we could manage, usually sandwiches and takeout. I feel hungry, but when food is placed in front of me, I can barely stomach a bite.

"Anything," I reply, heading upstairs.

Iris must feel so lost. I don't know if she's had much contact with her friends, but I do know I haven't seen her on her phone at all. She needs them now, probably more than she needs me and Dad.

I climb the stairs, tying my long wavy hair in a knot on top of my head, and knock on her door. "Iris, it's me. Can I come in?"

"Sure," she replies.

Okay, I was expecting some resistance.

I open the door and offer a small smile as I head into the room. She's sitting on the edge of her bed, doing nothing. Her long hair fans around her body like a cloak.

"Dumb question, but . . . how do you feel?" I ask.

She shrugs one shoulder. "I'm not sure there's a word for it."

Her eyes are sunken, ringed with dark circles that make her look a lot older than she is. I don't think she's sleeping well either.

We have the same shade of dark blond hair and the same pale blue eyes.

"Well, do you need anything?" Besides the obvious.

"I'm good."

Raising my eyebrows, I move deeper into her room. "Are you?"

She meets my gaze. "Are *you*?"

"No, I'm not." I wring my hands. "We can talk . . . if you want?"

We don't talk, not about real, deep stuff, anyway. She has her friends for that, and I have mine. It's actually kind of sad how we've missed out on that close twin bond. It's the only thing I regret about staying with Dad when Iris moved away with Mom.

She tilts her head. "Can we talk?"

"Well, I know that's not usually our thing, but it can be. I mean, I'm willing . . . and we are twins."

"We shared a womb, share a birthday and DNA, but I've never felt like a twin. We never talk."

Okay, ouch. We used to talk when we were little. I remember being five and sneaking into each other's room at night. We didn't share because we were too different—her room candy pink and mine ocean blue. But it didn't matter after dark; we would make a den out of blankets, grab our flashlights, and talk about random fairy-tale things our imaginations would conjure.

Iris was going to marry a British prince and eventually become queen, and I was going to travel the world in an old Mustang like the one our grandad used to own.

Somewhere over time and our parents' separation, our silly dreams died, and we stopped sharing any new ones.

"Do you want to talk, Iris?"

Her haunted eyes look right through me. "I want so much more than that."

Don't miss
Natasha Preston's

THE FEAR

Coming Spring 2022